P9-DEG-523

Jake shoved his hands in his pockets and started walking away.

He'd barely gone two steps when he felt Anne's hand on his arm. He froze in his tracks. The scent of her body, the soft fragrance of her perfume, filled his senses.

"Jake, you're a good man," she said.

"Not by a long shot."

"You are." She moved closer. "You've done a fine job with—with your daughter. She couldn't have turned out to be as sweet and loving as she is if you weren't decent."

He spun toward her so quickly, she didn't have time to move back. He told himself he was a fool, that come morning he would regret acting on this impulse. But that didn't stop him.

"If I'm so decent," he said, hauling her up against him, "why can't I stop thinking about this?" And then he lowered his mouth to hers....

Dear Reader,

Welcome to Silhouette Special Edition…welcome to romance.

The hot month of July starts off with a sizzling event! Debbie Macomber's fiftieth book, *Baby Blessed,* is our THAT SPECIAL WOMAN! for July. This emotional, heartwarming book in which the promise of a new life reunites a husband and wife is not to be missed!

Christine Rimmer's series THE JONES GANG continues in *Sweetbriar Summit* with sexy Patrick Jones, the second of the rapscallion Jones brothers you'll meet. You'll want to be around when the Jones boys bring their own special brand of trouble to town!

Also this month, look for books by some of your favorite authors: Celeste Hamilton presents us with an emotional tale in *Which Way Is Home?* and Susan Mallery has a *Cowboy Daddy* waiting to find a family. July also offers *Unpredictable* by Patt Bucheister, and *Homeward Bound* by Sierra Rydell, her follow-up to *On Middle Ground.* A veritable light show of July fireworks!

I hope you enjoy this book, and all of the stories to come!

Sincerely,

Tara Gavin
Senior Editor

Please address questions and book requests to:
Silhouette Reader Service
U.S.: 3010 Walden Ave., P.O. Box 1325, Buffalo, NY 14269
Canadian: P.O. Box 609, Fort Erie, Ont. L2A 5X3

SUSAN MALLERY

COWBOY DADDY

Published by Silhouette Books
America's Publisher of Contemporary Romance

If you purchased this book without a cover you should be aware that this book is stolen property. It was reported as "unsold and destroyed" to the publisher, and neither the author nor the publisher has received any payment for this "stripped book."

This book about a mother's love for her daughter could only be dedicated to my mother. For listening and encouraging me. For giving me the freedom to try and the support to risk failing. For never judging me. For always being there when I needed her.
With love.

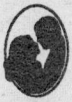

SILHOUETTE BOOKS

ISBN 0-373-09898-7

COWBOY DADDY

Copyright © 1994 by Susan W. Macias

All rights reserved. Except for use in any review, the reproduction or utilization of this work in whole or in part in any form by any electronic, mechanical or other means, now known or hereafter invented, including xerography, photocopying and recording, or in any information storage or retrieval system, is forbidden without the written permission of the editorial office, Silhouette Books, 300 East 42nd Street, New York, NY 10017 U.S.A.

All characters in this book have no existence outside the imagination of the author and have no relation whatsoever to anyone bearing the same name or names. They are not even distantly inspired by any individual known or unknown to the author, and all incidents are pure invention.

This edition published by arrangement with Harlequin Enterprises B. V.

® and TM are trademarks of Harlequin Enterprises B. V., used under license. Trademarks indicated with ® are registered in the United States Patent and Trademark Office, the Canadian Trade Marks Office and in other countries.

Printed in U.S.A.

Books by Susan Mallery

Silhouette Special Edition

Tender Loving Care #717
More Than Friends #802
A Dad for Billie #834
Cowboy Daddy #898

Silhouette Intimate Moments

Tempting Faith #554

SUSAN MALLERY

has always been an incurable romantic. Growing up, she spent long hours weaving complicated fantasies about dashing heroes and witty heroines. She was shocked to discover not everyone carried around this sort of magical world. After taking a chance on her dream, she gave up a promising career in accounting to devote herself to writing romances full-time. This prolific author lives with her husband in Houston, Texas. Susan also writes historicals under the name Susan Macias.

COLORADO
Denver
Colorado Springs
Jake's Ranch
NEBRASKA
KANSAS
OKLAHOMA
NEW MEXICO
TEXAS
Austin
Houston
MEXICO
All underlined places are fictitious.

Chapter One

"Your two o'clock is a hunk."

Anne Baker stared blankly at her assistant. "A hunk?"

"Yeah!" Heather clutched her notepad to her chest and sagged against the door. "Tall, dark, with big brown eyes that could melt you faster than..." Her voice trailed off. "I assume by the way you're looking at me that you're not happy with the news."

Anne fought the urge to bury her face in her hands. "It doesn't matter what he looks like. The fact is he's here. What am I supposed to do with him?"

"Talk?" Heather grinned. "You aren't scared of him, are you?"

"Me?" Anne firmly shook her head. "Of course not. I've worked with company presidents, relocated Fortune 500 companies."

"Leapt buildings in a single bound. You *are* scared."

Anne sighed. "Terrified."

"Should I send him away?"

Anne almost wished that was possible. No, that wasn't true. She didn't want to send him away; she desperately wanted to meet Jake Masters. With one phone call and a few carefully chosen words, the man had turned her world upside down. For the past two days she'd thought about nothing but his call. Now he was here, waiting to see her. She'd hoped for a connection—a way to undo the past—but she hadn't thought it would happen like this. Or happen this soon.

Anne glanced down at the slim gold watch on her wrist. It had been a gift to herself last month, celebrating both the completion of the electronics firm's contract and her birthday. Thirty-one. The day had made her think about many things, most of them revolving around her eighteenth birthday. Funny, less than a month later Jake Masters called. Had her thoughts been a premonition? She shook her head. Of course not. She thought about the same thing every birthday. She tried not to of course, but it was inevitable.

Anne looked up and forced herself to smile. "Is he really a hunk?"

Heather smiled back. "We are talking heartthrob city. Long, lean and luscious."

Anne's forced smile became genuine. "You are a wicked woman."

"It is one of my best qualities." Heather winked. "He's pacing back and forth like a caged lion. Do you want me to send him in?"

Anne's stomach lurched as if she'd just taken the last heart-stopping drop on a roller coaster. "Waiting is only going to make it worse." She drew in a deep breath. "All right. Here goes nothing. Tell Mr. Masters he can come in."

Heather nodded. Her blond hair bounced with the movement. "One hunk, coming right up." The oak door closed quietly behind her.

Just keep breathing, Anne told herself. She sat straighter in her chair and rested her hands on the desk. Her fingers shook. She thrust them onto her lap. She touched her hair to make sure it was still neatly smoothed in place, then wished she'd told Heather to give her a couple of minutes. She wanted to freshen her lipstick, to check the mirror for the hundredth time and make sure there was nothing in her teeth. She wanted to catch her breath and think about something other than Jake Masters and why he was coming to see her.

A knock on the door brought her out of her seat. She straightened, tugged at her suit jacket and called, "Come in."

Heather pushed the door open. "Mr. Masters to see you, Ms. Baker." She stepped back to let the man enter.

Anne's heart was already pounding in her chest, but at the sight of the tall, dark-haired man standing in front of her, it leapt into high gear and tried to lodge in her throat. Her palms grew damp.

The panic threatening to swamp her had a little to do with the reason for his visit and a whole lot more to do with the way he was dressed. Boots, jeans, tailored white shirt rolled up to the elbows and a black Stetson he'd removed when he came to her office. It took all her strength to remain standing. Jake Masters was a cowboy. She avoided cowboys at all costs—not an easy thing to do in Houston, Texas.

It shouldn't matter what he wore or did for a living, she reminded herself. But why did he have to be a cowboy?

"Would you like me to bring coffee, Mr. Masters?" Heather asked.

He turned to her assistant. "None for me, thanks." His voice was low and controlled with only the hint of a Texas drawl. He was a native, but not local. Dallas, maybe.

When Heather glanced at her, Anne shook her head. The younger woman gave her a thumbs-up sign and retreated.

The door closed. Anne returned her attention to her guest. His shadowed eyes held hers. Brown, she thought, with odd flecks of gold, but no expression. He might have been a hunk, as Heather had promised, but Anne couldn't judge from the impressions she gathered. Tall, brown hair, a firm mouth with no hint of a smile. Broad shouldered, slim hipped. Younger than she would have thought. Mid-thirties. Handsome? It didn't matter. Her gaze drifted back to his face and she saw he returned her close inspection. Her hands tightened into fists. What was he seeing? She resisted the urge to smooth her hair.

"Mr. Masters?" she said, raising the pitch of her voice so it came out as a question.

He nodded. "Thank you for seeing me, Ms. Baker." Those cool, oddly flecked eyes searched her face. "I still have the picture you gave us. You've changed."

Anne flushed. She knew the hot color would flare brightly on her cheeks, giving away her embarrassment. She ducked her head and pointed to the leather chair in front of her desk. "It was a long time ago."

"Thirteen years," he said as he sat down and set his hat on the edge of her desk. His hair was short, barely brushing the collar of his white shirt.

Anne lowered herself into her seat. She looked at the bookcases against the right-hand wall, at the sofa on the opposite side of the room, at the closed door, and suddenly wished she'd asked for coffee. She could use the momentary rescue, if not the caffeine.

"I know how much time has passed," she said. "It's not the sort of thing I would forget."

His eyes narrowed and his mouth drew even straighter. "I'll have to take your word on that."

She leaned forward. "You know nothing about me or my circumstances, Mr. Masters," she said curtly. "You have no right to judge me. If that's what this meeting is about—"

"It isn't." He cut her off, then rubbed the bridge of his nose with his thumb and forefinger. "Look, it's been a hell of a summer. First the move, then this whole situation with Laurel."

"Laurel?" Her voice quavered as she spoke the name.

He dropped his hand to the armrest. "Yes. My daughter."

Laurel. Anne blinked several times. She had often wondered what they'd called her child. Now she knew. No matter what, she would always know. Laurel. She pictured a towheaded toddler in a frilly pink dress. No, that wasn't right. Thirteen years had gone by; Laurel was a teenager now. A milestone in a child's life. Maybe that's why their shared birthday had struck a nerve this time. "It's a beautiful name."

"My wife picked it out." He watched her carefully.

"Is she here with you?"

"My wife passed away two years ago."

"I'm sorry. But I was asking about... your daughter."

He caught the slight hesitation. "I thought we should speak alone first," he said.

She hadn't known how much she'd hoped to meet her—to meet Laurel—until this moment. To have come so far, to be so close. It was more than she'd ever dared to hope for, and yet she *had* hoped. The chance had been snatched away and she wanted to cry out her pain. She rose slowly and walked around her chair to the floor-to-ceiling window.

Downtown Houston stretched out before her. The double-glazed glass protected her from the weather and the noise, but she could see the August heat shimmering on the streets and sidewalks.

Heather had opened the vertical blinds that morning. Anne stared out at the city. "You have the advantage here, Mr. Masters."

"How?"

"I don't understand why you're here or what you want from me. From your reaction a minute ago I would guess you might not want to believe me, but I'm having a difficult time with this. When you called, I agreed to meet with you because—" She paused. The ache in her chest deepened. She drew in a breath and told herself she was strong enough to get through this. She had no choice; she was in this alone. "Because I couldn't say no. I've spent thirteen years wondering about her. The private adoption arranged by the attorneys meant you could have contacted me at any time. Why now?"

"She wants to meet you."

The opposite of pain was joy. Happiness flooded her, chasing away the darkness and the fear. Tears she'd managed to ward off before filled her eyes. She covered her mouth with her hand to hold in her cry of relief. The window in front of her blurred as she remembered a day thirteen years ago.

It had been summer then, too, but July instead of August. Paradise was too small a town to have a hospital, so her mother had driven her the forty miles to the nearest community facility. On her eighteenth birthday, surrounded by strangers, with only her mother's hand to hold, she'd given birth to a daughter. She remembered little of the pain, although the smells stayed with her, as did the cold stare of the nurse who had taken the baby from the doctor and carried her from the room. Later, the woman had returned, her arms empty. Anne had cried out to see her child. The woman had refused. "If you give 'em up, you can't see 'em. Hospital policy."

She had begged for hours. The stern-faced woman refused to budge. Later, the night nurse had taken pity on her and told her the baby—her child, her daughter—was already gone. The new parents had whisked her away.

Anne wiped at the tears on her cheeks. "She wants to meet me," she whispered, barely able to believe her good fortune.

"I think it's a mistake."

She spun to face him. Sometime while she'd been lost in the past, he'd risen from the chair and approached her. He stood only a foot away. She had to tilt her head back to look into his eyes. Coldness radiated from him. And anger.

"Why?" she asked, fighting the urge to step back.

"Laurel is having some problems right now and—"

"What's wrong? Is she sick? Tell me what I can do."

"It's nothing that concerns you."

"But it does. I'm her—"

He grabbed her shoulders. Strong fingers bit into her. "Don't you dare say it. You're *not* her mother."

She wanted to contradict him, but she knew he spoke the truth. She'd given up all rights to that title the day she'd given up her child. Another tear rolled down her face.

He briefly tightened his hold on her, then released her. He cursed under his breath. "Ms. Baker—"

She turned away and fumbled for the box of tissue in the bottom drawer of her desk. She glanced at him.

Jake Masters looked as uncomfortable and confused as she felt. "I need a drink."

She wiped her face, then glanced down at the streak of makeup and a black smudge staining the white tissue. "Me, too." She pointed to the center cabinet in the bookcase. "Please pour me one of whatever you're having. I'll be right back."

She escaped through the door opposite the bookcase and into the small powder room off her office. When she was safely alone, Anne braced her forearms against the vanity and exhaled. Her whole body ached, as if she'd been beaten and left for dead. Her eyes burned and her hands still trembled. She'd thought she'd been prepared for this meeting.

"Not very," she muttered softly as she forced herself to stand upright.

After clicking on the overhead light, she stared into the mirror. The summer humidity had already done its damage to her hair as the sleek pageboy crinkled into an unruly mass of waves. Mascara and eye shadow collected below her eyes, and what was left of her lipstick didn't begin to cover her mouth.

"Good thing he didn't bring Laurel. Seeing me like this would probably scare her back to—"

She paused in the middle of turning on the faucet. Back to where? She didn't know where her daughter lived. Didn't know where she'd grown up or what she looked like or if—

She closed her eyes. To see her, to hold her, just once, she prayed silently. One time. To look into her face. To know that she was all right.

Anne swallowed and blinked away fresh tears. After opening the single drawer on the right of the sink, she took out her emergency makeup kit and used a headband to pull her hair away from her face. She always got red and puffy when she cried, but it could all be cured with a little cold water and a lot of denial.

Jake stared at the shot of brandy, swore briefly, then tossed it back with a single gulp. The fiery liquid burned down to his stomach. He filled the snifter again, but this time he carried it over to the coffee table in front of the leather couch. He set the glass next to the one he'd poured for Anne, then looked around the room.

He knew all about executive offices. She was one step away from the prized corner slot. A high-powered lady on her way up. She'd come a long way from that tiny west Texas town. She'd probably forgotten all about her little mistake in high school. He must have shocked her when he'd called. The tearful scene today had been a nice touch. He shook his head. If he had his way, he would walk out that door and never come back. She didn't deserve to know his daughter. But Laurel wasn't giving him a choice.

Why now? he wondered for the hundredth time. Why this? He'd asked Laurel, had argued with her, but she'd refused to listen. Meeting her birth mother—he hated that phrase—had become the only thing she cared about. He didn't know how to talk to her anymore. Laurel wasn't grown-up yet, but she wasn't the little girl who had spent so many evenings curled up on his lap. Was he making a mistake?

He paced the area between the coffee table and the window. She was his daughter. And Ellen's. Only Ellen was gone. It was up to him to do what was right and to protect her. Especially from Anne Baker.

The side door opened and Anne stepped out. She'd cleaned up her face. Except for the slight redness around her eyes, no one would know she'd been crying. Probably had it down to an art form.

She walked over to him. "We have a lot of things to learn about each other. Laurel wanting to meet me must have been a shock for you, as well. I know I haven't been a part of her life, but you must believe I only want what's best for her. Let's start over." She offered him her hand.

Jake stared down at her. Unlike Ellen, who had stood only four inches shorter than his six foot one, Anne Baker's head barely skimmed his chin. He didn't want to shake hands, he didn't want to be friendly, he didn't want to do a damn thing but get the hell out of here.

He hesitated long enough to make her uncomfortable, but she didn't back down. Light blue eyes met his, refusing to look away. She'd put mascara on her top lashes, but the bottom ones were pale. He could see freckles across the bridge of her nose.

It wasn't politeness or his mother's training that caused him to reach out and engulf her small fingers in his. It was the memory of Laurel staring up at him, confused and scared and desperate to find something—and someone—to belong to.

As he took her hand, he felt it. A jolt of electricity flashed up his arm, igniting a spark that flared low in his belly. He fought to steady himself. The anger inside fed on the heat and burned hotter. She pumped his arm once. He withdrew from her and retreated to the edge of the couch.

When she sat at the far end, he lowered himself down to the leather seat and picked up the drink he'd poured. Instead of gulping down the brandy, he stared at the liquid.

He'd sensed it—the attraction. From the moment he'd walked into this room. Whether it was scent or instinct or some great cosmic joke, he didn't know. But he did know the meaning of that jolt. Ellen had been gone two years. In all that time, he'd never felt the surge of need, had never wanted to—

He looked at Anne Baker. She sat in the corner of the soft leather sofa. The supple material surrounded her, the light peach color highlighted the pale red of her hair and made her skin appear translucent. Oh, she'd planned this right down to the slight gap in her navy suit jacket that allowed him to see the lacy edge of her blouse.

"How much do I have to pay you to meet with Laurel?" he asked abruptly.

She gaped at him. "What?" Fury straightened her spine and darkened her pale blue eyes. It shot out at him, heading straight for his heart.

Unperturbed, Jake took a sip of his drink and rested one arm on the back of the sofa. He didn't trust her. She'd disappeared from her daughter's life once already. Why should anything be different now?

"Mr. Masters, you don't know what you're talking about. I agreed to see you because I care about—"

He stiffened, but she stumbled on without saying "my."

"—your daughter. I don't see what money has to do with it." The fury abated. Her full mouth trembled slightly. "I just want to see her and t-talk to her."

"You expect me to believe that?"

"Why would I lie?"

"You took money easy enough the last time."

She flushed. The bright color didn't complement her freckles or her hair. "It was necessary. I needed it to pay the medical expenses. My mother couldn't afford insurance."

A poor girl with a struggling single mother. He didn't want to buy into the lie. The point was she had taken a large sum of money. He frowned, trying to remember the report he and Ellen had read so many years ago. Had Anne Baker had a father? He vaguely recalled the mention of the man running off. Ellen had said that was why she'd gotten pregnant in the first place. Jake had told his wife it was more likely that Anne Baker hadn't bothered to say no some night in the back of a pickup.

He leaned forward. "Just so we understand each other. I've checked with my attorney. You have no legal or financial rights to me or my child."

She reached for her glass of brandy. When she picked up the snifter, her hand shook so badly the liquid sloshed up the sides. She set it back down and looked at him. Pain straightened her mouth. "I know."

"And?"

"And what, Mr. Masters? You're the one who contacted *me*. You had to go through several people to get my name and number. I'd left the channels open because I wanted Laurel to be able to find me if she ever wanted to." She smoothed her pleated navy skirt, then clasped her hands together to stop their shaking. "So far you've bullied me and accused me of wanting your money. Anything else you need to get off your chest before you tell me about the problems you're having with Laurel and what I can do to help?"

He would have walked out the door. He was in fact ready to leave, except she raised her head and her chin jutted forward defiantly. Recognition clawed at his gut and with it, pain. Laurel stood up to him much the same way. She squared her shoulders and tilted up her head until her chin thrust out. With her hands planted on her hips, she would say, "Dad," stretching the word out to two syllables.

Until this past summer, he'd thought the gesture cute. But now, between the tears and stormy arguments, the door slamming, the threats, he didn't know what to do anymore. Ellen could have guided him, but Ellen was gone. He'd come here because he had nowhere else to go. And because he would do anything for Laurel, no matter the cost to him.

He rose to his feet and walked to the window. The view of the city stretched out before him. He ignored it. Turning to face the woman, he shifted until the afternoon sun hit her full in the face. He knew the light at his back would keep his expression in shadow. That's what he wanted. For Laurel's sake he had to know everything Anne Baker thought, dreamed or lied about.

"I told you my wife passed away two years ago," he said abruptly.

Anne watched him warily but didn't speak.

"Laurel took her death pretty hard. They'd always been close. She started running with a bad crowd."

The corner of Anne's mouth twitched slightly, as if a spasm of pain had caught her off guard. This was hard for her, he realized, then squashed any thought of compassion.

He folded his arms over his chest and continued. "We moved recently. It seemed the best solution for both of us. Laurel hasn't adjusted to our new home yet. She misses her friends. I'm sure that's why in the past couple of months she's started talking about her birth mother. She wants to meet you."

"As easy as that?" She rose to her feet and approached him. "Why don't I believe you? It's been thirteen years. Tracking me down is obviously the last thing you wanted to do. Why did you agree to this?"

She was close enough that he could feel the heat of her body. He told himself to ignore it, but he couldn't. Something flickered in her pale blue eyes. It took him a minute to identify the emotion, then he realized why. He'd never seen an open wound before—nothing as raw and exposed as the haunted emptiness that flashed through her eyes. She looked away quickly, then back, and by then, the feelings had been shuttered. But he'd seen them. It was her pain that allowed him to speak the truth.

"I didn't handle Ellen's death any better than Laurel did," he said. "Her grandfather, Ellen's father, also fell apart." He thought about his last conversation, then forced the older man's harsh words from his mind. "We've all spent the past two years missing her. I thought moving would make it better for Laurel and me. Get her away from those kids and bring the two of us closer together."

"But it hasn't?" she asked.

"No. If anything, it's worse. She didn't want to move and now she hates the new place. About two months ago there was some program on TV about adopted kids finding their birth mothers." He shoved his hands into his pockets and walked over to the bookcase.

"She knew then?"

"Yeah. We talked about it from the beginning. She probably doesn't remember not knowing. Anyway, after this show, she started mentioning that she wanted to find her—you." He studied the titles of the books, seeing the words, but not really reading them or understanding what they said. Just thinking about Laurel made the knot in his gut double in size. She was his baby—he couldn't lose her.

But she was slipping away before his eyes. Day by day she pulled back until he worried he wouldn't be able to reach her ever again.

"She seems a little young to make that kind of decision," Anne said, from somewhere behind him.

He didn't bother to turn around. He didn't want to see the look on her face. Compassion would be more than he could handle, and triumph, well, he didn't want to distrust her any more than he did.

"She ran away."

Silence.

"She was gone overnight. Hid out in a neighbor's barn. When we found her, she was fine, but it made me realize she wasn't kidding. That's when I called the attorney." He fingered the thick volumes. Something about zoning laws, he noticed. "Just meet with her one time. That's all she wants. Then we'll be out of your way."

"I'll do anything I can to help."

"How about dinner tomorrow night?" he asked.

"W-where—" she had to clear her throat "—where would you like to meet?"

Not the hotel, he thought, knowing he was being a jerk but not able to help feeling he had to protect his own turf.

"How about my place?" she asked.

Why not? he thought. At least he would be able to see where she lived. There might be some clues as to the kind of person she was. Despite his claims of a single meeting, he knew Laurel wanted more. He could only pray the two of them wouldn't hit it off.

"That's fine." he said.

She scribbled her address on a piece of paper and handed it to him. He took it from her, careful to make sure they didn't touch. But she didn't let him escape that easily. She rested her hand on his bare forearm. Hot need bubbled to the surface. He tried to ignore the sensations, tried to step back away from her. He didn't want this in his life, not from a woman like her.

Her eyes held his, their gazes locked until the entire world faded leaving only the sound of their breathing to fill the silence. Her scent teased him. It was just a popular expensive fragrance. It wasn't special. But on her the perfume became something different, more tantalizing. He tore his gaze away from hers and studied the pale red of her hair. Strawberry blond? No, that wasn't right. Definitely red, but a lighter color. The thick blunt cut had begun to curl slightly, spoiling the smooth style. He could see the freckles on her nose and cheeks. He didn't like freckles. Never had. But he couldn't help wondering if they stopped at her chin or continued down farther toward her—

He wrenched his arm free of her light touch. Stop! he commanded himself. It had been too long since Ellen passed away. It wasn't Anne Baker, it was the fact that she was female. Dammit, it couldn't be her.

"Seven o'clock?"

"Seven o'clock," he said curtly, and turned to leave.

"Mr. Masters?"

He paused, his hand on the door.

"Do you have a picture?"

A simple request. Reasonable. But his irrational anger returned. He didn't want her to see what Laurel looked like. It was too much like giving in. That made no sense, he told himself, even as he knew it made perfect sense. He wanted to put off the inevitable as long as possible. Fate, and his teenage daughter, were forcing his hand.

He reached into his jeans pocket and pulled out his wallet. The front slot contained her seventh-grade school photo. Without looking at the sweet smiling face, he extracted the snapshot.

"Here." He half turned and thrust it out toward her.

Anne stepped forward and took it. He told himself to leave now, while she was occupied. He shouldn't watch this private moment. But he couldn't stop himself.

He stared at her small hand. It shook slightly. He raised his gaze. She stared down at the photo. Her lips trembled and her white teeth worried her lower lip.

A single tear fell on the picture. She carefully wiped it away. "She's very beautiful."

"Yes."

"She has my mother's eyes."

The simple statement caught him like a pistol shot. He grabbed his Stetson, then blindly reached for the door and yanked it open. He heard Anne call his name, but he didn't stop moving. Past the curious secretary, into the main foyer, then to the elevators. When the bank of doors remained stubbornly closed, he sprinted for the stairs and out toward the street.

Chapter Two

"What does she look like, Daddy?" Laurel practically skipped with impatience as they walked along the street.

Jake brushed her bangs out of her eyes. "You need a haircut."

"Da-ad!" Laurel shook her head. "You're avoiding the question. Is she pretty?"

He didn't want Anne Baker to be anything. Especially not important to his daughter. But it had already happened. Yesterday, Laurel had pounced on him when he'd returned to their hotel suite. He'd told her he'd met with her birth mother and that the three of them would be having dinner tonight. Now, walking along the wide street in front of Anne's high-rise condo, Laurel continued the barrage of questions that had flowed since the moment he'd announced the meeting.

"Does she look like me?"

He glanced down at his daughter's upturned face. She'd sprouted in the past couple of years, and almost reached his shoulder. Her hazel eyes, wide and framed with dark lashes, gazed up at him.

She has my mother's eyes.

Anne's phrase echoed over and over again in his mind, as it had since he'd escaped from her office. He didn't want the reminder that Laurel wasn't completely his. With her medium brown hair, easy smile and tall, lean body, there'd been enough physically to let him and Ellen pretend she was really theirs.

Now, he took his daughter's arm and tugged her to a stop. He cupped her face in his hands. He studied her wide full mouth and the dusting of freckles on her nose, then the dark hair hanging long and straight down her back.

He wanted to lie and say she and that strange woman had nothing in common. Only he'd never lied to his daughter. He wanted to tell her it didn't matter, but her determination told him it did.

"Do you look like her? A little I guess," he said. "Not so much your coloring, but other things. She said you have her mother's eyes."

As soon as he spoke the words he wanted to call them back. "You showed her my picture?"

He nodded.

Laurel's smile faded. "Did she like me?"

"I didn't discuss that with her. I left right after I gave her the photo." He bent down and kissed her forehead, then pulled her close for a hug. She was still young enough to allow the embrace, but he knew that in a year or two it wouldn't be cool to hug her dad in public. "She can't help but like you, Laurel."

"Promise?"

Those wide hazel eyes he'd always thought so beautiful stared into his. He watched the shifting colors of blue and green and brown and knew that he would never look at them again without hearing Anne Baker's words. Another woman had given her those eyes. Another family's blood coursed through his child's veins. Another—

He forced the thoughts away. "I promise," he said, squeezing her briefly, then releasing her. "Everything is going to work out."

As they approached the high rise, Laurel craned her neck to see to the top. "I wonder which floor she's on. Do you think she can see us?"

He shrugged and buzzed the button by the glass door.

"Hello?" a soft voice said.

Beside him, Laurel froze. "It's Jake Masters. I've brought—" He had to clear his throat. "My daughter is with me."

"Come in."

The door buzzed and he pulled it open. Laurel walked in beside him. When they stood in front of the elevators, she reached for the button and pushed.

"Do I look all right?" she asked, glancing down at her dress, then up at him.

It had taken her the better part of the day to choose her outfit. Last night, after he'd told her about meeting Anne, Laurel had insisted on going shopping to find something to wear. The huge Galleria was just off their hotel. She'd tried on dozens of outfits, only to reject them all and decide on something she'd brought with her.

He'd hated to see her so frantic to please, but told himself she was only a little girl. Her desire to make a good impression was natural under the circumstances. Yet it didn't feel natural, he thought as he gave her a quick smile.

"You look terrific."

"Thanks." She smoothed the skirt of her green dress. The drop waist made her look taller. There weren't any sleeves, but a ruffle began on each side, above her waist, and went up over her shoulders and down the back. A matching headband held her hair away from her face. Small gold earrings glittered from her ears. They'd had an ongoing fight about makeup; he wanted her to wait until she was twenty-five and she wanted to wear it all today. Their compromise showed in the pale gloss on her lips.

When the elevator doors opened, he stepped inside. Laurel hesitated. He had to push the button to hold the doors open.

"Laurel?"

She shifted her weight from one leg to the other. Her mobile mouth straightened, then one side tilted down.

"I'm scared."

"We can leave, if you'd like." Oh, God, had he sounded too eager?

She didn't notice. "No. I want to meet her. It's just—" She shrugged and stepped inside.

As the elevator began to rise, Laurel slipped her hand in his. The warmth of her small hand and the trust behind the gesture eased the knot in his chest.

She watched the flashing numbers above the door. When the light reached fifteen, the elevator stopped. They walked out into a long hallway.

Anne's door was on the end. It would have a perfect view of the city, he thought as he reached up to push the bell. It sounded loud in the silence.

Laurel squeezed his hand tightly, as if she'd never let go. "I love you, Daddy."

"And I love you."

The door opened.

Anne stared at the tall man and the young woman beside him. She wasn't sure what to expect. Nerves had kept her stomach jumping all day and she hadn't been able to form a coherent thought since noon. She offered Jake a quick smile and wasn't surprised when he didn't return it. The man didn't like her, but that was the least of her problems. She drew in a breath and turned to the teenager.

"Hello, Laurel."

Even prettier in person, she thought with pleased surprise. A couple of inches shorter than her own five foot four, her daughter stood stiffly at her father's side, her hand holding on to his. Anne could see the white around her knuckles and the worry in her hazel eyes. Her mother's eyes.

She'd studied the picture for hours last night, searching for something of herself in the snapshot. She had found it in the way Laurel held her head as she looked at the camera.

Laurel gave her a smile that faded quickly. "Hi."

Anne fought the urge to pull her close and hug her. Laurel was obviously nervous. They all were. But none of that mattered. Her child, *her* beautiful child. The thought echoed over and over until she was afraid she would say it aloud. After all this time, she could see her and speak to her. It was more than she'd dared to dream.

"Come in, please." Anne stepped back and searched her mind for small talk. "Did you find the building easily?"

"Yes," Jake said curtly. He held on to his daughter's hand as if he had no intention of letting go.

The trio paused awkwardly in the foyer of the two-bedroom condo, then Anne ushered them toward the living room. At 7:00 p.m. in August, the sun was just beginning to slip below the horizon. Heat and haze created a shimmering blanket that separated the light into all the colors of a kaleidoscope. She'd opened the blinds, but left the sheers closed to diffuse the glare.

She glanced around her decorated living room and wondered how it looked to Jake Masters and Laurel. As she waved them toward the overstuffed white sofa, Laurel at last released her father's hand and stepped past him to one end of the sofa. She perched on the edge of a cushion. Jake walked over to the window and stood in front of it, a trick he'd used on their previous meeting to hide his expression from view. Anne hovered uncertainly, wondering what she was supposed to say. Part of her had foolishly hoped to be welcomed with open arms. She held in a sigh. It was too soon.

"Would anyone—"

"This is—"

Anne and Laurel spoke at the same time. Awkward silence followed.

"Would you like anything to drink?" Anne asked.

"A soda, please."

Anne looked at Jake. He shook his head. She walked toward the wet bar in the corner of the living room. After filling a glass with ice, she opened the small refrigerator. "What kind?"

Laurel glanced at her father. When he didn't say or do anything, she rose slowly and approached the wet bar. She offered Anne a shy smile and pointed at the red-and-white can. "That one, please."

"Sure." Anne poured the drink and handed her a glass. "You're very polite."

"Thank you. My mom—" Laurel stopped talking and took a sip of her drink.

Anne felt the flash of pain deep inside, then told herself she was being foolish. Laurel was right. The other woman—Ellen Masters—*had* been her mother. Ellen might not have given birth to the girl, but in every other way, she'd been her mother.

"Yes," Anne encouraged. "Your mother what?"

Laurel shrugged. "She always made me say things like please and thank you. You know, dumb stuff like that."

Anne studied the teenager. In her green dress with her dark hair swirling around her face, she looked more like a changeling than a young lady. All long legs and big eyes. She would grow to be a beauty. And she was *here*. Close enough to see and hear and touch.

Laurel looked around the living room. "This is nice," she said. "I like the white. Do you like it, Dad?"

"It's very nice."

He sounded thrilled, Anne thought sarcastically, then glanced at the bleached wood floor and white overstuffed furniture. "I had a decorator do it. I was so busy at work that I never got around to unpacking boxes after I moved. As much as I love decorating, I never found the time. Finally I gave up and called someone to get the place together for me."

"We just moved," Laurel said, then took a sip of her drink. She ran her fingers along the metal sink. "I haven't finished unpacking. We don't have a lot of furniture yet." She shifted her weight from foot to foot.

Compassion flared in Anne. She wanted to make the teenager comfortable. She leaned toward her slightly. "It's not much fun, is it?"

"No." Her expression brightened then, and she grinned. "I have a horse. I mean, I've always had a horse, but now I take care of her. I'd rather be riding or reading than unpacking—" The grin faded. "But there's not much else to do. I used to spend a lot of time talking with my friends, but they're so far away."

"Where do you live?"

"Colorado. It's pretty, but—"

"It's not home," Anne said.

"Yeah." Laurel looked surprised. "How'd you know?"

"I left home once."

Those hazel eyes so like her own mother's met and held hers. "You ever go back?"

Anne shook her head. "Just to visit sometimes. I live here now."

"I'm going back." Laurel darted a glance at her father. Anne suspected the girl was trying to look defiant, but only succeeded in appearing young and lonely.

"I'm sure you'll make new friends," Anne said.

"Maybe. But they won't be the same."

"Different doesn't mean they won't be as much fun."

Laurel didn't look convinced. Jake stepped away from his place by the window and approached the wet bar. Anne looked up at him, then quickly turned away. The anger flaring in his eyes was hot enough to burn wood. He stopped behind his daughter and rested his hands on her shoulders. The possessive signal came in loud and clear. He didn't want or need her running interference with his child.

Anne tilted her chin up a notch. She refused to be intimidated by the likes of him. But the sensation of her heart's rapid pounding told her that as with Laurel's attempt at defiance, her bravado was only a facade. Still, *he* didn't have to know that.

"Would you like a glass of wine?" she asked.

He nodded. Despite his obvious ill temper and combative stance, he was, Anne had to admit, attractive. Perhaps not the hunk Heather had claimed, but certainly a man easy to look at. Yesterday, she'd noticed his appearance, but simply as a collection of features. Now she saw his sharp cheekbones and strong jawline made him look aristocratic. His well-shaped mouth that had yet to smile in her presence suggested a sensual nature, although she didn't want to think about that. He wore his brown hair short, not touching the collar of his pale blue shirt. New jeans skimmed over slim hips and hinted at muscular thighs concealed by the denim. All in all, a very impressive package. He'd left the Stetson home tonight so no shadows diffused the intensity of his gaze. She shook her head and fought the urge to sigh. A cowboy. Just her luck.

She managed to open the bottle and pour without spilling more than a drop or two. When she handed him the glass, he took it carefully, as if he were trying to make sure they didn't touch. The tension between them was obvious. Anne glanced down at Laurel. The girl stared up at her.

"Do I pass inspection?" Anne asked, forcing herself to speak with a teasing tone.

Laurel smiled slowly and nodded. "I wondered what you would look like. Sometimes I'd like stare in the mirror and think about if we had the same hair or something. Daddy says I have your mother's eyes."

"That's true. You and I both have freckles."

Laurel wrinkled her nose. "Do you hate them, too?"

"All my life." Anne grinned, then walked over to the entertainment unit and picked up the small photo she'd been given the day before. "I think you and I have the same smile."

Laurel moved to her side and glanced down. "Really?"

"Yes." Anne could feel the teenager's warm arm casually brushing hers. She wanted to pull her close and hold on forever. She forced herself to act calmly, all the while fighting new and wonderful maternal urges.

Laurel looked at her. "You have to smile now so I can see if we do."

Anne laughed.

"Gee, you're right." Delight flashed in her eyes. She sipped her soda. "I can't wait to call my friends and tell them about meeting you."

Anne caught her breath. This moment, more perfect than she had ever imagined, made her want to cry out with gratitude. She'd never thought she might actually meet the child she'd given up all those years ago. She'd never allowed herself to do much more than mourn. Of course she'd left information available so that Laurel could find her. But she'd half feared her child wouldn't be interested in her birth mother. She'd never thought she'd be with Laurel any sooner than her eighteenth birthday.

Laurel looked at her father. "What do you think, Dad? Same smile?"

"I see the similarity." His words sounded stiff.

"Similarity." Laurel chuckled. "I know that one, but he's always using big words to improve my vocabulary." She shook her head. "I have to ask him what they mean and he tells me to look them up in the dictionary. But I can't spell the words enough to find them, and I *never* learn what they mean." She rolled her eyes.

Anne returned her conspiratorial grin, then made the mistake of glancing at Jake. He stood beside the wet bar, clutching the glass of wine so tightly she feared he would snap the delicate stem. Their gazes locked and his cold rage threatened to freeze her into oblivion. His intensity shocked her and her laughter died. She fought the urge to step closer to Laurel and protect her from her father's wrath. She understood his need to stake his claim, even as she resented his selfishness. Would it be too much to ask him to share her for an hour?

"I should see about dinner," she said, then ducked into the kitchen.

Once alone, she pressed her hands against her flushed cheeks. She didn't want to know that this was difficult for Jake Masters. Just thinking about his assumption that she would expect to be paid to see her own daughter made her want to march right back into the living room and tell him to leave.

But she couldn't. Partly because she *had* taken the money they'd offered thirteen years ago. Even knowing that she'd had every right to accept the payment and that she had needed it to pay her medical bills didn't stop the feeling of shame.

Anne checked the oven. Despite the summer heat, she'd chosen to make a roast. The built-in rotisserie made the entrée foolproof, and the way her apprehension had shattered her concentration, she'd been concerned she wouldn't be able to handle anything more complicated. The meat was almost ready. She sniffed the pleasing scent and closed the door.

From the refrigerator, she pulled out green salad and the vegetables she wanted to steam. She'd already prepared her mother's famous potatoes and had them simmering on the back of the stove. After putting the vegetables into a pot, she walked into the dining room and set the salad in the middle of the table, then returned to the living room.

Jake stood by the window again, staring out at the view. She wondered what he was thinking. Laurel bounced up from her perch on the sofa.

"You don't need any help in the kitchen, do you?" she asked, obviously hoping for a refusal.

"It will just be a few more minutes," Anne answered. "I have it all under control. But thanks for asking."

Laurel looked at her father as if to show him she'd done as he requested, then turned back to Anne. "It sure smells good. Back home—Dallas, I mean, not where we live now—we had a housekeeper who did the cooking. She was okay, but she wouldn't fix any good stuff. You know, like cookies. My mom—" Laurel suddenly stopped talking and stared at her empty glass.

Anne drew in a breath to fight the unexpected tightness in her chest. Silence filled the room. Laurel fidgeted. Damn. She was obviously uncomfortable. This was difficult for all of them, but as the child, Laurel was the least equipped to handle the situation. Anne glanced at Jake, but he had his back to them. Apparently she was on her own. She took Laurel's glass and walked over to the wet bar. The teenager trailed along behind.

"Ellen Masters was your mother in every sense of the word," Anne said as she popped the top on another can of soda. "I don't mind if you talk about her."

She handed the girl her drink. They looked at each other. Pain flashed through Anne as she stared at eyes so much like her mother's. The older woman had been gone eleven years, but she still missed her. Laurel must feel even worse about Ellen. "I know that you loved your mother very much," she said.

Laurel blinked in surprise.

Anne perched on the end table between the sofa and the wet bar. The teenager took a step closer. Anne drew in a deep breath, then reached forward and briefly touched the girl's arm.

"I'd like us to be friends, Laurel," Anne said. "We don't know each other very well so we're both going to say things that make us feel funny. I think we should keep trying until we get it right. What about you?"

"Okay." Laurel gave her a quick smile, then took a sip of her soda. "I'm glad you're not mad or anything. I don't talk about her much, but sometimes things just kinda slip out." She darted a glance at her father. Her voice dropped to an audible whisper. "Daddy gets upset if I talk about her."

Anne followed Laurel's gaze. Jake Masters remained in front of the window, staring out at the city. The sun had slipped below the horizon and lights twinkled all around. With his hands shoved into his pants pockets and his legs braced, he seemed more conquering hero than mere visitor in her home. At his daughter's words, his shoulder's tightened, but he didn't turn around or otherwise acknowledge that he'd heard the confession.

Anne decided it was best to return to a safe topic of conversation. "I'm not much of a cook," she said. "I don't get home from work before seven, and by then it's so late that I don't want to bother."

"Mom cooks—" Laurel glanced at her father and worried her bottom lip. Then she took a deep breath and spoke very quickly. "My mom *used* to cook a lot. She made special things. You know, like gourmet foods? I didn't like all of it, but it was fun to try. There used to be parties with lots of people and I'd help sometimes. Once for my birthday, my mom decorated a cake with—"

"Laurel, I'm sure Ms. Baker doesn't want to hear this," Jake Masters said, without bothering to turn around.

"But, I—"

"Laurel." The tone of his voice made even Anne sit up and take notice.

The girl shrugged. More silence. Anne searched her mind for a topic of conversation. She didn't know very much about teenagers. Most of her friends had chosen the career path rather than marrying and having children. A few had recently changed their minds, but they were still in the pregnant stage or had infants and toddlers. Her cousin, Becky Sue, had teenagers, but Anne couldn't ask her for advice without getting a lot of questions in return. Questions she wasn't ready to answer. Anne didn't watch much TV, and she had a feeling her taste in music and movies was light-years away from the girl's.

In the kitchen, a timer rang. Anne sprang to her feet and raced toward the other room. "Dinner is almost ready," she said. "I'll be right back."

But her escape was short-lived. Laurel followed her into the kitchen and leaned against one of the counters. Like the other rooms in the condo, this one had been professionally decorated and the predominant color was white. The counters, floors and appliances gleamed. Copper pots provided contrast, while the bleached wood cabinets softened any glare.

Laurel watched with interest as she poured the steamed vegetables into a serving bowl. "Daddy called you Ms. Baker."

"I know."

Anne thought she was lucky that was all he'd called her. His distrust and anger radiated like a giant beacon, circling through the room and lighting up all the corners. She felt so exposed having him in her house. It was difficult to act normally knowing he sat in judgment of every word she said. She half expected him to decide that she was an inappropriate role model and march his daughter out of her presence. If it were up to him, there never would have been a meeting at all.

Anne looked at the young woman glancing around the room. Curiosity brightened her hazel eyes, turning the multicolored irises more green. Long brown hair bounced and swung with each turn of her head. So alive, Anne thought. Bright and pretty and interested in everything. Pride swelled within her. She savored the sensation before allowing her practical nature to firmly squash it. Laurel was her child by birth, but not by environment. She had no justification for her pride; she'd done nothing to earn it. And yet—

She stuck a serving spoon into the bowl of vegetables and handed the container to Laurel. "Put this on the table, please. Through there." She motioned to the dining room, off the opposite end of the kitchen.

And yet, she didn't want to lose her. Not after just meeting her. One meeting, Jake had said. But was that Laurel speaking or was it his own agenda?

Laurel returned. "Should I call you 'Ms. Baker'?"

"My name is Anne," she said.

"Anne," Laurel repeated. "Okay." She said it again. "Does anyone call you Annie?"

Anne smiled. "My mother used to. My cousin still does. Just family members I guess."

Laurel propped her elbows on the center island and rested her chin in her hands. "Can I call you Annie?"

"It's 'may I.' Not 'can I.'"

Anne hadn't heard Jake enter the kitchen, but he stood just inside the room, leaning against the cabinets.

Laurel straightened. "*May* I call you Annie?"

Anne hoped she didn't look as flustered as she felt. She understood that Jake wouldn't want her to be alone with his child for too long. Heaven knows what sort of corrupting influence she could be in two or three minutes. But did he have to be so obvious about it?

"I'd like that, Laurel." She thought about telling Jake Masters he could continue to call her "Ms. Baker," but figured he wouldn't appreciate her minor attempt at humor. "Here. The potatoes are ready to go into the dining room. Then if you'd like to wash your hands, the powder room is down the hall on the right."

"Be right back."

Laurel moved forward and picked up the dish. As soon as the swinging door closed behind her, Jake straightened. "You're handling this very well."

Anne pulled open the stove and shut off the rotisserie. "If anyone else were saying that, I'd think it was a compliment."

"It's not?"

She slid the rack out toward her, then began to move the heavy roasting pan closer to the edge. "I know it's not. You made your decision about me thirteen years ago. There's nothing I can do to change your mind." She lifted the pan and placed it on the counter. She stepped back and glanced up at him. The bright overhead lights caught the gold flecks in his brown eyes. She'd been right. Anger flared there, right alongside distrust and a few other emotions she didn't want to name.

"My main concern is Laurel."

"That much is obvious."

He raised his eyebrows, as if surprised she'd admit that.

"Oh, you don't make it *easy* to dislike you, Mr. Masters. You're judging me based on some very out-of-date information. Even this minute you're standing over me waiting to pounce in case I say something inappropriate." She tossed her oven mitts onto the counter and rubbed her hands on her silk trousers. "Your only saving grace is that you obviously love Laurel very much." She took another step back.

"Look out!" he said. "The oven is open."

He leapt forward and grabbed her arms, jerking her hard against him. One of her hands got caught between their bodies and she felt the cold metal of his belt buckle. Her breasts flattened against his hard chest. His thighs brushed hers. Their breath mingled as she exhaled sharply with the impact.

"What are you—?"

Their gazes locked. Something dark and hungry flared to life in his eyes, and the flames turned the flecks of gold almost iridescent. The fingers holding her arms tightened their grip. It hurt and she told herself to pull away but she couldn't. Whatever had exploded in him sparked a response deep within her body. The need, the want, raced through her like a fire storm consuming dry brush. Everywhere they touched—his hand on her arm, her breasts mashed against his chest, their legs trembling against each other—electricity arced. The scent of his body—clean, masculine, he was not a man to wear cologne—made her wonder what he would taste like if she were to kiss him.

"Oh, my God." Gathering the last of her rapidly dwindling strength, she slipped free of him and leaned against the counter. The cool tile contrasted with her overheated body. They were both breathing heavily, as if they'd run five miles.

As if they had kissed.

Kissed. Involuntarily, she licked her lower lip. His mouth pulled into a straight line. No, she cried silently. Not him. Not now. Not like this. She swallowed and forced her eyes closed. Only then was she able to break the spell.

"You almost stepped into the open oven door," he said. She opened her eyes. He pointed. "You would have been burned."

She shook her head to clear it. "Thank you," she murmured. "I appreciate what you..." Her voice trailed off as she looked up at him. The fire continued to burn inside him, but the heat of flames had changed from desire to hate.

She saw the contempt steal across his expression. He blamed her for that moment between them. He thought she'd done it on purpose.

"Everything smells so great," Laurel said as she entered the kitchen. "When do we eat?"

Her presence dispelled the last of the tension between them. Anne turned her back on Jake. It didn't matter what he thought of her, she told herself. This night was about Laurel, and not about the handsome stranger who had adopted her.

Chapter Three

"The beach house is really big, with lots of windows and stuff. We lay around by the ocean. My dad and great-uncle go fishing sometimes, and my great-aunt takes me shopping." Laurel paused long enough to take another bite of potatoes.

"Sounds lovely," Anne said.

Jake remained silent. Anne told herself she shouldn't be surprised. He'd been nothing but silent since they'd sat down to eat almost an hour before. Laurel had chattered on about school and the friends she'd left behind in Dallas. Anne had explained a little about her job, but Jake hadn't said a word.

"We'll spend a week there," Laurel said after she'd wiped her mouth with her napkin. Her smile faded. "Then we're going back to Colorado."

"You make it sound like you're going back to prison," Anne teased.

"Worse. At least in prison you get time off for good behavior." Laurel stared at her plate.

Anne toyed with her wineglass. "I think you might surprise yourself," she said at last. "And you do have that great week by the beach."

"Do you like the ocean?"

"Sure. I love the smell of the salt water, and seeing all the people on the sand." She wrinkled her nose. "Hot dogs always taste the best on the beach, don't you think?"

Laurel laughed. "Yeah. And ice-cream sandwiches. At home, I never eat them, but there—" she shrugged "—I get one every day." Her hazel eyes widened and she turned to her father. "Daddy, can Annie come with us for a couple of days? You said I could bring a friend."

Anne was glad she'd spent the evening toying with her wineglass rather than drinking from it. If she'd been swallowing at that moment, she would have choked. She looked at Jake.

His tanned skin darkened, and his mouth pulled even straighter. She hadn't known it was possible for a man to look completely furious and devastatingly handsome at the same time. She clenched her hands into fists and waited for the explosion. Laurel stared hopefully, never realizing what she asked.

"I don't think that would be a good idea," he said, calmly.

Anne didn't know she'd been holding her breath until she exhaled it in a loud rush.

"But why?" Laurel asked. "They've got extra bedrooms. You *said* I could bring someone."

"No."

The teenager sprang to her feet. Her brown hair swirled around her face and she brushed it back impatiently. "You're *always* like this. I never get to do anything I want. You *always* decide. I didn't want to move. I didn't want to leave my friends behind. You say it's for me, but it's *al-*

ways what's easiest for you." Laurel threw her napkin on the table and stormed out of the room. There were a few seconds of silence, then Anne flinched as she heard the bathroom door slam shut.

"I'm sorry," she said softly. "I didn't mean to start anything."

"Yeah, I'll bet." He stood up. "It takes her about five minutes to cool down, then she'll be out. I'd appreciate it if you wouldn't encourage her. We're spending the week with Ellen's aunt and uncle. I don't think they would understand if you came along." With that, he turned and left the room.

Jake was off by two minutes, but Laurel did finally emerge from the rest room. Her eyes were puffy and her face blotchy, but other than that, she seemed to have recovered from her outburst.

"I'm sorry," she said as she walked into the kitchen.

Anne put the last plate into the dishwasher. "It's okay, Laurel, but I'm not the one you hurt."

"I know. It's just he's so—" She scuffed her white flats against the wood floor. "He makes me so mad, sometimes. He doesn't understand."

"Maybe you don't understand so well, either."

Laurel looked at her. "You think so?"

"He's your father. He loves you."

The mouth so much like her own tilted slightly at one corner. "Then why's he always telling me what to do?"

"That's what dads are for. He's doing what he thinks is best." She looked at the young woman who, except for a decision made thirteen years ago, could have been hers. Funny, she would have thought she'd give up missing her a long time ago. She'd been wrong. "From where I stand, he's doing a fine job."

"Thank you." Laurel flushed at the compliment. "Maybe I should go tell him I'm sorry."

"Maybe you should." Anne wiped her hands on the dish towel and gave the girl a gentle push toward the door. "Now is a good time."

"I can't."

"You can. I know you can." Anne held open the door.

Jake had returned to stare out the window. At the sound of her voice, he turned and looked at them. She'd lived in her condo long enough to know that noise and conversations traveled fairly easily from the kitchen to the living room and that he'd probably heard everything they'd said. Not by a flicker of his thick lashes did he give that away. He stood, waiting. Laurel hovered by the door.

Anne gave her another nudge. The girl stepped forward. "I'm sorry, Daddy." Then she flew across the room and into her father's embrace.

Jake pulled his daughter close and held her tightly against him. "I know, sweetie."

From her place in the doorway to the kitchen, Anne looked at the two of them. Jake knew he should be grateful that she'd been so generous with his child, but he couldn't bring himself to say anything. She stared at him, at the way he held Laurel, with all the intensity of a starving person staring at bread. He read the hunger in her eyes, and the loneliness.

Laurel stepped away and gave him a brilliant smile. He forced himself to return it. When he looked up, Anne had returned to the kitchen.

Damn. He didn't want to like her. He sure as hell didn't want to feel sorry for her. And he certainly didn't want to remember what had happened that moment when he'd pulled her away from the stove.

"It's late," he said. "We should probably be going."

Laurel looked like she was about to protest, then seemed to think better of it. "Okay. When can I see Annie again?"

He should have been prepared. All the signs had been there. But he'd pretended that it would only happen this one time. Refusing another meeting was the best solution for all of them, but he couldn't. Not only because Laurel would fight him, but because he couldn't tell her why she couldn't see Anne Baker. He didn't trust the woman, but more than that, he didn't want to risk losing his daughter. Not when he'd just found her again. Neither of those reasons would make sense to Laurel. He had to decide what to do based on what was right for her, not what was easiest for him.

"We're leaving for the beach early in the morning," he said.

Laurel nodded. "I know Annie can't come with us to the beach, but I have to see her again, Dad. She's my birth mother."

That fact had haunted him ever since Laurel had first said the words. As long as he lived, he'd never forget the slash of pain when she'd told him she wanted to contact her "real" mother. He was grateful Ellen hadn't ever heard Laurel say those things.

"Can't we stop before we go back to Colorado? Just for a couple of days." Hazel eyes pleaded.

"One day. We'll stay overnight, then head back home."

"Thanks, Daddy." She reached up and kissed his cheek, then scurried toward the kitchen. "Annie, Annie."

Anne came out of the kitchen. She looked from the teenager to him and back. He tried not to notice how the pale peach silk shirt she wore brought out the color in her cheeks and darkened her hair to a more auburn shade of red. He looked away from the hopeful expression in her pale blue eyes, and the way her hands balled into fists at her side. If he'd been able to hear her conversation with his daughter when they'd been in the kitchen, it stood to reason she'd heard what Laurel had said. But she still looked nervous, as if she was afraid he would take it all away.

"We're coming back to Houston after our week at the beach," Laurel said, bouncing from foot to foot. "I can see you again." She became very still. "If you want to."

Anne smiled. "Of course I do, Laurel. I'd like very much to see you again."

"Great."

"We need to get going," he said. "It's late and we have to get up early tomorrow."

"Okay." Laurel hesitated, then ducked toward Anne.

Jake forced himself to watch the two women embrace. He saw Anne's eyes close as emotions chased across her face. He saw the tender smile, the brief kiss on the cheek, heard the promise to not forget their plans. He saw Anne scrawl her phone number down, Laurel take it and stuff it into her pocket. He saw his daughter approach him, happiness shining so brightly from her face, it almost blinded him. He saw it all and knew that he was close to losing everything to a woman whom he didn't like, or trust.

"Wait for me by the elevator," he told his daughter.

She waved once, then disappeared out the front door. Anne stared after her.

"You can be busy," he said.

Anne stared at him. "I don't understand."

"When she calls you don't have to see her if you're not interested."

A spot of color flared on each cheek. "I *want* to see Laurel again."

He shoved his hands into his pockets to make sure he didn't give in to the temptation to strangle her, then moved forward until he was directly in front of her. The kitchen door prevented her from backing up, although she didn't seem inclined to give any ground. The soft light from the lamps made her freckles stand out. He stared at the random pattern and told himself he'd always hated freckles.

"Why do you care?" he asked. "If Laurel is so damn important to you, why did you give her up in the first place?"

He might as well have slapped her. The color drained from her face and her eyes widened with disbelief.

"That's none of your business," she said, her voice low and angry.

"If it's about my daughter, it's my business."

"Get out!" She pointed to the door.

"If I leave now, I'm never coming back."

She parted her lips to draw in a breath of air. He didn't like the man he'd become these past few days. He was beginning to believe that Anne Baker's pain was as real to her as his was to him. He almost wanted to take it all back. But he couldn't. Laurel was his responsibility. The bottom line was this woman had once given her child away. Who was to say she wouldn't get involved with Laurel, only to dump her a second time when the relationship became inconvenient?

"What do you want to know?" Anne asked, her voice resigned.

"Why did you give her up, and why do you want anything to do with her now?"

She seemed to collect herself. The color returned to her face and this time she was the one to step closer. Less than a foot separated them. She had to lean back to look him in the eye.

"You're quite a bastard, Jake, aren't you?" She folded her arms over her chest. "You can threaten me all you want. You're the one holding all the cards anyway. I can't make you let Laurel see me. There's nothing I can say to explain my actions to you. There's nothing to justify what I did. You've already passed judgment on me. If I'd known the name of the family adopting my daughter, I would have gotten in touch with them, with you, right away. I didn't know. Not a day went by that I didn't hope and pray Laurel would want to follow the trail I'd left and find me." She walked to the front door and gripped the knob. "You go ahead and believe what you want. Just don't be too surprised when you find out you were wrong."

With that, she swung the door open. Laurel stood in the doorway. "Dad, the elevator's come and gone. I thought you said we were in a hurry."

He stared at Anne. From the rapid rise and fall of her chest, he could see that she was still furious.

He brushed past her as he walked through the door. Sparks flew between them, sending liquid need pouring through his blood. He gritted his teeth and kept walking. Behind him, he heard Laurel say goodbye again and promise to call. As the elevator doors opened, he swore Laurel would never have any contact with that woman again.

"Then we need to see to the executive homes. I think three should be—" Anne put down the papers she was holding and glanced at Heather. Her assistant continued smiling. "Why are you grinning at me like that? Do I have lipstick on my teeth?"

Heather shook her head. "You gave me this information two hours ago, Anne. What *is* the matter with you?"

Anne groaned. "My concentration is completely gone. The RCR Company relocation committee will be here at the end of the week and I'm not even close to prepared."

Heather leaned forward from the seat opposite Anne's desk. "Man trouble?"

"Don't sound so excited. No, it's not man trouble. At least not the way you mean it." She pushed her chair away from the desk and slumped against the back. "Laurel called me again last night." In spite of herself she smiled. "Told me all about this movie she'd seen. Boy meets girl. Girl turns out to be a vampire. They don't make movies like they used to."

Heather tilted her head and frowned. "But if your daughter is calling you every other night, what's the problem? I thought you wanted to stay in touch with her."

"I do. I love hearing from her. We talk about movies and clothes and she tells me everything she's doing." Anne picked up a pen and fiddled with it. Just thinking about Laurel was enough to give her a warm feeling inside. She wasn't sure if it was genes or the way she'd been raised or both, but Laurel had turned out to be a fun, sweet, charming young woman. Their phone conversations were equal parts pleasure and pain. Pleasure at the relationship they were building and pain at what she'd missed all these years. "It's not her, it's her father. He doesn't trust me. The worst of it is, I almost don't blame him. If she were my child—"

"Isn't she?"

"Good question. I've been wrestling with the same one for almost a week and I still don't have an answer. All I did was give birth. Jake and his wife raised her."

"So where does that leave you?" Heather asked.

"Confused."

"What are you going to do?"

Anne tossed the pen back on the desk. "The only thing I can do. Keep working on the RCR bid. Try not to let the situation destroy my job performance."

Heather placed her hands on the desk. "When Wilson retires in four months, you're right in line for the vice presidency."

Anne nodded. "I know. If I can get RCR to sign, I've got the promotion. If not, Tim the Turkey gets it." She jerked her thumb to the office next door. "He's always hated the fact that I've done better than him and I'm just a woman."

Heather chuckled. "That does make him cranky, doesn't it? I'll go get you the figures for the RCR project."

"Thanks."

"When do you see Laurel again?"

"Day after tomorrow. I'm hoping Jake will have cooled off enough so that I can arrange to visit her in Colorado from time to time. I'd like to stay in touch. She's important to me."

"Sounds like everything is going to work out."

"I hope so." Anne shrugged. "I wish I knew how much of her wanting to be with me is because she needs a mother figure in her life and how much of it is to get back at her father. If I get too involved before I figure out the situation, I could really get hurt. I want a second chance with Laurel, but I'm not sure how reasonable that is. Or if I even deserve one." She rose to her feet and straightened her white linen jacket. "I know that my real life is here, with the company. Work is the only thing I can count on. I'm so close to that promotion, I can't afford to let it go."

Heather looked at her. "You've got it under control."

"It only looks that way." Anne smiled. "Still, I'm going to keep pretending I know what I'm doing until I figure it out."

"I think denim is going to be very hot this year," Laurel said as she fingered the cropped jacket.

Anne looked at the price tag and winced. "This isn't very practical, honey. It snows in Colorado and this isn't even lined."

Laurel grimaced. "Now you sound like my dad."

"Maybe your dad has a point."

Jake didn't bother entering the discussion. He didn't like shopping and given a choice, he would have stayed in the hotel bar and watched the football game on the big screen TV. But Laurel wanted to go shopping with Anne, as part of their day together. He was determined not to let the two of them spend any time alone. He wasn't concerned about Anne kidnapping the girl, or anything that extreme, it was more an issue of trust. Or lack of trust.

After the way they'd parted company a week ago, he'd expected Anne Baker to be uncivil, or at the very least, ignore him. She'd done neither. Except for a slight tension in her body and the way she paused before speaking, as if considering her words carefully, she'd treated him as if they were old acquaintances. She included him in the conversation, spoke highly of him to his daughter and consulted him on every clothing purchase. It was driving him crazy.

"But it won't be cold during the day. Not for a couple of months. And I'll be taking the bus to school, so I won't need a warm coat. Besides—" Laurel pulled the jacket off the hanger, "—it goes great with that skirt we saw at the other store."

"The one that's too short?" Anne asked.

"I'm thirteen."

Anne grinned. "That doesn't make the skirt any longer."

"But it's in style."

"But you're still not buying it."

Laurel looked mutinous. "I'm the one who has to wear these clothes to school. You probably don't even own one denim skirt."

"True, but if I did, it would be bigger than a bandage." She touched Laurel on the nose. "Give in graciously. It's easier for all of us." Her smile remained teasing.

Laurel turned to him. "Da-ad."

He hated to agree with Anne, but he had no choice. He shook his head.

Laurel sighed heavily. "You guys have no sense of style."

"I know." Anne took her arm and steered her over to a selection of jeans. "How about something like this to go with the jacket?"

Laurel frowned. "You said it was impractical."

"Compromise."

"You're the best."

Laurel rose on her toes and kissed Anne's cheek. The older woman flushed with pleasure, then darted him a glance. "I hope you don't mind," she murmured.

He didn't know if she meant the jacket or the kiss, but it didn't matter. He was too busy trying to remember how to breathe again. Laurel had accepted Anne so easily.

The kicker of it all was that Anne was either a superb actress or not the bitch he'd thought her to be. In the last—he glanced at his watch—six hours, Laurel had run the gamut of her emotions. Anne had handled them all well. Not always easily, but well. Even the potential squawk about the short skirt had been averted by the judicious use of humor.

They came to a kiosk selling fudge. He bought three pieces and passed them out. The rich chocolate required drinks and by the time everyone had finished their snack, they were too tired to do more than sit on the level above the ice skaters and watch the antics below.

Anne picked up her purse. "I have to call the office," she said. "I'll be right back."

He watched her walk away. Laurel chatted on about clothes and accessories, but he didn't pay attention. He was mesmerized by the sway of Anne's hips and the way her tailored cotton trousers outlined her generous curves. The soft silky shirt she wore clung to her breasts and emphasized their fullness. So different from Ellen who'd had the height and figure of a fashion model.

He preferred long and lean to petite and curvy, he told himself. Besides, whatever it had been that had sparked between them was nothing more than nerves. They'd both been tense about that first meeting. Today, nothing like that had happened.

He leaned back on the bench and nodded at what Laurel was saying. Of course he'd been careful to never touch Anne, so his theory remained untested, but he was confident the problem had been solved.

"Oh, Dad, look at the girl down there." Laurel pointed to one of the skaters. The young girl jumped into a high turn, then landed and spun around several times. "She's so good. Can I go down and watch?"

Jake glanced around the rink, then nodded. "Stay by that bench there," he said. "No shopping."

"Okay." Laurel piled her purchases on the seat next to him. "I won't be long." She gave him a quick kiss, then hurried to the stairs. By the time Anne returned from making her call, Laurel had already found a seat in front of the skaters.

"Where's Laurel?" Anne asked.

"Down there." He pointed.

"Oh, aren't those kids incredible? I always wanted to learn how to skate but there wasn't an indoor rink where I grew up and we certainly never got cold enough weather to freeze a pond."

He shifted the packages and made room for her on the bench. Anne glanced anxiously from him to the seat, then carefully sat down on the far end. She held her purse on her lap. He could see the apprehension in her pale blue eyes. He didn't blame her; now that they were alone, he could feel his own concerns returning.

He shifted until he was facing her. "Everything all right at the office?"

She nodded.

Most of her lipstick was long gone. He studied her mouth, especially her full lower lip. The corners trembled, then curved up. He found himself smiling in return.

He raised one arm and rested it on the back of the bench. "What do you do?"

"I would have thought you'd have had me investigated."

He shrugged. "I did a little checking. I was mostly concerned about a criminal record."

The trembling stopped and she grinned. "Just from that bank robbery last year."

"So what do you do?"

"I work for a relocation firm. We help other companies move to the Houston area. We handle everything from permits to housing." She shifted toward the center of the bench, sliding one leg under the other. "Once I've signed a company, the whole team takes over to make the relocation flow smoothly." She moved her hands as she spoke and leaned forward. "There are all sort of details to be worked out."

"I can imagine."

Her eyes glittered with enthusiasm. "The hardest part is recruiting the company. A lot of them are moving out of the Northeast and California, but they don't all think of Houston as their first choice."

"You convince them?"

"I do my best. There's nothing like a little Texas hospitality to persuade the unbelievers." She raised her eyebrows. "Doesn't everyone want to live in Texas?"

He glanced down at the rink. Laurel perched on the edge of her seat and watched the skaters. "My daughter sure does."

"I know the move has been hard for both of you, but it'll get better."

"I'm not so sure."

"Once school starts and she makes a few friends, everything will change."

He rubbed the bridge of his nose. "I hope you're right. I couldn't take another summer like this one." He sensed she was about to start asking questions he didn't want to answer. "How long have you worked for the company?"

"Since I graduated from college. There's been a lot of opportunity for advancement. I'm up for a promotion. To vice president."

He glanced at her. Now, with her red hair curling to her shoulders, with the casual silky blouse draping the curves of her breasts, with most of her makeup worn away and a tentative smile tugging at her lips, she didn't look like anyone's example of an executive on the way up. But he remembered her cool confidence in her office, and the way she'd stood up to him. No doubt Anne Baker could play hardball with the best of them. And win.

"Good luck," he said sincerely. A hard-won promotion would keep her firmly located in the Houston area and away from his ranch in Colorado.

"Thanks." She moved her purse off her lap and onto the bench. One of the packages went sliding toward the ground. She grabbed it and set it back on the pile. "Do you think Laurel is going to need anything else?"

Jake eyed the bags. "I can't imagine anything, but I'm sure she'll think of something. I still have to buy her a decent jacket and some boots, but we'll do that back home."

Anne nodded. "I, um, I had a good time today. Thank you for letting her call me."

"Look..." Jake cleared his throat and glanced around at the crowds in the shopping center. Teenagers walked together in groups. Rich matrons clustered around the expensive boutiques and young women pushed strollers through the open walkways. Conversation filled the multistory center, but their bench, tucked in front of the railing overlooking the ice rink, offered an illusion of privacy. "About last week—" He cleared his throat again. He'd been thinking about it for days, but that didn't make saying it any easier. "I was out of line. You've been great with Laurel. You could have made me pay for some of the things I said, and you didn't. I appreciate that."

Instead of looking pleased, or at least superior, Anne surprised him by flushing and staring at her lap. "Don't thank me. I want to see her again."

Jake stiffened. "We're leaving in the morning."

"I know." The words came out as a whisper. "I can't let go. I've spent all these years wondering about her, and now, to have met her and spent time with her..." She drew in a breath. "She's wonderful."

"Yes, she is."

Anne leaned forward. Her hair swung out and shadowed her face. "I don't mean big visits. Not alternating weekends or anything. I understand that I have no legal rights, but maybe just a couple of days over Christmas break or in the summer. A phone call now and then. Just to stay in touch."

The fear deep inside him grew with each word. He wanted to grab Laurel and disappear into the crowd. He wanted to take back ever meeting this woman, ever letting Laurel know she'd been adopted. But he couldn't. Not for Anne, even though he was finding it harder and harder to hate her, but for Laurel. She would want the same thing Anne did. Laurel would want more.

He looked down at his daughter. She was talking to another girl her age and they were pointing at the skaters. As if she sensed his gaze, she looked up, smiled and then waved at him. He waved in return. He couldn't refuse her what she needed simply because he was afraid of losing her. But by God, he wanted to.

"I'll let Laurel call you," he said slowly, not looking at her. "I would appreciate it, however, if you didn't initiate the calls or talk about a visit. I believe it should be Laurel's decision."

"Yes, of course." Anne smiled brilliantly. Her pale blue eyes practically glowed with happiness. She tilted her head. "Why are you being so accommodating?"

"Do I have a choice?"

"I think so." She folded her arms over her chest. "Oh. I get it. You're hoping that by giving Laurel what she wants, she'll get tired of the whole thing. By taking away the forbidden, you eliminate one of the attractions."

"Maybe."

Her smile faded, and with it the light in her eyes. "You could be right."

"Look, Anne, don't take this personally."

"Hard to take it any other way." She shook her head. "Jake, I know you don't like me very much. I understand that. I even understand what you're doing and why. If Laurel was my daughter—" She stared at him for a second. "If I had raised Laurel, I'd probably be doing the same thing. That doesn't mean I have to like it."

It was a victory of sorts, and he could afford to be generous. "This isn't about you, Anne," he said.

"But if you had your way, I'd disappear from her life, never to be heard from again?"

He looked at her. "Do you want me to lie?"

"That answers the question."

"I guess it does. If it makes you feel any better, you've changed my opinion some."

Her delicate brows raised slightly. "For the better, I assume. You could hardly think worse of me."

Now it was his turn to feel a little uncomfortable. He resisted the urge to shuffle his feet. "Maybe if you'd robbed that bank."

"Right." She held out her hand. "Truce?"

"Truce." He reached out and engulfed her small fingers in his.

Immediately electricity shot up his arm, through his chest and down into his groin. He wanted to jerk his hand back, but that would mean admitting she affected him. Yeah, right, as if he was supposed to ignore the practically visible sparks flying between them.

Her smile faltered, then faded altogether. They stared at each other. Awareness flashed between them, and a growing horror that they were both experiencing the same physical reaction. He released her hand. She pulled her arm close to her chest and massaged her fingers as if they'd been burned.

This wasn't happening, he told himself. It couldn't be. Not with Anne Baker. Ellen had been gone two years. In all the time he'd been alone, hell in all the time he'd been married, he'd never felt like this with anyone. Never. Not even with Ellen.

"Jake, I—"

"Don't say a damn thing," he commanded. He turned until he was facing straight ahead and rested his elbows on his knees. It didn't make sense. It wasn't anything. Just weather, or static electricity or—

"I'm sorry," she said softly.

"There's nothing to be sorry about."

"Are you denying—?"

"Yes." It was, he decided, an aberration of nature. He didn't care for curvy women, he hated freckles, except for Laurel's, and had never been attracted to a redhead. He glanced at Anne. Her hair wasn't even red. It was a paler color.

She folded her arms over her chest. "Have it your way."

"Can you explain it?"

"No, but at least I'm willing to admit it exists."

Before he could answer, Laurel came up the stairs and walked over to them.

"How was the skating?" he asked, grateful for the interruption.

"Terrific." She spun in a circle. "I wish I could do that." When her turn was complete, she leaned against the railing and stared at him. "Dad, I've been thinking."

Ever since Laurel had mentioned wanting to find her birth mother, he'd been carrying around a knot in his gut. At her casual phrase, the knot tightened a notch.

"About?"

"I'm not ready to leave."

He glanced at his watch. "It's not even six. I thought we'd have dinner here before—"

She slowly shook her head. "I'm not ready to leave Houston."

He shot Anne a glance, but her confused expression told him this was as much of a surprise to her. "School is starting in a few days," he said. "We have to head back."

"I don't want to go back. I love you, Daddy, but I want to stay here. With Annie."

Chapter Four

Anne told herself to close her mouth. She could feel it hanging open. No doubt she looked as shocked as she felt. She couldn't move or speak. Good thing, because the malevolence in Jake's gaze was enough to send her running for cover. Laurel wanted to stay with her?

"Please don't be mad," Laurel said to her father and twisted her hands together.

"I'm not." The anger faded from his expression, leaving behind intense pain, then he blinked and there were no emotions at all. "What brought this on?"

"I just met Annie, and now we're going to leave." Laurel gave her a smile that quivered a little at the corners. "I know you have to go back because of the ranch and all, but I could stay. I could go to school here. I know you didn't like my friends back home, but I'd be getting new ones here. Just for a little while, Daddy. Just so I can spend some time with Annie." She spoke quickly as if she could convince her father by the volume and speed of her words.

Anne stared down at the pile of packages, then at the people walking by, and finally at Jake. She waited but he never jumped up and accused her of having planned this with his daughter. She was grateful for that. Laurel wanted to stay with her. She had to bite down hard on her lower lip to keep from grinning like a fool. Her daughter wanted to stay with her. It was a dream come true. Better than a dream because it was actually happening.

She glanced over at Jake and saw he was leaning back on the bench as if everything was fine. Her gaze dropped to his lap where his hands rested on his worn jeans. His fists were clenched so tightly, she thought his skin might split. Confusion, hurt and a desperate need radiated out from him. She could feel his emotions pounding against her like waves against the shore. Suddenly her own lighthearted joy began to fade. What would Laurel's staying do to Jake?

"Anne has a full-time job," he said, his voice low and controlled.

Work. Anne shook her head. She hadn't thought about that.

"So do you," Laurel said. She shifted until her feet were spread, then placed her hands on her hips. "Da-ad," she said, drawing the word out to two syllables. "I'm old enough to stay on my own until Annie gets home from work. I've done it before."

"It's more than just child care," Jake said. He ignored the way his daughter huffed at the phrase. "She probably goes to her office early and stays late. Who's going to take you to school? Cook your dinner? Help you with homework? What about your horse?"

What about me? He didn't ask that question, but Anne heard it all the same. What about him? What about her taking in a thirteen-year-old who she knew nothing about? The sense of responsibility overwhelmed her. Yet even as she thought of a hundred reasons why it was a bad idea, a part of her screamed *Yes, I want the chance to get to know my daughter.*

"Your father is right," Anne said, speaking for the first time since Laurel's announcement. "There are a lot of practical considerations."

"You have a spare bedroom," Laurel said. "I know. I checked when we were at your place for dinner." She looked pleadingly at Anne. "Don't you want me to be with you?"

"I—"

Jake cut her off. "Laurel, I've tried to explain why it's not possible for you to stay with Anne Baker. We're leaving for Colorado in the morning. End of discussion. Now finish your shopping or go up to the room. I don't want to hear any more about it."

The cold anger in his voice made Anne want to cower back against the bench, but Laurel was unaffected. She leaned closer to her father.

"I'm not going back with you," she said loudly. "You can't make me."

A couple of shoppers gave them odd looks, then hurried past.

"Dammit, Laurel." He rose to his feet. "Stop acting like a child."

"You just *said* I was a child. That I needed someone to take care of me after school." Tears threatened. "Annie, you want me to stay with you, don't you?"

Father and daughter turned to look at her. Brown eyes flecked with gold dared her to interfere and promised swift, angry retribution if she did. Big hazel eyes framed by thick lashes begged for a hint of caring and support. Slowly Anne rose to her feet. She told herself she was the stranger here, and it was up to her to remain calm. It wasn't easy. Part of her wanted to pull Laurel close and admit she would love the girl to stay with her. Part of her was practical and wondered what on earth she was going to do with a thirteen-year-old. And a small part of her, a piece of her heart, back in the place that was familiar with pain and loss, ached for Jake.

"Laurel, this isn't something we should be discussing right here and now. Let's go back to your room and we can—"

Laurel turned on her father. "You're making her say those things. I know you are. She *wants* me to stay with her. I know she does." Tears streamed down her face. She brushed them away impatiently. Several people stopped to stare.

"Laurel, he's not making me say anything."

"I don't need your help," Jake said, glaring at her. "You've done enough." He moved close to Laurel and put his arm around her shoulders.

She shrugged it off. "You're doing this on purpose, Dad. I know you are." Her voice caught. She sniffed and wiped her face again. "I know the truth. You didn't think I would figure it out, but I did. Annie loves me. She's always loved me. You stole me from her. She didn't want to let me go, but you made her. You and Mom." She stood stiffly, with her arms at her sides. Fresh tears flowed down her cheeks. Her skin was blotchy and her freckles stood out like painted dots.

Anne's heart went out to her. So much pain in one teenage child. They were all hurting in different ways.

Jake spun toward her. "Is this what you tell her when my back is turned? What the hell kind of lies are you—?"

"Don't talk to Annie that way," Laurel said, coming to stand in front of her father. "She didn't have to tell me. I figured it out on my own. You stole me from my birth mother."

The crowd around them was getting larger by the second. Anne felt a heated blush climbing her cheeks. She didn't like being the center of attention. She bent toward the bench and grabbed an armful of packages. "Here." She thrust them at Laurel. Quickly she picked up the rest, then slipped her purse strap up over her shoulder. "Can we please continue this upstairs in your hotel room?"

Jake glanced around as if just realizing the interested group hovering nearby. He took Laurel's arm and led her through the crowd toward the elevators. Anne followed behind.

The ride up to the room was accomplished in silence, except for Laurel's muted sniffs and the rustling of paper bags. Jake opened the hotel room door, then stepped inside. He walked over to the window overlooking downtown Houston and stood there, his back to the room.

Must be a favorite position of his, Anne thought, dropping her packages into a wing chair. Staring out into the great beyond like some cattle baron of the 1800s. Damn. Now what was she supposed to do?

Laurel let her bags fall to the floor. "Annie?" she said, then burst into tears.

Anne reacted without thinking. She opened her arms and, when Laurel threw herself against her, she hugged the girl close. "It's going to all work out," she said softly, hoping she wasn't lying.

"No, it's not," Laurel said between sobs, her voice muffled against Anne's shoulder. "It's not. He won't let me stay with you. But I have to." She raised her head. Those familiar hazel eyes, her own mother's eyes, stared back at Anne. "Don't let him take me away *again.* Please."

"Oh, baby." Anne brushed her fingers against her daughter's cheek. For the first time in her life, she felt the warm skin and the dampness of Laurel's tears. She squeezed her tight, loving the lankiness of her daughter's growing body. She was going to be a beauty, but right now she was a confused, overemotional teenager.

"You look like a wet chipmunk," Anne said, teasingly.

Laurel raised her head. "My eyes and mouth get all puffy when I cry, huh?" She wiped her face with the back of her hand.

"I get puffy, too," Anne said. She touched her arm, briefly. "You've really dropped a bomb here, kid. I need to talk to your dad. Why don't you take your new clothes into your room, wash your face, then try everything on again to make sure you really want to keep it."

Laurel's eyes started to fill with tears again. "You're going to make me go back with him, aren't you?"

"I'm going to talk to your father."

Laurel gave him a quick glance, then gathered her bags together and escaped through a door at the end of the room. When she was gone, silence filled the elegant salon.

While she was trying to figure out what on earth to say to Jake, Anne glanced around. The suite was obviously expensive. She figured a three-night stay would be more than her mortgage payment for an entire month. The huge parlor held two couches, a large entertainment unit, a wet bar by the powder room, two blue wing chairs and a dining room set in the far corner. Big windows filled one entire wall, giving a perfect view of downtown Houston. She stared out past Jake and figured if she was standing right by the window and looked to the left, she would be able to see her office building. She wondered if he knew that.

"I had no idea what she was thinking," she said when it became obvious he wasn't going to speak.

Jake turned away from the window, but he didn't answer. He walked over to the wet bar and pulled open the refrigerator. After removing two cans of soda, he popped the tops on both of them, then handed her one and sat on the floral-print sofa across from the entertainment center. He stretched out his long jean-clad legs and rested his cowboy boots on the coffee table. He hadn't worn his Stetson for their shopping trip, but despite the omission, he still looked like a cowboy come to the city.

She'd always been a sucker for a man who could fill out a pair of button-fly jeans. There was something lethal about the combination of hard man and soft denim. Even with the crisis Laurel had thrust upon them, Anne found herself itching to rub her hands up and down his thighs. Denim could transfer body heat just about better than any material she knew. That's why she never wore it. The fabric was too much of a reminder of her weakness. Cowboys. She took a long drink of the cold soda and wondered if the day could get any worse.

"She's only thirteen," he said at last. He leaned his head back on the sofa and closed his eyes. Lines of stress and pain tightened around his mouth. "I can't let her go."

"I'm not asking you to. I swear I didn't know what she was going to say."

He tilted his head forward and looked at her. Something dark and untrusting swirled in his brown eyes. "You'll have to forgive me if I don't believe you."

Anne turned away and started walking around the room. A couple of teen magazines lay scattered by the dining room table. Pumps and athletic shoes formed a pile by Laurel's bedroom door. An oversize T-shirt bearing the likeness of a popular cartoon cat was slung over one of the wing chairs. Anne touched it.

"I don't know her," she said, stroking the nightshirt. "We've talked on the phone three or four times. We've met twice. I don't know why she thinks you and your wife stole her from me." She looked at him. "I never said anything about that. We've never even discussed the adoption. I give you my word."

"I don't know you well enough to know if your word means a damn thing."

He wasn't making this any easier, but then he wasn't trying to. She drew in a deep breath and tried to stay calm. "I'd wondered why Laurel wasn't asking any of the hard questions. Now I know the reason."

"Hard questions?"

"You know. Why did I give her up for adoption? Why didn't I try to find her? That sort of thing. I was pleasantly surprised she was so accepting."

"At least one of us is happy," he said sarcastically. "Guess it's all going your way. Don't expect it to last. I don't know where Laurel got her ideas, but you and I both know she wasn't stolen out of her mother's loving arms. You decided to give her up."

He spoke the truth, but that didn't make it hurt any less. Still her discomfort would have to wait. Laurel was what mattered. She walked over to the sofa and sat on the far end. "Laurel must have seen something on TV or read it in a book," she said, ignoring his bad temper. "I know you don't like me or trust me. I know you didn't want me to meet her in the first place. That's okay. But I'd never ever do anything to hurt Laurel." She stiffened. She'd almost said "my daughter." That would have sent Jake over the edge for sure. "I'm sorry you have to go through this."

He grimaced. "I'm sure you'll understand if I don't believe that one, either."

She resisted the urge to throw something at him. "I'm *not* the enemy." She tucked one leg under her and shifted until she was facing him. "We have to work together and decide what's best for Laurel."

"We don't have to work together at all. You don't have any rights here. She's coming home with me."

"You're just going to tell her that?"

"Yes."

She put her soda down on the coffee table. Leaning toward him, she said, "Then you'll lose her. Don't let your anger at me and your fear cloud your judgment." She reached out to touch his arm. "Please, Jake—"

Without warning, he grabbed her wrist and held it tightly. She could feel the strength of his fingers and the heat from his body. He turned toward her, his brown eyes blazing with fire.

"Don't you tell me what to do with my daughter. You lost that right the day you gave her up."

Despite the anger and dark emotion swirling between them, her body responded to his touch. Her quivering skin betrayed her. Sparks arced between the two of them. She could feel the individual imprints of his fingers as if the fire in his gaze reached down to sear her wrist.

He hated her more than he could say, he thought she'd conspired to turn his daughter against him, he correctly reminded her that she'd lost all claims to Laurel. And he could turn her on with the slightest touch. In her belly, wanting swelled, flowing higher to her breasts, and lower between her legs.

He dropped her wrist as if the fire that had been consuming her suddenly turned on him. Before she could say anything, the bedroom door opened and Laurel stepped out.

She'd washed her face and tied her hair back into a ponytail. With her scrubbed skin, and wearing a matching shorts set, she looked more like a child than a young lady. But there was a knowing sadness in her eyes.

"Daddy, don't be mad at me."

"I'm not mad," he said, sounding weary.

"But you don't want me to stay with Annie."

"No, I don't."

Laurel lifted up her chin. "You don't understand. And you won't give her a chance." She looked helplessly at Anne. "Can you explain it to him?"

"Come here, honey." Anne beckoned the girl over. Laurel stepped between them and settled on the coffee table. She angled her body away from her father. Anne straightened in her seat and took Laurel's hands in her own. She studied the short nails and stubby fingers. "You have

Bobby's hands," she said without looking up. "He was a boy I liked in high school."

"My—" Laurel glanced at Jake. She couldn't say the word, but Anne knew what she was thinking.

"I dated him for almost two years. I thought we were in love." She gave Laurel a quick smile but didn't dare look at her father. "He was three years older than me. He rode in the rodeo."

"Really?" Laurel sounded pleased. "A professional cowboy. Cool. What did he do?"

"He rode bulls."

"That's dangerous."

"I know." With the telling, the memories threatened. It was easy to keep them locked up day after day, until she almost forgot she had them in storage. Now they came forward into her mind, a kaleidoscope of moments. Bobby so tall and handsome, laughing. His hot, eager young body. Her inexperienced desire to please. The devastating pain when he'd left her.

"He started doing well at local events," she continued, "so he left to go on the national circuit. When I found—" She cleared her throat.

Laurel squeezed her hands, then released her. "It's okay."

The sofa cushions shifted. Anne risked a quick glance and saw Jake leaning forward to grab her soda, then he handed it to her. His brown eyes gave nothing away, but the set of his mouth was kind. He, too, was handsome. But where Bobby had still carried the soft lines of youth, Jake was a man. Hard muscles defined his broad chest and arms. Lines fanned out from his eyes. Scars marred the male beauty of his large hands, and five o'clock shadow darkened the unyielding line of his jaw.

"Thank you," she said, taking the can. They didn't touch and she was grateful. The soft drink soothed her throat. "When Bobby left Paradise, he also left me. Us."

She touched Laurel's leg. "I had a full scholarship to Vassar. I'd always promised my mother I'd make something of myself, use the opportunities that she'd never been given. I promised her I'd have the life she couldn't provide. Nobody stole you, Laurel. I gave you up."

The girl seemed to fold in on herself. Her shoulders drooped and she rested her forearms on her legs. Jake surprised Anne by scooting forward on the sofa, picking up his daughter and pulling her onto his lap. Laurel snuggled against him, but didn't cry.

Now Anne fought the tears. The lines had been drawn and she'd been left on the outside. Still, there was more to the story. Laurel deserved to know the entire truth.

"My mother had a friend who was an attorney. He told me I could choose a private adoption. That way I'd get the chance to know who was taking my baby, plus it would be easier to leave information so that if you wanted to get in touch with me when you were eighteen, you could."

Laurel raised her head and smiled hopefully. "Really? You wanted me to find you?"

"Of course."

Jake kissed the top of Laurel's head. "When you're not being a brat, you're an okay kid. Why wouldn't she want to know you?"

"Da-ad!" His daughter gave him a mock punch in the arm, then wiggled out of his embrace. "I understand now, Annie. Thanks for telling me."

She looked surprisingly calm, Anne thought, and wondered when the other shoe was going to fall. "What did you understand?"

Laurel grinned. "I know my mom and dad didn't steal me. You had to give me up. You didn't want to, though." She turned to her father. "See, Daddy, Annie needs me to stay with her. She's been waiting all this time for me."

Anne stared helplessly at Jake. "I'm only making this worse. I'm sorry. You're her father, you tell her."

"Tell me what?"

Jake rose from the sofa and walked over to the wet bar. He opened the small refrigerator, but instead of soda, this time he pulled out a beer.

"Laurel, you're too young to understand this."

She spun to face him and planted her hands on her hips. "I *am* not. You just don't want me to stay here with Annie."

She had him dead to rights with that one, he thought. He didn't want her to stay. He didn't want her out of his sight ever, but that wasn't an option. He could try to keep her safe, but he couldn't keep her from growing up.

He took a long drink, then set the can on the counter of the bar. He had to be honest—it wasn't her growing up that scared him, it was her growing away. These last two years. Damn.

"I know the move has been hard for you, Laurel," he said finally "It's been hard for me, too. But staying with Anne Baker doesn't solve any of that."

"Why do you have to say her name like that?" Laurel asked. "'Anne Baker,'" she said, her voice low and mocking. "Why don't you like Annie?"

Because she scares me, he answered silently. Anne Baker could finish what his two years of emotional withdrawal had started. She could steal away his child. His guilty conscience told him that Laurel's actions were a punishment for not being there when she needed him. But it had been so hard to keep it together after Ellen had died. On top of those feelings had been the nagging need for the one thing he could never have: a child of his own. What the hell kind of a man couldn't even father a child?

"Your dad is being cautious with you, Laurel," Anne said, rising and standing behind the girl. She rested her hands on his daughter's shoulders. He hated the possessiveness of the gesture. "You should be pleased he cares so much."

Jake was about to inform her that he didn't need her help when Laurel twisted free. "He doesn't care about me. If he cared he wouldn't have taken me away from all my friends. He wouldn't take me back to that horrible house. He wouldn't take me away from you. I'm staying with Annie, Daddy."

"You're not and that's final." He slammed the can on the bar.

Father and daughter stared at each other. His heart broke in the face of her anger, but he wouldn't let her see how she was tearing him apart. How in God's name was he going to raise a teenage girl on his own? When had loving her more than anything ceased to be enough?

"You can't make me," she cried. "I'll run away and keep running away until you can't find me." She tore across the room and slammed her door shut behind her.

He closed his eyes at the harsh sound. He'd earned her wrath, he acknowledged to himself. The shock of Ellen's death, his guilt at being free of their failing marriage, the second-guessing about what he could have done differently had taken their toll. Too many nights he'd stayed alone in his study wondering, mourning, not paying attention to his growing daughter. She'd become a stranger to him. She was the only thing good and decent in his life, and he'd lost her.

"I can fix this," Anne said. She crossed the carpeted floor to the bar. With her head held high and her chin thrust out defiantly, she looked like a warrior preparing for battle. "I'll tell her that I don't want her to stay with me."

"Is it the truth?"

"No." Anne gave him a faint smile. "But as you pointed out earlier, there is a lot of work involved with raising a child, even a half-grown one. It would require me to make changes in my life. I'd like to think that I would handle it all beautifully, but that's not true."

"I appreciate the offer," he said, "but it won't work."

"Why? She won't want to come if she thinks she's not welcome."

"Laurel doesn't need another rejection in her life. Especially not from you." He grimaced. "As her birth mother you've been vested with almost magical powers. If that image was destroyed, I don't know what would happen to her. Whatever my feelings on the matter, Laurel comes first." He was tempted by her offer, but he owed his daughter better than that.

"The problem is time," Anne said. "If only it was the beginning of summer rather than the end. I'm sure that after a few weeks of hanging around with me, Laurel would see that I wasn't the answer to all her problems."

"You start to wear a little thin after the honeymoon stage, Baker?" he asked.

She folded her arms and leaned one hip on the bar. "Not always, *Masters,*" she said, then grinned. "But I think I might lose my magical powers."

He relaxed a little. She was right. Laurel wouldn't take all that long to become disenchanted. It didn't even have to go that far. He was willing to compromise and let Laurel visit Anne. She just couldn't live there permanently.

"Why would you be willing to lose status with her?" he asked, resting his forearms on the bar.

"Because I want a real relationship with Laurel. Not a pretend one. She has fantasies about me. I'm bound to disappoint her." She shrugged. "Once that happens and is behind us, then we can get on with the business of being friends."

He wanted to believe her, but he couldn't. There was too much at stake. "That's all you want?"

"That's the only place left in her life. Ellen was Laurel's mother. I know that."

"You're ignoring the fact that you're everything Laurel wants to be. Attractive, successful and independent." He'd spoken without thinking and now wanted to call the words back.

Instead of taking advantage of his slipup, Anne blushed. "Maybe we can work something out."

He was angry at himself for complimenting her. He let the energy of his displeasure fuel him. "There's no time. Laurel's school starts in a week. I have horses being delivered and a ranch to run. I can't wait around for a thirteen-year-old girl to get her head on straight."

"All right," she said, leaning toward him. Her pale blue eyes flashed with defiance. "What do you plan to do about our little problem then?"

"Take you with us."

Chapter Five

"You're going to *what?*" Heather asked, staring at Anne as if she'd lost her mind.

Anne smiled at her. "Take a two-month leave of absence."

"From work? You? I can't even remember the last time you took a vacation."

"I went to Cancun last year."

Heather shook her head. "That was over a long weekend. Taking off two extra days doesn't count as a vacation. What about the RCR contract?"

Anne glanced down at her notes, then looked back at her assistant sitting in the leather chair in front of her desk. "I've got most of the information mapped out. I'm going to have you meet with them in my place."

"Me?" Heather looked horrified. "Alone?"

"You'll be fine."

"But I've never done anything like that alone. I can't—"

Anne held up her hand to silence her. "I've spoken with Mr. Wilson and he's in complete agreement. We both think you're ready. Besides, if I get offered the promotion to vice president, don't you want a shot at my job?"

Heather wrinkled her nose. "I guess."

Anne grinned. "I'm overwhelmed by your enthusiasm."

"I'd like the big raise and the office," Heather said, looking around. "But I don't want to work the hours you do, Anne. I have a little boy who wants to see his mother now and then."

"I understand. You wouldn't have to put in all the hours I do. You have different priorities. I've always wanted to get to the top." Anne leaned back in her chair. Her need to get ahead wasn't just about earning more money or the prestige of being a vice president at the firm. She worked hard because work was the only place she ever really fit in. Now all that was at risk. Of course she was pleased about spending two months getting to know Laurel, but she had a sense of ambivalence about the whole situation. What price was she going to pay career-wise? Was she a horrible person for even thinking that? She told herself that of course Laurel had to come first, but that didn't mean she wasn't worried.

"Two months is a long time to be gone," Heather said, as if she could read her mind.

"I know." Anne sighed. "But the choice is between my career and my child. How can I choose my career? Laurel needs me, and I welcome the opportunity to get to know her. Selfishly, I can't help wishing all of this could have taken place in Houston."

Heather winked. "At least you'll be spending two months with her hunky father."

"He doesn't like me very much."

"Why?" Heather sounded shocked. "Everyone likes you."

"Except Jake Masters and Tim the Turkey," Anne said, jerking her head toward the next office.

"Tim's scared he's going to lose the promotion to a woman." Heather stood up and smiled. "For what it's worth, I think you're doing the right thing, Anne. You're getting a second chance with your daughter, and that's worth any price. I know your career is the most important part of your life, but maybe these two months will show you there's more to living than convincing companies to relocate in Houston."

"Bite your tongue." Anne laughed. "I'll be checking in regularly. You have the phone number there if you need me. Don't be afraid to call."

Heather walked to the door, then turned back. "Have a good time finding out how the other half lives. It wouldn't kill you to let a man into your life."

Anne waved her out of the room. "Get back to your desk before I give the RCR account to someone else."

"I'm trembling with fear." Heather chuckled, then pulled the door shut behind her.

Anne turned her chair until she was staring out the large window. Ten days ago if someone had told her she would be taking a two-month leave of absence from her job so that she could get to know the child she'd given up for adoption thirteen years ago, she would have assumed that person was crazy. Now she was starting to question her own sanity. Was she making a huge mistake or was she setting everything right?

She still remembered the shock she'd felt when Jake had told her she was coming with them to Colorado. She'd started to tell him that it was impossible for her to leave work and just pack up for two months. But she hadn't. Maybe it had been because she'd thought about what Heather had said. She was getting a second chance with her daughter. Maybe it was because she wanted to store up memories for the times when she was alone. But mostly it was because of guilt. Although she'd missed Laurel and had never stopped thinking about her, giving up her child had allowed her to get on with her life. She'd never had to balance a baby and school, or a toddler and a career. She'd never had to worry about working late, child care, measles, or any of the problems of being a single mother. She'd taken the easy way out. She owed Laurel, regardless of what it cost.

She swiveled around to face her desk, then picked up the phone. After punching in a familiar number, she waited until she heard a voice say, "Hi, hold on," followed by a stream of instructions that included telling her youngest to stop chewing on the dog, and promises that yes, they were having hot dogs for dinner.

"Hi, Becky Sue."

"Annie. How are you darlin'? I haven't heard from you in forever. You callin' me from that fancy office of yours?"

"Yes."

"I bet you've got the air-conditionin' set just right. Out here it's hotter than a— Little Joey, I told you to stop chewin' on that dog. You're gonna make yourself sick. Stop it before I paddle you good. Sorry. These kids are driving me crazy. I can't hardly wait for school to get started."

Anne leaned back in her chair and smiled. Becky Sue, her only cousin, had stayed behind in their small west Texas town. She'd married a local boy and had five children.

"I have some news," Anne said.

"You've gone and got yourself another promotion?"

"No. I've heard from my daughter."

She heard a loud thump as something was knocked over by one of the children, then Becky Sue's voice laced with excitement. "Why, darlin' that's just wonderful. I'm happy for you. You must have been surprised. What happened?"

Anne quickly explained about Jake's visit and the subsequent meetings with Laurel.

"Stolen," Becky Sue said. "I wish someone would come and steal some of my kids."

Anne laughed. "You know you don't mean that."

"It's true, but some days, I sure wouldn't mind. So you gonna live with this man and your little girl? What about your fancy job?"

"I'm taking a leave of absence." Anne picked up a pencil and toyed with it. Becky Sue would do anything in the world for her, she knew that. Anne wasn't afraid her cousin would say no to the favor she was about to request. She was afraid of what she would hear along with the agreement. Becky Sue had the disconcerting habit of telling everyone exactly what she thought of a situation. "We're driving from Houston to his ranch in Colorado. I thought we could stop by for a bit."

"You're always welcome here, Annie Jo. You know that. There's plenty of air mattresses if you all want to spend the night." Her voice grew muffled. "Joey, I'm gonna smack your behind. Leave that dog alone! You hear me?"

A loud squawk of displeasure followed by a woof from the oversize dog filled the receiver. Anne grinned. It was almost like being there. Sometimes she missed her old home.

"You sure you want to come back to all this?" Becky Sue asked.

"I'm sure. I was forced to give her up. I thought if I brought her to Paradise, she might realize I made the best decision for both of us."

"You know, darlin', I think the world of you. I've always been so proud of your education and your job. You've been real generous with clothes for the kids. And I know you're putting money away for trade school, or even college, but only little Dolly seems to have the brains. Stop it," she screamed, then sighed. "I doubt little Joey's gonna live to grow up if he keeps chewin' on that dog. Anyway, you're a good friend, just like a sister to me. I've always wanted you to find some happiness. I'd like to meet your girl. But you be careful, Annie Jo. You say you want to show her that you made the right choice. Seems to me you're the one who needs convincin'."

The knot in her belly was from nerves and the early hour, Anne told herself as she zipped up her suitcase. It was completely normal and would go away as soon as they got going. A sharp buzz made her jump. She hurried over to the security panel and spoke. "Yes?"

"Annie, we're here," Laurel said, sounding awake and cheerful despite the fact that it wasn't even seven o'clock a.m. "Are you ready?"

"Sure. Come on up." She pushed the release button.

After taking one last look around her bedroom, Anne pulled the suitcase off the bed and rolled it into the living room. Her makeup, a change of clothes and a nightshirt were in a carry-on bag. She rubbed her damp palms against her shorts and tried to stay calm. It wasn't working.

After what felt like an eternity, there was a knock. She pulled open her door. Laurel practically danced into the room.

"You're really coming with us," she said, grinning. Her brown hair was pulled back into a ponytail that bounced with her movements. She wore white shorts with a bright neon orange tank top.

Anne pointed at the suitcase. "Looks that way."

Laurel stepped close and gave her a hug. Jake followed his daughter into the room, but his greeting was more controlled. Anne knew he wasn't happy about the situation. She had just as many reservations as he did, but for different reasons. Still, they were going to be spending the next two months together. They had to find a way to get along.

"Where's your luggage?" he asked.

She motioned to the single suitcase standing in the center of the room. "I have this and that overnight case." She pointed.

"That's it?" He sounded surprised. "Have you changed your mind about staying for two months?"

"No. I don't have any cold weather clothes, so I'll get a couple of sweaters there. It's a horse ranch, right? There's not going to be any fancy parties in town, so I didn't think I needed much."

Jake didn't say anything; he simply nodded and picked up the suitcase. "I'll take it and wait for you downstairs."

Laurel wasn't so circumspect. "Gosh, you hardly have any luggage. Whenever we went anywhere, Mom brought tons of stuff." She grinned. "She had this set of matching suitcases. There were four of them. The really big kind. Once, when we went to New York for a week, Mom brought twelve pairs of shoes. Dad and I counted. She had lots of pretty dresses and jewelry." Laurel's smile faded and her expression turned sad. "My mom was beautiful. Daddy and Grandpa always told her she could have been a fashion model."

Anne glanced down at her generous bust and wide hips. She wasn't overweight, but at five foot four and almost a hundred and twenty pounds, she wasn't anyone's idea of a fashion model. She picked up her carry-on bag, then her keys and ushered Laurel out of the condo. "She sounds lovely," she said, and locked the door.

"Oh, she was." Laurel pushed the button for the elevator. "She had dark hair, like Daddy's. It was long and pretty. She used to wear it up and then put on diamond earrings." Laurel looked at Anne. "Daddy says I'll get the earrings when I'm old enough. I want to wear makeup, but he doesn't like it." She grimaced. "Mom wore a lot of makeup all the time. She always liked to look put together."

She said the last two words with an affectation, as if playfully mocking her. When she giggled, Anne smiled with her. The elevator doors opened and they stepped inside.

On the trip down, Laurel continued to chatter on about the charms Ellen Masters had possessed. Anne started feeling more dowdy and inadequate by the minute. Maybe she should have packed some better clothes, she thought as they stepped into the foyer of the building. She didn't own much jewelry. A good portion of her extra income went to Becky Sue to help with the five kids. She'd thought about packing that silk dress, but had decided against it.

They stepped into the sunshine. Jake was waiting at the curb. Her suitcase had already been stored in the back of his black Ford Explorer. He took her carry-on bag and stowed it in the back seat. Laurel climbed in after it. He held open the passenger door and Anne stepped up into the vehicle.

Jake walked around the front, then slid in next to her. As always he wore jeans. Today his broad chest was covered by a polo shirt that hugged his hard muscles. The bright red knit fabric brought out the deep color of his tan. The Stetson shaded his eyes, but she didn't mind that. He had invited her to join them because there wasn't any other easy solution. It didn't matter what kind of clothes she wore or the fact that she would never be as pretty or well dressed as his late wife. She would only ever be a thorn in his side.

They pulled out into traffic, then headed for the freeway that would take them west. Laurel continued to talk about clothes. Anne glanced down at her own outfit of cream-colored shorts and a pale peach T-shirt. She had broken down and bought jeans for her stay at the ranch. They were the only practical attire for that sort of environment. After all, she was going to be living with a cowboy.

She shot Jake a glance. He concentrated on the road. Mirrored sunglasses hid his eyes from view, but she suspected he was staring straight ahead. He drove confidently, relaxed, but with both hands on the wheel. There was something about the set of his head. It gnawed at the back of her memory. What was it?

Suddenly she had to turn and glance out the passenger window so Jake wouldn't see her smile. He reminded her a little of Bobby. She looked over her shoulder at Laurel. No wonder they looked like father and daughter.

They stopped for an early lunch. Laurel continued to keep the conversation going. Anne nibbled at her hamburger and salad. She had to talk to Jake, but didn't know how to get him alone. She didn't want to get Laurel excited about stopping to see Becky Sue and cousins she didn't know she had, only to have her father veto the idea.

In the end, fate and Laurel intervened. "I'm done," Laurel said, pushing away her plate. "Dad, I need some new batteries for my Walkman and video games. May I have some money?"

He reached in his front pocket and pulled out some bills. "Buy plenty of batteries," he said, then winked.

Laurel rolled her eyes. "Dad *hates* my music," she told Anne. "He makes me listen to tapes using my headset."

"I like that," Anne said. "I think my taste is a little closer to your father's than to yours."

"That's 'cause you guys are old." Laurel took the money he offered and headed for the convenience store that shared the parking lot with the gas station and restaurant.

Anne watched her go. "She's a good kid."

"I know." Without his sunglasses and Stetson, Jake looked more approachable. He'd even joked with his daughter. But whenever he glanced at her, he iced up.

"You're going to have to do a better job of pretending," she blurted out.

They sat across from each other in a booth at the back of the restaurant. He raised his dark eyebrows. "Pretending what?"

"That you don't hate me."

Jake leaned back in the booth. He stretched one arm across the red vinyl seat. "I don't hate you."

"You don't trust me."

"In my position, would you be any different?"

"No," she admitted. "But we're going to have to learn to get along. Otherwise the two months will be unbearable."

"Agreed."

This would be the time to say something conciliatory, she told herself. Instead she was about to throw the fat into the fire. She glanced at him. He looked casual and in control. A lock of dark hair fell onto his forehead. The hollows of his cheeks emphasized the firm lines of his mouth and jaw. He was much too good-looking. If he ever turned his charming smile in her direction, she would melt. Not only because she found him attractive and they seemed on the verge of starting a fire every time they touched, but because he was a cowboy. Everyone had a weakness, she just wished hers could have been ice cream or gin.

"I'd like to make a detour," she said, then stared at the table. She began folding her paper napkin back and forth, pleating the white square into a long thick length.

"A historical site?" He sounded faintly amused.

"Paradise. It's a tiny town near El Paso. My cousin Becky Sue lives there."

Both his hands slammed onto the table. She jumped. "What the hell are you up to?" he growled.

She risked looking at him. Fire leapt from his eyes, but these flames weren't caused by casual contact. They were fueled by rage.

"I thought—"

"I won't allow you to manipulate my daughter for your own purpose. If you think introducing Laurel to a bunch of relatives will further your case, you're dead wrong. The only reason you're here today is because I care about my daughter. But don't push me, lady. I have the law on my side."

She fought the urge to shrink back in her seat. Instead she forced herself to stare him directly in the eyes. "Have you ever been to west Texas?"

He frowned. "What does that have to do with anything?"

"Paradise is miles from anywhere. The population is about a thousand. It's hot, dusty and poor. Most everybody lives in a trailer. Some of them are lucky, because theirs is a double wide." She paused and glanced down at the table. She was systematically shredding her napkin. She let go of the paper and pushed the mess to the side of the table. "Laurel is still confused about what happened when she was born. I thought if I showed her where I grew up, if she could see that it was poor and ugly, she might be grateful for what she has now."

She folded her hands in her lap and looked at him. He leaned his forearms on the table. "That sounds good, but I don't believe you. There must be another reason you're doing this."

His assumption that she had something to gain pushed all her buttons. Her temper overrode her desire to get along with Jake. "Who dumped on you so badly you can't recognize a decent act for what it is?" she asked hotly. "What could I possibly gain by this? Even if Laurel falls in love with Becky Sue and her kids, there's no way *I'm* going back there to live. I worked damn hard to get out of that town." She shook her head. "I'm tired of you judging me. You've had months to get used to the idea of Laurel wanting to meet me. I've had less than two weeks. My entire life has been turned upside down. I've risked a promotion that I've worked toward. I've tried to be fair and do what was best for everyone. I've put up with your innuendo and bad temper. Yes, I gave Laurel up for adoption. Yes, I have a certain responsibility to her. I am doing the best I can with what I have. If you can't see that, you're a bigger fool than I thought, and you deserve to lose your child."

With that, she started to slide out of the seat. Before she could, he reached out across the table and grabbed her arm.

"Wait," he said. "Please."

Jake didn't release his hold until she settled back in her seat. Only then did he let go. But even after he'd propped his arm up on the back of the vinyl booth, he could still feel the softness and heat of her skin. As always when he touched her, need flared to life inside him. He hated his body's betrayal. If only he'd returned to the land of the living with any woman other than her. But he hadn't. And she was right. He was going to have to get over his problems with her or it was going to be a long two months.

He shifted to ease the pressure in his crotch. "I don't mean to be a complete jerk," he said.

"Only half a jerk?"

Her smile was tentative. She was always willing to meet him partway. He had to give her that.

"Only half," he agreed, letting go of his anger.

"I know you're afraid."

"It's hard not to be."

"You're not going to lose her."

He rubbed the bridge of his nose. "She might already be gone."

"No." Anne shook her head. "Laurel loves you. You're a good father."

If only that were true. But Anne didn't know about the last two years. She didn't know about how he'd withdrawn from his child so that he could mourn Ellen and figure out a way to deal with his guilt. She didn't know about how he wanted a son to carry on the Masters name. She didn't know that he was the reason they'd had to adopt in the first place. She didn't know he wasn't enough of a man.

"Not good enough," he said bluntly, "or she wouldn't have gone looking for you."

"Maybe it won't be such a bad thing."

He studied her. "Maybe not."

She wasn't unattractive, he admitted to himself. Just different from Ellen. Anne had let her strawberry-colored hair go wavy today. A headband held it away from her face with only a fringe of bangs falling on her forehead. Her pale peach T-shirt brought out the color in her cheeks. She had freckles on her arms. Maybe they weren't so bad, either. He'd noticed her legs were nice. She was more curvy than his late wife had been. His gaze lowered to her full breasts. A lot curvier. The clinging knit of her shirt outlined her shape. She would fill his hands. The thought made his fingers curl into his palm and the ache in his groin deepen. He sighed. There were a few single women not far from the ranch. He was going to have to consider taking up with one of them. He might not hate Anne Baker, but he sure as hell didn't trust her. The last thing either of them needed was to complicate their relationship with sex.

"You really think letting Laurel meet your cousin and her family is a good idea?" he asked.

Anne shrugged. "I don't see how spending the night in Paradise is going to make anything worse. Hopefully she'll see that I made the best decision at the time."

"You sound as if you regret that decision now."

She slid out of the booth. He followed. Before heading for the door, she looked up at him. "I've always regretted it. That doesn't mean I've figured out if I did the right thing or not."

"You've got the job you wanted, and soon you'll have your promotion."

"I know."

She started walking. The scent of her perfume trailed after her like a seductive call. It whispered against his skin, making him break out into a sweat. He tried to ignore the sway of her hips in her shorts and the way her hair bounced as she moved. He had a sudden desire to know if her creamy skin tasted like peaches.

When they stepped outside, Anne slipped on her sunglasses. "I'd like to get sodas for the next leg of the drive."

"Fine by me." He moved into step beside her. "There's a cooler in the back. We can buy a bag of ice and keep them cold."

Before they entered the convenience store, Anne stopped. "What about Becky Sue? Are we going to go by there?"

He was torn between wondering if it would help or somehow make things worse. "When the two months are over, you're still going back to Houston."

It wasn't a question. "I know."

"She's my daughter, Anne. Nothing can change that."

Her mouth twisted. "I know that, too."

"Then we'll stop."

"So Becky Sue's five kids are my cousins, too?" Laurel asked from her place in the back seat.

"I'm not sure. They might be your second cousins," Anne answered. "I've never known how that works."

"Dad, do you know?"

"Nope."

"Well, I guess it doesn't matter, just so long as they're relatives. I haven't had many relatives before, have I, Daddy?"

"Just your grandparents," he said. And now, not even all of them. He didn't want to remember what Ellen's father, Michael, had said and done, but he couldn't forget.

They were miles from any large city, in the dusty west part of Texas. Instead of the dirt and scrub stretching out on both sides of the road, he saw the look on Michael's face when he refused to spend time with Laurel on her birthday.

"Why would I care about some bastard brat? I only dealt with her for Ellen's sake. She's your problem now. Keep her away from me."

Jake had been stunned by his father-in-law's dismissal of his only grandchild. But Laurel wasn't his by blood. Michael had taken great pains to remind Jake of that fact. So Jake had lied to his daughter and told her that her favorite grandparent was out of town on business the day of her birthday. With his father dead and his mother remarried and living in Florida, it had been up to Jake to make the day special for his daughter. There'd been a pool party with friends, but the happy event had been marred by sadness. It had also been a going-away party. He and Laurel had moved to Colorado the following week.

Even as he listened to Laurel and Anne talking about her "new" relatives, he wondered what kind of reception she would get from Anne's family. Would they welcome her with open arms or would they hold back and hurt his child?

Laurel leaned as far forward as her seat belt would let her. "What about—?" She paused. He glanced in the rearview mirror and saw her troubled expression. "What about your old boyfriend?"

What about my real father. She didn't have to say the words. He heard them pounding in his head. His hands tightened on the steering wheel. Anne looked at him, but his sunglasses hid his pain from her. He swallowed. What if that boy—no, he would be a man now—staked some claim on Laurel? He didn't want to hear what she would tell Laurel, didn't want to know that another man was his baby's real father.

"He didn't have much family," Anne said. "I think they're all gone. Either passed away or moved somewhere else."

That was something, Jake thought grimly. That only left the man himself. He shook his head. Funny how all this time he'd been grateful that Ellen wasn't around to hear

Laurel talking about her birth mother. He'd never thought about himself. About the man who had given life to his child. About the man who might now take her away. What good was the law when this stranger might steal her heart?

He should have left, he thought with sudden clarity. He should have left the marriage and taken Laurel with him. Those last years with Ellen had been horrible for all of them. The fights, the stony silences. Her bitter accusations that he had better not leave her, not after she stayed all those years, not when she'd adopted a child when she could have easily left him and had her own baby with another man. How many times had she thrown his sterility in his face? How many times had he raged at God for depriving him of a son?

"Is B-Bobby still there?" Laurel asked quietly, stuttering over the name.

Anne turned in her seat and smiled gently at Laurel. "A couple of months before you were born he was killed by a bull at a rodeo."

The relief was sweet. Jake let out the breath he'd been holding and relaxed.

"Oh."

Jake watched Laurel in the mirror. She dropped her chin to her chest and flopped back in the seat.

"At least I've got you," she said.

"And your dad," Anne said quickly.

"I'll always have him," she said matter-of-factly, then slipped on her headset. She flipped on the tape recorder and started bouncing with the beat of the music.

Anne shifted to face front. She reached out her fingers and gently touched his forearm. "You okay?"

"Fine." Except for the heat boiling between them.

"I probably should have told you about Bobby sooner. I didn't think that you'd worry."

"I wasn't worried."

She chuckled. He glanced at her.

"You're a lot of things, Jake," she said. "But not a very good liar."

He checked the mirror, but Laurel was involved with her music. "Maybe I *was* a little concerned about having to fight some rodeo cowboy for my kid."

"Bobby burned too bright to live very long. I always thought he was destined to die young. I think that was part of his appeal." She looked out the window. "The turnoff is in about twenty miles."

"We're really in the middle of nowhere."

"Tell me about it. I grew up here."

As they got closer to Paradise, he could feel her tension growing. Soon they turned off the highway onto a two-lane road. It was late afternoon, but the sun beat down unmercifully. The car's air-conditioning was set to high, but the temperature inside continued to climb. Up ahead he could see a cluster of tired buildings, surrounded by dirt and a few low-lying bushes. There was an elementary school, a diner, a gas station. The general store looked about a hundred years old. An old couple sat on their front porch rocking. Several of the side streets were paved, but some weren't.

"Welcome to Paradise," Anne said. She held herself so stiffly, he wondered if she would snap if he touched her.

"You want to keep going?" he asked when he saw a sign pointing back to the highway.

"More than you know. There's something about coming back that makes me feel—" She gave him a quick smile. "Ghosts. Can't seem to shake 'em. It's through here." She pointed to a narrow lane that dead-ended in a trailer park.

A few limp trees grew in the dust. Rusting cars sat on blocks. Barefoot kids played around a scraggly bush. His new Ford Explorer was as out of place as a Thoroughbred at a mule sale.

He heard a burst of music as Laurel pulled off her headset. "You grew up here?"

"I spent seventeen years in Paradise. All I ever dreamed about was getting away. Becky Sue's trailer is at the end."

He drove slowly to avoid the children and dogs crowding the dirt trail. Jake had assumed Anne wanted Laurel to see where she grew up as part of some master plan to steal her away. Now staring at the sun-bleached trailers, the frayed curtains and dirty children, he knew he'd misjudged her. He thought about her big office and her hopes for a promotion. He thought about her white-on-white condo, another lifetime from here.

"Park over there," she said, pointing to a spot past the last mobile home. A lone tree provided a fair amount of shade. As he came to a stop, a group of people rushed out of the trailer. A woman about Anne's size led the way followed by several children and two mangy-looking dogs. He opened the door and got out slowly. Anne and Laurel followed suit.

The woman stopped a couple of feet away. Her hair was several shades darker, a true auburn. It was pulled back in a braid, revealing features much like Anne's, but a little older. Her smile was wide and genuine. A clean but faded sleeveless blouse had been tucked into a loose skirt. He wondered if she'd dressed up to meet them. "Annie Jo Baker, you are lookin' mighty pretty. Is this beautiful young lady your little girl?"

Anne took Laurel's hand and led her forward. "Laurel, this is my cousin, Becky Sue."

"Laurel. Ain't that a lovely name." She moved closer, then touched her cheek. "Oh, my. You've got Aunt Rose's eyes." She held open her arms.

Laurel looked at him for guidance. He felt as if someone had sliced his belly open and was now twisting the knife. He wanted to drag Laurel into the car and drive so far that they both forgot about Paradise and Anne Baker and birth mothers and being adopted. But he couldn't. He nodded his approval and his daughter stepped into Becky Sue's embrace.

"Welcome home, Laurel Baker. Welcome to the family."

Chapter Six

"Now are you sure you don't want another piece of pie?" Becky Sue asked, rising from the table.

"Not for me," Anne said. "I'm stuffed. Jake?"

The man beside her shook his head. He'd been silent through their meal. Not that she blamed him. It was hot and sticky; even talking was an effort. The air conditioner in the mobile home had long since given up. Even though she'd showered and changed before dinner, Anne could feel the sweat dripping down her back. Her normally curly hair was lying flat from the heat. Jake's tailored white shirt clung to him in patches. Only Becky Sue looked comfortable in her loose floral print skirt and blouse.

The three adults sat at the old table in the kitchen. The six kids were scattered throughout the trailer. Two dogs and an assortment of cats wove between their legs and generally added to the heat and din.

Anne glanced at the cherry pie sitting in the center of the table. Becky Sue would have gotten up early to bake it herself. The fried chicken and biscuits had been from a family recipe, the corn picked that morning. This was the home she remembered. It was all the same; she was the one who had changed.

"I'm sure sorry J.T. couldn't get home early," Becky Sue said as she cleared the table. Anne rose to help, but her cousin pushed her back in place. "Now I know you're family, darlin', but today I'm gonna treat you like company."

Her familiar open smile eased the pain in Annie's heart. Becky Sue could always put her world right.

"Anyway, he wanted to meet your little girl, but he can get to it in the morning. He's got an extra half shift down at the gas station." She looked around the trailer. "We sure could use the money to fix up this place." She moved efficiently around the small but clean kitchen. When one of the dogs walked in front of her, she easily stepped out of the way.

"Annie Jo and her mother had a real nice mobile home," she said, then gave Jake a wink. "'Course it was only the two of 'em. Kids have a way of wearing a place out."

Anne shifted uncomfortably in her chair. She wasn't ashamed of where she'd grown up. There might not have been a lot of luxuries, but there'd been plenty of love and understanding. Still, what did Jake think of all this?

"You must be very proud of Anne," he said, taking the cup of coffee Becky Sue offered.

"Oh, we are. She's got that important job of hers. And her place. Have you seen it?"

He nodded.

"Ain't it pretty? All white." Becky Sue gave her a grin. "She tried to buy us a new mobile home, but I wouldn't let her. This one might be a little worn, but it still works for us."

"I'm sure Jake doesn't want to hear this," Anne said, starting to get uncomfortable.

Jake ignored her. "That was very generous."

"She is. She gives me money for the kids. College, she says, if they want to go." Becky Sue glanced over at her brood. "I think only little Dolly will take advantage of that, but the others might want to learn a trade." She sat down and patted Jake's shoulder. "Your little girl comes from strong stock. We ain't fancy, but we're good folks."

Anne felt the blush climbing her cheeks. She glanced down and smoothed her skirt. If Jake was half as uncomfortable as she was, he'd probably pay her to get him out of the sweltering kitchen. She looked at her cousin and smiled. "It's going to be a pretty night. Would you mind if we took a walk?"

"Go right ahead."

"Jake?"

He looked over at her. A puzzled expression wrinkled his brow. "Sure. I'll tell Laurel." He headed for the big family room.

"He's nice," Becky Sue said before Jake was out of earshot.

"He's Laurel's father. Don't get any ideas."

"But you haven't been out with a man since before my youngest was born."

Anne tried glaring at her cousin, but it was impossible to get or stay angry at her. She grinned instead. "Don't go matchmaking."

"I'm not. But you must admit, he's nice lookin'."

"I'll admit to that, but nothing else."

Becky Sue started to speak, but Anne saw Jake returning and jabbed her in the side with her elbow. She led the way outside. Here the temperature was about ten degrees cooler than inside the trailer. The night sky hung low.

"I'd forgotten about the stars," she said, staring up at the thousands of twinkling lights. "I never could wish on that first star. As the sun set, there weren't any, then I'd look up and the sky would be like this." She waved her arms toward the heavens.

"It's like this on the ranch, too," Jake said as he walked along beside her.

"But not so hot." She fanned herself with her hand.

"You got that right."

By silent agreement, they headed away from the trailer park. Quickly the sounds of the children and the dogs, the bang of pots on the counter and the blare of the televisions faded. Soon all Annie could hear was the soft hooting of an owl and the crunch of Jake's boots on the small rocks underfoot. Her own sandals were quieter as she stepped on the familiar, uneven ground.

The smells of cooking faded more slowly, but soon she could inhale the scent of the desert, the clean air and the musky fragrance that belonged to Jake. Her arms hung loosely at her sides. They moved in the same direction to go around a small boulder, and they brushed together.

Hot skin seared hot skin. The slightly sweaty contact sent excitement rippling through her body. The waves of need alerted all her senses, then settled low in her belly. She fought the urge to fold her arms over her chest. She didn't want him to know he got to her.

She cleared her throat. "So tell me, is Paradise what you expected?" she asked, more to distract herself than because she wanted to start a conversation.

"Not exactly. You said the town was small, but I was expecting—"

"A little more life?"

"Yeah."

His voice sounded friendly. She wanted to know if he was smiling at her, but she was afraid to turn her head and look at him. What if he was smiling? How would she control the impulses that flooded her? Worse, what if he wasn't? She would rather die than make a fool of herself in front of Jake Masters. He already had her at a disadvantage.

"It's not a bad place," he said, stopping beside a large rock the size of a dining room table. When she would have followed him close to the boulder, he held her back with a raised arm. "Wait a minute." He walked around the rock, then kicked at a small burrow. "Okay, you can come closer."

"What were you doing?"

"Checking for rattlers. I'm wearing boots, you're not."

She knew the desert snakes thrived around Paradise, but she was surprised Jake had thought of it.

"I might have grown up in Dallas," he said, as if he could read her mind, "but I've always been a country boy at heart."

"I never thought of you as a boy at all," she blurted out, then could have cheerfully thrown herself off a cliff. Unfortunately there weren't any around for hundreds of miles. She settled for sitting on the rock and staring at the stars. At least it was dark and he couldn't see her blushing.

"I like your cousin," he said as he sat next to her. They weren't touching, but she could feel the heat from the rock, and the heat from the man. The temperatures were about the same, but her reactions were very different. She was hyperaware of her body. Of the dampness of her skin and the way her breasts swelled uncomfortably against her cotton bra. Her nipples puckered. Between her thighs the ache grew. She could feel her damp panties. He hadn't even touched her, but she was ready.

"Becky Sue is very sweet," she said, hoping the conversation would distract her. "She's only ever wanted to get married and have kids."

"Then she sure got what she wanted."

"I'm not going to apologize for her," Anne said sharply.

"No one's asking you to. I meant what I said. I like her. She's very straightforward."

"Sorry." She sighed and folded her hands on her lap. "I guess I'm a little tense about being back. There are so many memories." She studied the familiar stars. "My mother and I used to sit out on our porch at night and look at the sky. We'd wait for the moon to rise and talk about the future. She had so many dreams for me. She used to tell me that I'd leave Paradise and find something better."

"And you did."

"Sometimes it feels like I never lived here at all."

He leaned back on the rock and supported himself on his elbows. "I'll admit I have trouble reconciling you with the girl who grew up here."

"Oh, I was here." She half turned until she was facing him. She tucked one leg under her and smoothed down her light cotton skirt. "I graduated top of my class and seven months pregnant. Imagine what everyone thought of that."

"Tell me about Bobby."

She laughed. "He was the hottest thing around. Bobby was going to be a champion bull rider. That's all he aspired to in life." Her smile faded. "I thought he was perfect. I didn't even care that we were doing it in the back of a pickup. My mother didn't like him, but she wasn't angry when I found out I was pregnant. She just held me and told me she wasn't going to let Bobby interfere with our plans for my future."

"Did you want to marry him?"

"I don't know." She shrugged. "In a way, I think I did. But I'd always known I was going to college, and by the time I was willing to admit to myself I was pregnant, he'd left me for another woman. Guess who?"

"I can't imagine."

"A barrel racer. They met on the circuit."

Jake chuckled. His low laugh seemed to find its way into her belly and curl up into a soothing glow. She wanted to capture the sound and hold it close to her heart. She turned away and faced the horizon.

"Did he know about the baby?" he asked.

"Yes, but he didn't care. A friend of my mother's, an attorney, arranged for a private adoption. I never knew the name of the couple." She paused. "I never knew your name, but he promised you were nice and that you'd take care of my child. So I gave her up. It wasn't too horrible," she said, wondering if he heard the lie. Her throat tightened, but she forced herself to go on. "I had a full scholarship to Vassar. The baby was due in the middle of August, and I wasn't showing that much. Everybody knew, but no one said anything. After Laurel was born, I went off to college, acting like nothing ever happened."

But something had. And she'd carried around that hole in her heart for thirteen years.

"You've done very well for yourself," he said. "Your mother must be very proud."

"She was." She thought of how her mother had sat listening each summer break. She'd made Anne tell her everything she could remember about her year at college. "She died my last semester. She never saw me graduate, but at least she knew I was going to make it." She drew in a deep breath and forced herself to sound cheerful. "So, where did you say you grew up?"

"Dallas."

She felt him shifting on the rock beside her, but she didn't look. If he said something nice to her, she would break down completely. All the memories were hard to resist. She could hear her mother's gentle voice telling her that a baby would only get in the way. In her head, she knew her mother was right. It was only now that she realized her heart had never been convinced.

"My father was in construction," he continued. "He was very successful."

"Let me guess. A big white house with a swimming pool."

"And horses."

She looked around. The moon had risen. In the distance she could see the lights from the mobile homes. Some laundry hung limply in the warm night. A dog barked.

"That's a lifetime from here," she said.

"About as far from Paradise as you are now. You've come a long way yourself."

"That I have." But what was the price? Giving up her child had been so logical. Her mother had always told her she didn't have to pay for that one mistake for the rest of her life. But was getting pregnant the only mistake she'd made? "You moved away, as well. Why Colorado?"

He shifted on the rock until he was sitting up next to her. His long legs swung back and forth. She heard the *thunk* as his boots hit the rock.

"My grandfather had a ranch there that he left to me. I always wanted to try to make it successful, but I was expected to go into my father's business. I never thought about trying to make a living with horses. I told myself it was a dream."

"You're doing it now."

"Yeah, and it's a lot more hard work than I'd realized."

He grinned. The flash of white made her own lips curl up. In the faint light of the moon, the details of his face blurred until she could forget he was good-looking enough to make her nervous. She could forget why they were here, and the distrust and awkwardness between them. Maybe this was their chance to become friends.

"You love it," she said, hazarding a guess.

"That I do. I should have done it years ago."

"Why didn't you?"

She felt him stiffen. She wanted to grab his arm and keep him with her, but she didn't. He had to make the decision on his own. He stared straight ahead into the darkness of the desert. The stars twinkled overhead. At last he exhaled and relaxed.

"Ellen and I were best friends in school. Both our families encouraged us to marry. There I was with a wife and a child. Chasing dreams wasn't an option. I had responsibilities."

"Do you always do the responsible thing?"

"Don't you?" Jake asked, and wondered when he'd stopped hating her. Maybe it was the night, or seeing how she'd grown up. But sometime in the last couple of hours, Anne Baker had ceased to be the enemy.

"I try to do what's right," she said.

"Is that why you send Becky Sue money?"

She shrugged. The movement brought her shoulder in contact with his arm. The faint brush, gone almost before he registered the sensation, made him want to haul her close to him and press his hard body against her soft one. Being next to her, smelling the scent of her perfume, knowing that if he could just bury himself inside her he could get rid of this damn need, made him half crazed. He wanted to touch her and taste her. He wanted to forget himself inside her—he wanted to forget she ever existed.

"She's my family. I want to help her. I do as much as I can."

It was a hell of a lot more than his family had done for him. Or Ellen's father. He pushed away the thoughts of Michael. "It shows."

She turned toward him. "I think that's the first nice thing you've said to me."

"What have I said that hasn't been nice?"

She laughed. "How much time do you have?"

"Okay, maybe I've been a little difficult."

"A little? Oh, please. You've practically accused me of harboring all seven deadly sins."

She was teasing, but her statement made him uncomfortable. He stared out into the desert. "I protect what's mine."

"Don't ever stop doing that."

He looked at her in surprise. "I would have thought you'd get all huffy and accuse me of being a male chauvinist or at least a barbarian."

"No. There were a lot of times I wished for someone to protect me. Mama tried, but she was gone so much. She worked two jobs to support us."

The moonlight reflected in her eyes turning the light blue irises to the color of sapphires. Her skin glowed as if lit by candles. He couldn't see the freckles anymore. Her hair brushed against her shoulders with each turn of her head. Would the strawberry-colored waves be soft against his fingers? He had to ball his hands up into fists to keep from finding out.

He forced himself to think of other things. Of a young girl waiting alone in a trailer for her mother to get home from work. Of the studying it must have taken to get a full scholarship at a prestigious school.

"You didn't fit in here, did you?" he asked.

"No."

"And at Vassar?"

She laughed, but it sounded hollow and sad. "I was a country hick with homemade clothes. I sounded just like Becky Sue," she said, falling back into the accent. "'Hi, ya'll, I'm Annie Jo Baker, from Texas.' You can imagine how well that went over." She stopped talking and swallowed. He watched the movement of her throat and wondered if she fought against tears. "The farthest I'd ever been from home was to the county hospital to give birth to my illegitimate child. I'd seen exactly five movies, I'd never eaten in a restaurant that had tablecloths. I'd never owned a hardback book."

For the second time in as many minutes he wanted to touch her. But this time the urge was about comforting rather than sex. Still he kept his hands on his lap.

"How many do you own now?" he asked.

"A lot." She smiled. "I have a whole bookcase of them in my bedroom at home."

"So you made it."

"I did. At work I've finally found a place to fit in. I'm successful and I know where I'm going."

She pulled up her knees close to her chest. Her full skirt reached down to her ankles so she was completely covered, but there was something provocative about the pose. And something painfully young. She might have made it financially, but in her heart she was still that young girl from Paradise.

"It must be hard for you to come back here," he said.

She looked at him. "I wanted Laurel to see where I grew up. I don't want her to have any fantasies about me. I want her to care about me. I want to be a part of her life, but she's too young for regrets."

"What about your regrets?"

"Do I get to have them?"

"I don't know. Do you?" he asked.

"Don't you hate me too much to care about my regrets?"

"I don't *hate* you."

She sighed. "You don't like me much. I suppose that's an improvement over being hated, but not one I can get excited about."

The night allowed them to speak freely. Perhaps he would regret telling the truth, but she deserved to hear it. "I don't trust you. There's a difference."

"Not a big one." She rested her head on her knees. "The trick is," she said, her voice slightly muffled, "that you never get to know what could have been. How would my life have been different if I hadn't gone to Vassar? What would have happened if I'd given up the scholarship and kept the baby?"

He didn't want to think about that, but she forced him to examine the alternatives. "I wouldn't have been Laurel's father." Or stayed married to Ellen.

The thought caught him off guard. But it was true. He would have left his wife. Without the responsibility of a child and her tearful claims that he owed her because she stayed when she could have left and had a child of her own, their marriage would have ended after a couple of years. If not for missing Laurel, that scenario would have been better for both him and Ellen.

"It's hard, isn't it?" she asked. "Trying to figure out what would have been. I could have gone to a local junior college, worked somewhere. You would have—" She looked at him. "What would you have done, Jake?"

He couldn't tell her the truth. She wouldn't understand. Besides, he'd only admitted half of it. The other half was that he would have still wanted a child of his own. A son. The one thing he couldn't buy, earn or achieve, no matter how hard he tried. He was sterile, and no wishing in the world could change that fact.

"I would have moved to the ranch sooner," he said at last.

"Did Ellen want to go there, too?"

"No. She liked Dallas and being in the city. After she was gone, I stayed for Laurel and because of my obligations to my father-in-law."

"What changed your mind? Laurel's new friends?"

He was surprised she'd remembered that conversation. "She was getting into trouble, but it was more than that. My father-in-law, Ellen's father, didn't want—" He hesitated. Anne might as well know, in case Laurel ever mentioned her grandfather. "After Ellen passed away he decided he didn't want anything to do with Laurel. She wasn't a blood relative and he disowned her."

Anne gasped. "His own granddaughter?"

He nodded. He could still feel the rage swelling inside him. It had taken every ounce of his self-control not to beat the crap out of the older man. Only his respect for Ellen's memory had kept him from attacking her father.

"Does Laurel know?" she asked.

"I don't think she's figured it out," he said. "He didn't come to her birthday party, but I told her he was out of town on business. I bought a gift and said it was from him." He shrugged. "That was probably a dumb idea, but I couldn't tell her that her grandfather didn't want anything to do with her. She would never understand. I'd already started the move to Colorado. What he said that day convinced me that getting away was the best thing for both of us. Even if Laurel doesn't believe it right now."

"She'll understand," Anne said. She leaned closer and smiled up at him. "One day she'll realize she has a wonderful father who loves her very much."

"I haven't been much of a father at all," he said, turning away from her. "After Ellen was killed in a car accident, I had a hard time dealing with her death. I pulled away from everything, including her."

"I'm sure she understands."

"Dammit, she was eleven. How could she understand?" He pushed off the rock and stood up. "I don't understand. She's a stranger, Anne. I have a thirteen-year-old daughter and I don't know what the hell she's thinking most of the time. She hates me for taking her away from her friends. Her grandfather has turned his back on her. She wants to live with you in Houston. The best news I've heard all day is that her real father is dead. I was glad when you said that. I don't need any more competition. What the hell kind of bastard does that make me?"

He shoved his hands into his pockets and started walking away. He'd barely gone two steps when he felt her hand on his arm.

"Wait, Jake."

He froze in his tracks. Her palm burned his skin. The scent of her body, the soft fragrance of her perfume, filled his senses.

"You're a good man," she said.

"Not by a long shot."

"You are," she insisted, moving closer. "You've done a fine job with Laurel. She couldn't turn out to be as sweet and loving as she is if you weren't decent."

He spun toward her so quickly she didn't have time to move back. In the moonlight he could see the shape of her head and body, but not the individual features. He couldn't see the expression on her face or read what was in her eyes.

He told himself he was a fool, that it wasn't about anything other than sex and that come morning he would regret acting on the impulse. But that didn't stop him.

"If I'm so decent," he said, grabbing her arms and hauling her up against him, "why can't I stop thinking about this?" He lowered his mouth to hers.

Chapter Seven

His kiss was as sweet and hot as the Texas summer. His firm mouth softened when it touched hers. He moved his lips back and forth as if testing her, then his hold on her arms loosened. Anne knew if she pulled back, he would let her go in an instant. She told herself that she *should* pull back, or at the very least be angry with him. But she didn't, and she wasn't. She couldn't be. Not when every inch of her body cried out for his touch. Not when she trembled within his gentle embrace. She had longed for this from the moment they'd first met. Damn that cowboy curse.

But even as she leaned against his broad chest until her breasts flattened against him she knew it was more than her weakness for cowboys. It was her weakness specifically for this man.

One of his hands reached up to cup the back of her head, the other moved down to the small of her back. She raised her arms to rest them on his shoulders and buried her fingers in his hair. The coffee-colored strands felt like cool silk, contrasting with the warmth of the night and the heat of their bodies.

He angled his head and pressed more firmly on her mouth. She tried to hold back, but it was no use. Her body clamored for him. Before she could think that she shouldn't, her lips parted, begging for his invasion.

He didn't disappoint her. His tongue swept past her lips, pausing only to tease the delicate skin with a quick swipe. A shudder rippled through her. At the first brush, a moan started low in her throat. His hand on her back moved lower to the curve of her derriere. The tiniest hint of pressure caused her to flex her hips forward. Her hips and stomach cradled his pelvis. The rigid proof of his excitement surged against her.

She told herself this was wrong, or at the very least, insane. She barely knew this man. There was already so much going on between them. Sex would only complicate a difficult situation. But when his tongue circled through her mouth, she ceased to care about anything but the sensations he created.

She clutched at his shoulders. His fingers touched her jaw then moved to her ear and traced the curves there. He pulled back from her mouth and licked her lips around and around. Her breasts ached with need. Between her thighs, the dampness grew as her cotton panties clung to her.

He lowered his arm so both his hands cupped her rear. He squeezed and pulled her against him. She rotated her hips, needing more, so much more. He kissed her jaw, her neck, down to the first button of her shirt. His hot breath seared her skin. She arched her head back, begging silently for more. She needed this. It had been too long. More than that, no one had ever made her feel this way before.

"Annie," he murmured against her skin. He spoke the word as if it was an endearment. He'd never called her Annie before. Maybe he didn't hate her.

Oh, God, he was Laurel's father. It was all too complicated. She had to stop. They had to stop. Now, before it became too late.

He touched her breasts. She bit her lip hard to keep from moaning aloud. His big hands cupped her sensitive flesh, taking their weight in his palms. He brushed his thumbs over her hard nipples. Through the blouse and bra, the contact burned. And it was too late to think.

Even as he fumbled with the buttons of her blouse, he stepped back the way they'd come, bringing her with him. As he pulled the thin cotton free of her skirt's waistband, her thighs touched the rock they'd sat on. Jake grabbed her by the waist and raised her up onto the flat surface, then he pulled off her blouse and lay it down behind her.

Her thighs parted and he stepped between them. His denim jeans rubbed against her bare skin. She told herself this wasn't happening, but she knew it was. Maybe it was those damn jeans, she thought as she reached for his shirt. She'd always been a sucker for a man in jeans. And his were button fly, the style that made her weak in the knees.

She quickly worked his shirt buttons, but before she could touch his chest, he reached for the center clasp on her bra. She caught her breath in anticipation.

He bent down and kissed her again. This time there were no preliminaries. He plunged his tongue inside, sweeping around her mouth, tasting every part of her, letting her taste him. She closed her lips in a tight O and sucked. With her hands on his shirt, she felt his muscles stiffen. He groaned. His fingers toyed with her nipples, flicking quickly over the hardened tips until her gasp released him and he, too, let her go.

He pulled back and opened the clasp. Gently he drew the bra back. The cups caught on her nipples. He bent over and with his tongue, freed each side. Then he drew the straps down her arms, leaving her bare to him. He stared for so long, she started to feel self-conscious. She glanced down and saw the way the moonlight reflected off her skin. Her nipples were dark tips on alabaster skin. In the darkness, her freckles didn't show. She almost felt beautiful before him.

He moved closer and his groin brushed against her damp panties. She wanted him, wanted this, more than she'd ever wanted anything. He lowered her back onto the rock. Her shirt protected her from the rough surface. He kissed her mouth, then licked her ear. He trailed a wet line down her collarbone toward her breasts. She arched up toward him, impatient for his touch.

He cupped her in his hands and held her still for his tender assault. He licked the sensitive nubs over and over until her world consisted only of fiery sensation and a need that burned so hot, it threatened to consume her. She rocked her hips against him. Her hands clutched at the rock, but she couldn't get any hold on the stone. She eached for his warm chest and felt a light dusting of hair. She rubbed her fingers against him, finding the flat male nipples and teasing him as he teased her. He punished her with a gentle bite. She moaned.

Everything felt perfect. The night. The heat of the rock below her, the fire of Jake's body above her. His hands and tongue continued to ply their magic. She wanted him, she could feel how he wanted her.

He nibbled along her midriff to the waistband of her skirt. She raised her hips. He reached down and began pushing the filmy fabric up her legs. His hands were hot on her thighs. His work-roughened skin grated deliciously. She could hear the soft rasping sound and it excited her more. She brought her arms back to brace herself and banged her elbow. The sharp pain made her cry out.

"You okay?" he asked, his voice gruff with passion.

"I just hit the rock. It's being outside. I haven't done anything this wild since..." Since she was seventeen. Since

Bobby and doing it in the back of his pickup. Since she got pregnant.

Remembering that was like being doused in cold water. She struggled to sit up. What on earth was she doing? Was she crazy? They both had to be. His hand continued to climb her legs. His thumb brushed perilously close to the apex of her thighs and she stiffened against the pleasure that flooded her.

"Jake, stop."

"Why?" The night caught the flare of his lazy, self-satisfied smile. He touched her panties, and she knew he felt the moisture. "You feel ready enough to me."

Oh, she was ready. Too ready, and far too willing. "We don't have any protection."

"Is that all?" He bent down and nibbled the inside of her knee. "I haven't been with anyone in over two years. About six months ago I had to give blood to a friend. They checked and I'm fine."

"I'm okay that way, too," she said. "What I meant was, I'm not on any birth control. I'm right in the middle of my cycle and probably as fertile as a rabbit."

He reacted as if she'd slapped him. He straightened up and glared down at her. The moonlight caressed the skin exposed by his open shirt. She wanted to touch him and feel his warmth again, but he held himself stiffly, as if in terrible pain. She folded her arms over her bare breasts.

"Jake?"

"You don't have to worry about getting pregnant," he said grimly. "I'm the reason we had to adopt a child instead of having one of our own. I'm sterile."

Now it was her turn to be shocked. Sterile? She stared at him. She'd never given much thought to why Jake and Ellen had adopted. She supposed that if she had, she would have assumed it was Ellen's fault. Which was foolish. She had no way of knowing why they couldn't have a child.

He stood silently before her, his chest rising and falling with each breath. She had time to become aware of herself, of what they were doing. All she wanted to do was put her bra and shirt back on and escape to the safety of Becky Sue's mobile home. She didn't want to be out here like this. It was a huge mistake. But she couldn't just walk away and leave Jake in such emotional pain. She could feel it radiating from him. It showed in the set of his shoulders and the tilt of his chin. He was waiting for her to scorn him. She had to tell him it didn't matter to her, although inside she ached for him.

He was such a proud man. Finding out he couldn't father children must have devastated him.

He started to turn away. Without giving herself time to think, Anne reached out and grabbed him. The only thing she could reach was his belt buckle. She pulled him hard against her. He moved forward reluctantly. She wanted to tell him she was sorry, but he wouldn't want to hear her words. There was nothing she could say, so when he was close enough, she wrapped her arms around his waist and pressed her lips to his chest.

He tasted all male with a combination of sweat and the unique flavor of his skin. What started out to be comfort rapidly became something else. She kissed him gently at first, moving her mouth across his chest with hard, hot kisses, then she began to lick him. She found his nipples and caressed them until his breathing became as rapid as her own.

His hands reached for her breasts. He touched her sensitive skin, kneading and rubbing until she quivered again with need. She'd had a half-formed notion that this was for him, to help take away his pain, but the second he reached under her skirt and touched her moist center, all thoughts of altruism fled, washed away by a flood of passion.

He jerked off her panties and pulled her skirt up around her waist. She undid his belt buckle and reached for the buttons on the fly of his jeans. To torment them both, she worked slowly, savoring the feel of his hardness against the back of her hand. Her knuckles brushed him with each button and his erection flexed at her touch.

At last he was free. She stroked his smooth length. He felt hotter here. Hard and ready. He quickly pushed down his jeans and briefs and moved between her thighs.

The velvet tip of him rubbed against her center, causing her muscles to clench rhythmically. When she was panting and desperately close to her release, he entered her.

She hadn't had a lover in several years and she was tight inside. He pushed forward slowly, stretching unused spaces, forcing dormant feelings to flare with sensation. She braced herself on her elbows and watched him move in and out of her body. She glanced at his face. He was looking at her. Their eyes locked.

They didn't speak, they didn't have to. Communication flowed between them as if they'd spent their whole lives waiting for this moment. Her hips flexed in time with his thrusts. She was closer, so much closer, but not close enough. She wanted more. He reached between them. With his thumb he gently stroked her. Up and down, double time to the movement of her hips. She felt him tightening, getting ready to explode and it was enough to send her to the edge.

He breathed her name and made her fall. Her muscles convulsed in release. It went on and on, forever it seemed. She felt his final thrust, heard the guttural cry, then he was still. He pulled her up against him, cradling her in his arms. She listened to the thundering of a heartbeat and wondered if it was his or hers. Perhaps now they only had one heart between them.

Reality gradually intruded and she could hear the night creatures around them, feel the hard rock jabbing her bare behind. She kissed Jake's chest and tasted him, but now her tongue was coated with the bitterness of regret. She sighed.

"That sounded pretty serious," he said, placing one finger under her chin and forcing her to look at him.

She flushed and was glad the darkness hid it from view. "You're Laurel's father."

"I know."

"This was all a mistake. I don't even know you. And you hate me."

"I don't hate you." He dropped his hand to his side. "I don't trust you."

"We just made love and you don't trust me?"

He stepped away. She pulled her skirt down and reached behind her for her bra.

"How did this happen?" she asked.

"I don't know." He didn't sound any happier than she did. "It was just hormones or circumstance." He pulled up his jeans and started fastening them. "We've both been without for a long time."

She slipped off the rock and grabbed her shirt. "So it was like taking a drink of water because you're thirsty?"

"Yeah."

The warm lover who had touched her was gone. Even his voice was different. Jake Masters was back. The man who, despite what he said, really didn't like her. And she'd just made love to him. In the desert. About fifty yards from Becky Sue's mobile home. On a rock. She wanted to die.

"I can't believe we did this," she said frantically. She tried to button her blouse, but her fingers weren't working. "We've never even been out on a date. I've known you less than two weeks."

"This isn't any easier for me," he growled. "Dammit, woman, I was married for fourteen years and I was never once unfaithful to Ellen."

"Golly, maybe you deserve an award for that," she snapped. "Blame it all on me, why don't you? That seems to be your favorite method for dealing with your problems anyway. Everything with Laurel is my fault, so make this my fault, too."

She was close to crying, so she clamped her mouth shut. By concentrating very hard, she managed to do up her shirt and stuff it into her skirt. She was about to walk away when he touched her arm.

"What?" she snapped.

Silently he held out his hand. He had her panties. The white cotton contrasted with his tanned skin. She covered her face with her hands.

"I just want to die," she whispered.

He pulled her close. "It's going to be okay," he said, his voice low and comforting. "We both reacted. I've never done anything like this, either. I'm not blaming you. It's no one's fault, Anne. Maybe it was for the best. We were both wondering about it. Now we know. It'll make the next two months easier for both of us. All we have to do is to pretend it never happened."

She stepped back and took her underpants. While he turned his back, she slipped them on. He was right. They had both wondered how it would be, and now they knew. But he was wrong, too. This wasn't going to make it easier. She knew that as surely as she knew he'd called her Anne again, instead of Annie.

They left Paradise early the next morning. Becky Sue got up before dawn and baked cinnamon rolls. After she'd filled them with coffee and the gooey confections, she gave them fifteen minutes of advice about the local highway.

Jake hovered in the background as Anne hugged her cousin goodbye. Laurel exchanged last frantic whispers with Becky Sue's oldest daughter and the two girls giggled together. He waited patiently while everyone got settled, then he headed toward the highway and home.

In the back seat Laurel fumbled with her portable radio. "I had a great time, Dad," she said, and yawned.

"I'm glad you enjoyed it. How late did you and Dolly stay up talking?"

She leaned back and yawned again. "Not late."

"Yeah, sure." He looked in the rearview mirror and winked.

She grinned at him. "Okay, maybe kinda late. But you know, not much past two."

"Yikes," Anne said from the seat next to him. "You must be tired."

"Maybe a little," Laurel answered. She slipped on her headset and started nodding to the beat. "I liked meeting everyone," she said. "Dolly's cool. We're going to write each other."

Jake's first impulse was to tell her that she would do no such thing. He didn't want his daughter corresponding with Anne's relatives. It was a knee-jerk reaction that would only get him in trouble with both Anne and Laurel. It was also unreasonable.

He rubbed his face with one hand, then shifted in his seat. He hadn't gotten much sleep, either. Not because he'd stayed up talking, though. He and Anne had immediately returned to the house. They hadn't bothered to linger in the desert. There had been awkward, mumbled "good-nights," then they'd fled for separate quarters. But even though she'd been out of sight, he hadn't been able to stop thinking about her or what they'd done. He was still thinking about it.

If it wasn't such a big mess, he'd have to laugh. After all he'd been the one saying they should just forget it. Yet every time he closed his eyes, he could see her naked body moving beneath his. He could feel her soft skin and taste her sweetness. Despite the release they'd shared, his body tightened over and over again in response to the memories. Even now, in the car, his groin hardened painfully, pressing against the button fly of his jeans. He prayed Anne wouldn't notice.

He glanced over at her. She was wearing a green tank top and matching shorts. Freckles dotted her skin. The shirt dipped low until he could see the hint of the valley between her breasts. Her perfume whispered through the interior of the Explorer.

She stared out her window and nibbled on her lower lip. He had a view of the elegant line of her neck. Last night he'd traced that line and tasted her skin. Not quite peaches, he remembered, but hot and sweet enough to drive a man to want more.

She drew in a deep breath, her breasts rising then lowering slowly. He could see the faint outline of one nipple. The tiny bud taunted him.

He glanced in his rearview mirror. Laurel had fallen asleep curled up on the seat, her head resting on Anne's carry-on bag. Thank God, he thought. Bad enough to have these kinds of thoughts, but it was disgusting when he considered his daughter was in the car with him. Her headset covered her ears. He could see the tape player was on. He thought about asking Anne to turn it off but he didn't want to wake the sleeping girl. She listened to the music all the time, anyway. It wouldn't kill her to sleep with it.

"What are you smiling at?" Anne asked.

He jerked his head toward the back seat. "She's out like a light. I was debating whether or not to ask you to take off her headset."

Anne twisted and looked over her shoulder. "I'm afraid I'd wake her."

"My thoughts exactly. She'll be fine."

"You're surprisingly cheerful." She faced front and smoothed her seat belt.

"Why wouldn't I be?"

"I saw the way you stiffened up when Laurel said she wanted to write Dolly. Don't you want to yell at me and get this off your chest?"

Nothing got by her. He resisted the urge to glance down at his erection. Maybe she hadn't noticed that. "Is that what I do?"

She shrugged. "I don't know you well enough to make a judgment. Let's just say that's what you've been doing with me about Laurel."

"This isn't easy for me," he admitted.

"It's not easy for me, either."

She looked at him. He quickly glanced over at her and their eyes met. Awareness flashed between them. The temperature in the car seemed to climb about twenty degrees. He swore silently. So much for forgetting. He returned his attention to the road.

They passed the next two hours in silence. Laurel slept on. Jake found a country station. The sound of steel guitars blended with his daughter's steady breathing. Anne stared out the front window. Occasionally he caught a glimpse of an emotion flickering across her face. He told himself he should ignore her. It wasn't any of his business. But he asked anyway.

"You're awfully quiet. What are you thinking about?" Part of him hoped she'd say "last night." Mostly because it was all he could think about.

"Becky Sue."

Jake shook his head. Guess he hadn't impressed Anne as much as he'd thought he had. "Why?"

"I was thinking about her life. Five kids in a double-wide trailer in the middle of nowhere. She couldn't be happier."

"You sound surprised."

She shifted until she was facing him. After adjusting her seat belt, she looked up and smiled. "I suppose I am. I spent most of my time trying to get away from there. It never occurred to her to do anything *but* stay. I'd always thought she was wrong."

"And now?"

"Now I'm not so sure. It was all so easy back then. I didn't even think about keeping Laurel." She glanced back at the sleeping girl. He saw her wistful smile. "I'm sorry, Jake. You're the last person I should be dumping this on."

"I don't mind," he said, and was surprised to find out he meant it. "I guess it's because all the wondering in the world isn't going to change the fact that you gave her up and we adopted her."

"I know." She leaned her head against the edge of the seat. "I always used to think that living in that tiny town and having just a few dollars above the legal poverty level would be a horrible life for a child. I didn't want that for my baby. Because I grew up that way. But so did Becky Sue. Her kids are doing it now. They all seem fine."

"Except for Joey chewing on the dog."

She chuckled. "Yeah, there is that." Her humor faded. "Don't be mad at me, but I can't help wondering if Laurel could have been happy there, too."

"Maybe she would have been."

She raised her head, her eyes wide with surprise. "I was sure you'd jump down my throat at that one."

"I'm not a complete jerk."

"I remember. Just half of one," she said, her voice low and teasing.

He gripped the steering wheel tighter. He liked this side of Anne Baker. He liked the quick mind and the gentle teasing. He liked the way her warm breath tickled his arm. He liked the sun catching a strand of her hair and turning the pale red color to auburn. He liked the feeling of family and it scared him to death.

"So you're having second thoughts," he said, returning to their original conversation.

"Maybe. But then I think about my career."

"And your promotion?"

"That, too. It's between me and this other guy." She sighed. "Tim the Turkey."

"Interesting title. Does it mean he's in management?"

She laughed. "Yes. And that he has a reputation for cornering secretaries in the supply room. No one's formally complained about sexual harassment, but the rumors have been running wild. He hates that I'm his competition."

"He doesn't like you?"

"He doesn't like the fact that I'm a woman." She looked up at him. "What kind of boss were you?"

"My dad made me work my way up through the ranks, so I knew what it was like to be forty stories up on a steel beam. I tried to be fair, to listen, then make the best decision. Pretty much an average kind of boss."

"Sounds a little better than average to me," she said, shifting until she was sitting straight in her seat. "I've worked so hard for this promotion. It was my goal from the time I hired on with the company right out of college."

"How is the leave of absence going to affect your chances?"

"I don't know. I'd like to think it won't matter, but I'd be kidding myself. Tim will be there every day, getting his work done."

Jake was surprised to find he wanted Anne to get the promotion, not because it would make his life easier, but because she'd worked hard and it was something *she* wanted. He was still a little wary, but the distrust was easing.

"I appreciate you taking the time to see this thing through with Laurel," he said.

"I want to spend some time with her, but I'm so scared."

"Of what? She thinks you're the hottest thing since hand-held video games."

"That's it, exactly." She glanced over her shoulder at the sleeping girl. Her lips curled into a smile. "Every day I spend with her, I grow to care more and more. Laurel is in the honeymoon stage. It's working now, but we're heading in different directions. Her case of hero worship is going to wear off. I think she'll still like me, but it won't be the same. I don't want to get my heart trampled by a thirteen-year-old girl, but I can't find a way to stop it from happening."

He'd never thought about Anne's risk in all this. He'd spent the past few days worrying about how Laurel's relationship with Anne affected him. But she was right. Laurel would get over her intense feelings and then life would settle down to some semblance of normalcy.

"She'll never want to let go of the relationship," he said. "She needs a woman in her life."

"She needs a woman, but that doesn't necessarily mean she'll need me. What happens if you remarry?"

"That'll never happen," he said without thinking.

"Why?"

"It just won't."

Get married again? He shook his head. Not in this lifetime. He'd barely recovered from his last marriage, and Ellen had been gone for two years.

It had all started out so well. He and Ellen had been best friends. Marriage had been a natural extension of that relationship. Everything had been fine those first couple of years. Until Ellen had decided she wanted to have a baby. They'd tried and tried, but nothing had happened.

Jake gripped the steering wheel more firmly. He could still remember the look on his father-in-law's face when he'd sat Jake down in his study.

"I've got some bad news, son." Michael had taken to calling him "son" when Jake's father had passed away. "It seems the problem is with you."

He'd gone on with an explanation about low sperm and lack of production, but none of it had made sense. He hadn't been listening, didn't even remember leaving Michael's large house. The next thing he knew, he was home and Ellen was crying. She hadn't said a word about it to him. She hadn't had to. He'd seen the sorrow and pity in her eyes. There would be no Masters son to carry on the family name. No child of his own to love and watch grow. That night Ellen had spoken to her father about adopting a child and within two weeks he'd arranged something private through a lawyer friend.

Jake glanced in his rearview mirror. Laurel shifted in her sleep. Her long brown hair hung over her shoulders. He couldn't see her eyes, but he knew they were hazel. Like Anne's mother.

Anne. He looked at her. She was staring at him. Their eyes met, then she quickly turned away. Bobby had given Anne what Jake could never give any woman. A child of her own.

He remembered the last years with Ellen. The arguments, the silences. Laurel's pale face as she witnessed her parent's marriage fall apart. He remembered last night and the sound of Laurel's laughter as she had played with her cousins. He remembered her insistence on spending time with Anne. With her birth mother. He remembered the last two years and the way he'd pulled back from his daughter. The nights he'd spent alone mourning his late wife and the future they were supposed to have had. He remembered the times he raged against God for denying him a son.

Anne was right. They were all heading in different directions. He could only pray they weren't on the road to disaster. He clenched his jaw. No matter what, he wasn't going to lose Laurel. She was all he had left.

Chapter Eight

The house stood in a shelter of pine trees. Behind it was a large barn and several corrals. Past them, Anne could see more buildings and a young man exercising a horse on the end of a lead.

"We're here," Jake said, turning off the engine. He glanced at her expectantly.

"It's beautiful," she said, staring at the peaked roof and wide bare windows. A big porch wrapped around the front of the house. The lawn looked new and a painfully bright green.

She stepped out of the Explorer. Her legs were stiff. She shook them and stretched. Jake hadn't rushed to get them back, so the drive had taken three days. Laurel unfolded herself from the back seat. She ripped off her headphones and tossed them back into the truck.

"Give me the key," she said, dancing around her father. "I want to show Annie *everything*."

He handed her his key ring. Laurel found the correct one, then took Anne's hand and pulled her toward the house.

"Come on," she said. "You've got to see the inside. It's *so* big. But empty." She climbed the porch stairs, let go of her hand and stuck the key into the lock. "I've been working on decorating it, but I don't know very much, and it's not that fun to do alone. You can help me now."

She got the door unlocked and pushed it open. She dragged Anne across the threshold. Laurel had been right. The house was huge. A stone fireplace dominated the living room. A couple of couches were pushed up against bare walls, but other than that there wasn't any furniture. Laurel showed her the dining room. Again, bare walls and floors, no window coverings. Just a tattered old table and four chairs.

"Dad says we should replace this," Laurel said, running her hands over the pitted wood. "Through here is the kitchen."

Modern appliances gleamed from their built-in spaces. Unlike her white-on-white, this kitchen was filled with color. The tiles were cream with a pale blue pattern. The oversize center island continued the theme with alternating blue and cream tiles. The bleached cabinets contrasted with the bright floral wallpaper. Plants hung in the corners. A cow-print table with four matching chairs sat in front of the bare window.

"I ordered this from a catalog," Laurel said proudly, standing behind one of the chairs.

Anne stared. The furniture was wood, all right. But it had been painted white with black marks. Like a cow. "Oh, my. What did your father say?"

"He wasn't very happy," Jake said, coming into the kitchen. He had her luggage in one hand and Laurel's bag in the other. "Where did you want to put Anne?"

"There's an extra bed in my room," Laurel said hopefully.

"Not a good idea," Jake said, before she could answer.

He shot her a glance as if daring her to defy him, but she had no intention of doing so. As much as she adored her daughter, she wanted her own room.

"How about that front bedroom?" Laurel said. "It's big and it's right next to me."

He looked at her for confirmation.

"Sounds fine," she said.

"I'll go ahead and take these up." He lifted the bags a few inches, then turned and headed toward the stairs.

Laurel took her hand and pulled her across the hall and into a library. "Daddy and I both like to read. Mom did, too. She liked to collect first editions. We've got bunches." There were piles of boxes, some of them open. Anne could see the books inside. The walls of the room were floor to ceiling bookshelves.

She remembered telling Jake that before she'd left Paradise, she'd never owned a hardcover book in her life. Had he thought of his library then? Had he secretly laughed at her or had he understood her desire to be more than she'd been born to?

A pair of leather wing chairs stood in one corner with a table and a reading lamp between them. Scattered throughout the room were smaller tables covered with framed photographs. Anne stepped closer to study the pictures.

The first one she picked up showed a much younger Jake and a beautiful, elegantly dressed dark-haired woman holding a baby. A newborn, from the look of the infant's scrunched-up face. The pain caught Anne like a blow to the chest. The air rushed out of her lungs and she had to gasp to breathe.

"That's when Mom and Dad brought me home from the hospital," Laurel said, blithely unaware of the hurt her words caused.

Anne stared. Her child. The baby they wouldn't let her hold that horrible day over thirteen years ago. She traced the cool glass, but she couldn't touch the infant's face, feel her warmth or inhale her baby scent. She wanted to weep and scream against a fate that had been so unkind. But it wasn't fate, she reminded herself. It was her. She'd made the decision to give Laurel up, and now she had to live with the consequences.

She swallowed hard and exchanged that photo for the one that had been next to it. This was a wedding portrait. Ellen looked stunningly beautiful in yards of white lace. The gown showed off her fashion-model's figure to perfection. She carried a cascade of flowers. Next to her, Jake stood tall and handsome. The look on his face as he stared at his bride made Anne's heart clench even tighter. There was so much love between them. It was as tangible as the cool silver of the frame.

The rest of the photographs showed the happy couple together. Some with Laurel, some just the two of them. Anne glanced down at her rumpled shorts and T-shirt. At her freckled arms and generous breasts. She was nothing like Ellen Masters. Even on her best day, she could never compete with the tall, slender beauty.

She told herself it wasn't a competition. She reminded herself that Laurel didn't care what she looked like, and that Jake hadn't minded her curves that night they'd made love. But it had been dark, a little voice whispered. Their joining had been about circumstance and mutual need. She had a bad feeling that he hadn't specifically been making love to her. Any woman would have done.

She took a moment to compose her features, then turned away from the photos. "I don't see any of your school pictures," she said to Laurel.

"Oh, Dad keeps those in his bedroom." She wrinkled her nose. "I hate some of them. There's a photo album of me somewhere in one of these boxes." She motioned to the stacks. "Maybe we can find it later."

"I'd like that." Anne drew in a deep breath to compose herself. "What's next?"

"Through here are all the catalogs and stuff." Laurel led the way into a smaller room. A long table stood against one wall. Decorating magazines, paint and carpet samples and catalogs from dozens of home furnishings manufacturers covered the surface. "I've been trying to figure all this out, but I don't know where to start." She brushed her bangs out of her face and sighed. "Dad told me I could do anything I wanted with the house, but everything is so expensive, and I *am* only thirteen."

"Oh, you are, are you?" Annie walked over to the table and gave Laurel a smile. She forced her feelings of inadequacy into the back of her mind and concentrated on her daughter. "A couple of days ago you were trying to convince us all you were grown-up."

"Maybe I am still a little, you know, young," Laurel said, then grinned. "Can you help me with this stuff?"

"I'd love to." If she really stayed for two months there wasn't going to be much else to fill her time, Anne thought as she stared at her daughter. "I used to do a lot of crafts when I was growing up. I also sewed."

"Really?" Laurel couldn't have looked more shocked if Anne had told her she was a spy for a foreign government. "With a sewing machine and everything?"

"It's a lot faster than doing it by hand. Why are you so surprised?"

Laurel shrugged. "I've never known anyone who could sew before."

Anne thought about the pictures of Ellen. In all of them she was wearing expensive designer clothes. It made sense that Jake's late wife hadn't taken the time to sew anything.

"I haven't done it in a while, but I think I could whip something up."

"Can you teach me crafts and stuff?"

"Sure. Next time we go into town, we'll find a crafts store and I'll get you started on counted cross-stitch. It's easy and the results can be beautiful."

"Cool." She motioned to the piles of catalogs. "Can we do my room first? I saw something in Dolly's room I'd like to do here. So can we?"

"If your father doesn't mind." Anne picked up a ring of paint samples. "Let's ask him tonight and then get started in the morning."

"You're the best." Laurel came up to her and wrapped her arms around her waist. "I'm glad you're here with me. We belong together."

Anne set down the samples and hugged her back. Despite her misgivings, it felt right to be here. She closed her eyes and concentrated on memorizing everything about this moment. When she opened her eyes again, she saw Jake standing in the doorway. From the look on his face, she figured he'd overheard Laurel telling her that she was glad Anne was here. A stark expression swept through his eyes, and she knew their fragile peace had once again been destroyed.

"Mom didn't do much regular cooking," Laurel said as she rinsed the green beans. "We had a housekeeper. Mom was really busy with her charity work a lot of the time. She didn't have a job. Mom said it was important for people with money to give something back to the community."

"That's a good philosophy," Anne said, and bit down on her lip to keep from screaming. While Laurel avoided mentioning Ellen around her father, she didn't feel that same restriction with Anne. In the past hour, she'd included the word "Mom" in almost every sentence.

They'd finished their tour of the house. Anne had a brief impression of large rooms filled with small amounts of furniture. In Jake's room, a king-size bed had dominated one wall. There had been a few scattered garments and his still-packed suitcase, but little else. Her guest room suffered the same fate. A bed, a small dresser and her suitcase. At least she had her own bathroom and some much-needed privacy. She adored her daughter, but she'd spent the past three days in close contact with Laurel and could use some breathing space.

Which probably makes me a crummy parent, she thought grimly as she searched for a casserole dish.

"They're in here," Laurel said helpfully, pointing at a shelf in the center island.

"Thanks." She rinsed off the chicken she'd defrosted in the microwave. On the way to the house they'd stopped at a local vegetable stand for fresh produce, but everything else in the meal would have to be either canned or frozen.

Anne dug around in the pantry for a package of rice. "I can't find the rice, Laurel."

"We don't have any. Mom didn't like it."

Anne started to stand up, but she bumped her head on a pantry shelf. The sharp pain brought tears to her eyes.

"I heard that crack," Jake said, silently appearing at her side. "You okay?"

"Fine," she said curtly, and turned away from him. She rubbed her head and willed herself to ignore him.

He'd been doing that since they'd arrived. Drifting in and out of rooms. Showing up in the middle of conversations, then leaving. She knew what he was doing; she knew he was checking on her. He didn't trust her not to say or do something in the presence of his daughter. Anne fumed. He just plain didn't trust her. But he could sleep with her.

She wasn't completely upset that they'd given in to the sexual tension between them. She wasn't happy about it, but it wasn't a total surprise. The attraction had been too powerful for their vulnerable states. It almost made sense. Almost. But what really steamed her was the fact that he was actually able to do as he'd suggested and put that night out of his mind. She hated that he was able to engage her in casual conversation as if nothing intimate had ever occurred. It took all her mental power and self-control to keep from blurting out something inappropriate, or reaching to touch him. Now that she'd tasted his male passion, she wanted more.

Laurel hovered nearby. "Do you want some ice for your head?"

"I'm fine," she said again. If there wasn't rice, she'd have to come up with something else. She remembered seeing a frozen potato dish in the freezer. She rummaged around until she found it and set it on the counter.

Laurel looked at the package. "Are we having that with chicken?"

Anne drew in a deep breath. "Is that a problem?"

"Well, Mom always served that with pork, didn't she, Dad?"

The threat of tears returned, but not just because her head was hurting. Ellen had been gone two years. Shouldn't Laurel have let go of all these little traditions? Anne rubbed her swelling bump. She didn't have a clue as to what was going on with Laurel. Maybe she clung to the rituals because they were all she had.

"I think we can have them with chicken this once," Jake said.

Anne didn't dare turn and look at him. She didn't want to see anything like compassion in his eyes.

"I don't expect you to take the place of a housekeeper," he said, leaning against the island.

Anne moved around him and picked up the chicken. She placed it in the dish and sprinkled on the spices. "I don't mind cooking," she said. "I never have much of a chance at home."

"Are you sure?"

No, she wasn't sure about anything. "Of course."

"I've put a call in to an agency. Because of our location, it may be a little while until I can get someone full-time. I appreciate your help."

She put the cover on the chicken dish and popped the casserole into the oven. After setting the timer, she forced herself to smile then turn toward him.

He leaned against the island, one hip resting on the tile with his opposite leg crossing over in front and the toe of his boot touching the floor. He'd folded his arms over his chest. The blue polo shirt hugged his broad shoulders, snuggling up to skin that two nights ago she had touched and tasted. His brown eyes studied her with equal thoroughness, and she wondered what he was looking for. Would he be pleased with what he saw or would she again come up short?

She thought about the pictures in the library and how perfect Ellen had looked in each of them. Even the candid shots. Anne became aware of her wrinkled shorts and T-shirt. She'd been in her clothes all day on the road and she looked like it. She brushed a stray strand of hair out of her face. No doubt her makeup had long since faded. She was a mess.

Laurel set the table, then excused herself from the room. When she was gone, the tension in the kitchen cranked up noticeably. Anne became aware of her breathing, of the heat from the oven, which was nothing compared with the heat from the man in front of her. And he was a man. Every lean inch, every masculine line. Her body cried out for what she had known. He might be able to forget what had flared between them, but she would remember long after these two months were over.

She wondered if he would take advantage of the moment of privacy. She wanted him to pull her close and claim her mouth. She wanted him to touch her and love her and—

"What time do we eat?" Jake asked.

"About seven."

He nodded. "I need to go talk to my manager and see how the horses got along." With that he, too, left the room.

She stared around her, at the unfamiliar room and furniture. She thought about the need filling her body. Apparently she'd been wrong about the tension. How could it have been there if only she could feel it? He didn't remember their lovemaking. He didn't trust her.

Anne checked the oven, then headed for the stairs and her room. She wanted a long shower before dinner.

As she stepped into the spray of hot water, she told herself she'd been a fool. Of course she'd expected some problems during the two months she'd planned on spending here. But it was even worse than she'd imagined. She'd forgotten what it was like not to fit in. She felt awkward and self-conscious about everything she said or did. She didn't know the right food or where anything was. She was entering another woman's domain. It didn't matter that Ellen Masters had been dead for two years and had never even lived in this house. Every item and every person in this house bore her mark. Everyone except Anne.

As the water poured down her face and mingled with the tears, Anne wondered if it was too late to go home.

Jake stared at the open ledger in front of him. Several of the mares were going to be ready to breed soon. He was still mentally debating about whether to cover them with his own stallions or go outside the ranch. He weighed the expense with the value of fresh bloodlines.

He leaned back in his wooden chair and glanced around the office. It still looked the same as it had when his grandfather had lived here. Trophies and ribbons covered most of one wall. The large window that overlooked the paddock gleamed from its weekly washing. Like the old man before him, Jake wanted to be able to see what was going on with his horses. The battered desk was close to a hundred years old. Only the computer equipment and table were new additions. He was a long way from his penthouse office in his father-in-law's executive suite. A long way from Dallas and the life he'd known before.

He heard a knock on the door.

"Come in," he called.

Anne stepped into his office. She was carrying a tray, which she placed on the corner of his desk.

"You've been in here all morning," she said. "I thought you might be hungry."

He glanced at the plate of sandwiches, the cut-up fruit and the pot of coffee. He already had a mug of his own, but there was a second one beside the pot. In the two weeks that she'd been at the ranch, they'd settled into a sort of routine. It consisted of him avoiding her and her letting him. He knew that she was spending her days alone now that Laurel was in school. He told himself he should encourage her to fix up the house if she wanted to. God knows he wasn't interested in picking out wallpaper. He even felt guilty about leaving her every morning while he came out to the barn or to his office beside the tack room. But it had been easier to stay out of her way and try to forget what happened every time they were in a room together. Now she had made the first tentative move toward a normal relationship and he couldn't throw it back in her face.

He picked up his mug. "Looks like you brought an extra cup. Why don't you sit down and keep me company." He motioned to the leather chair in front of his desk.

"I don't want to disturb you," she said, nervously wiping her hands on her jeans.

"I wouldn't have asked if I didn't want the company."

"Thanks." She smiled and took the seat.

She didn't wear much makeup. Just something around her eyes and a little lipstick. Still, when she smiled, her whole face lit up. He liked that. He was also starting to like the freckles. He noticed there were exactly eleven on her nose. He'd caught himself counting them at odd times.

Like when she sat across from him at dinner or when she earnestly asked if it was all right for her to bake a cake to celebrate Laurel's first day at school.

Even in southern Colorado, late September meant the arrival of fall, so she'd exchanged her shorts for jeans. The soft denim hugged her generous curves. Jake kept trying to picture Ellen in jeans, but he didn't think his late wife had ever worn them. He tried to remember her in any trousers so that he could use the memory of her slender hips and long legs as a talisman against Anne's sensuality. But he couldn't summon her to his mind. He was forced to admire the swell of Anne's hips and the way her breasts filled the front of her blouse. At least the table shielded him and she wouldn't be able to see the result of his erotic thoughts.

Anne poured herself a cup of coffee, then refilled his mug. She stared around the room, glanced quickly at him, then away. He sensed her apprehension. It made him feel like a complete bastard. It wasn't her fault he couldn't put the memory of their lovemaking out of his mind, so instead of continuing to try, he chose to avoid her. It wasn't her fault he couldn't bear to watch his daughter grow to love her more and more each day, so he hid out in his office. It wasn't even her fault that Laurel had wanted to meet her in the first place. For that last one, he only had himself to blame.

"This is really—"

"How are you—?"

They spoke at the same time. "Go ahead," she said shyly.

"How are you getting on?" he asked. "Do you miss work?"

She shrugged. "Some. The pace is certainly different. In Houston I generally work about sixty hours a week. With that woman coming in to clean twice a week, there's not much for me to do here." She grinned. "I can only bake so many cookies without all of us getting fat."

"I—" He drew in a breath. Hell, just ask her, he told himself. She deserved a little cooperation. "I'd appreciate it if you'd consider helping Laurel decorate the house."

"She'd mentioned wanting to do that," Anne said, staring at him intently. "But I didn't want to step on any toes."

He raised his hands in a gesture of surrender. "Don't sweat my toes. I don't know anything about furniture or color schemes or Berber carpet from shag. I'd prefer not to wake up to daisies in my bedroom, but other than that, I'm pretty easy to please."

She shifted in her chair and bit her lower lip. "If you're sure?"

"I am. Really. You'd be doing me a favor."

"Okay." Her blue eyes glowed with pleasure. "No daisies, I promise."

"Good, and I'd prefer to avoid any more cow-colored pieces of furniture."

She chuckled. "I'll admit I was a little shocked when I saw the table and chairs in the kitchen, but they're kind of growing on me."

He reached for the tray and pulled it closer to him. "Don't even try," he said with a mock growl. "You should have seen the look on my face when I opened that damned crate. I'm sure it was priceless." He took a bite of the sandwich.

"What did Laurel say?"

He finished chewing. "She was thrilled. I didn't have the heart to tell her it was the ugliest thing I'd ever seen. Who in their right mind would decorate their kitchen with cow-patterned furniture?"

She giggled and leaned forward, resting her forearms on his desk. "It's very trendy. All the best people are doing it."

"I've never been very trendy."

"Well, your daughter sure is. We had a 'discussion' this morning because she wouldn't wear a blouse. She'd had it a whole year and was convinced it was out of style."

He put down his sandwich and wiped his hands on the napkin. "How is she doing in school? She's told me she'd made some friends, but I worry she's just saying that to make me feel better."

Anne grew serious. "From what she's told me, I think she is fitting in. The students here are from a more rural background than she's used to, but she knows about horses and that makes a difference. I don't think she's hiding any big secrets. I know she's a little lonely, but a new girlfriend has invited her to a slumber party this Friday, so she's getting along."

"I appreciate your hand in all this," he said. "You've gone out of your way to help Laurel. You didn't have to."

"I wanted to." Anne drew in a deep breath. "This has been hard for both of us, I know. I didn't know what to expect when you asked me to spend two months here."

He grinned. "I don't recall asking you."

"All right. When you *ordered* me to spend two months here. Is that better?"

"Much."

Her soft giggle made him want to laugh in return. He'd been a fool to avoid her, he realized. The kicker was he'd been trying to punish her, but the person who had suffered the most was himself. She wasn't half bad. In fact, she was pretty okay. Not that he was going to tell her that. At least, not yet.

Anne reached over for the plate of fruit. Her hand hovered above a slice of cantaloupe. "May I?"

"Help yourself."

She picked it up. "I'll admit that I didn't expect to spend two months here. I thought I'd drive up with you two, fix whatever needed fixing, then fly home and get on with my life. I thought I'd see Laurel every few months, maybe for a week or so during the summer, and that would be it." She took a bite and chewed slowly. "It's not like that at all, is it?"

"No. You're building a relationship with her, and a bond. That's hard to ignore."

"Do you still hate me?" she asked.

"I told you I never hated you."

"I know, you say you just didn't trust me. But the truth is you did hate me. Admit it, Jake. Why wouldn't you? I would have hated you if the situations were reversed. But do you still?"

He thought about the sound of Laurel's laughter and how much he heard it these days. He remembered the look on Anne's face every time his daughter talked about her late mother and how she never told Laurel to stop mentioning Ellen. He stared down at his half-eaten sandwich and remembered how she consulted him before trying a new dish. She was always careful to, as she put it, not step on any toes.

What was in it for her? In a few weeks she would go back to her real life. Laurel would miss her and want to keep in touch, but the reality of the situation was that Laurel would probably now be content to stay with him. Anne would find her condo lonely without the chatter of a thirteen-year-old underfoot. He'd learned that in the few hours Laurel had been missing.

"Truth?" he asked.

"Truth," she answered.

"No, I don't hate you, Anne." He couldn't. She'd given too much unselfishly. She was going to pay a big price for that giving. He could afford to be generous. He didn't only understand what she was going to feel, he realized he, too, was going to miss her when she was gone.

"Do you think we can be friends?" She stared at him as earnestly as a schoolgirl.

He smiled. "I'd like that."

"Even if I decorate your bathroom with cow accessories?"

"That would put a strain on the relationship."

She grinned. "Okay. I just wanted to know where the line was."

He chuckled. Anne loved the sound of his laughter. He could make her knees quiver and her thighs go up in flames. Down, girl, she told herself. This was about building emotional bridges, not passion. In fact, in the past two weeks Jake had done nothing to indicate he was the least bit turned on by her. Apparently their little roll in the hay—more like their little roll on a rock—had been enough to appease him. He was calm, competent and completely impersonal around her. He couldn't have treated her any more asexually if he had been her brother. She, on the other hand, had all the subtlety of a cat in heat. Every time she saw him, she wanted to rub against his body and purr.

On that cheerful note, she was going to leave. She stood up. "I should be heading back to the house. I have to get dinner in the oven. Then I'm going to pull out those catalogs and think about ordering furniture. Is there a budget?"

He reached for the second half of his sandwich. "Try to spend less than it cost to build the house."

She raised her eyebrows. "That's it?"

"You seem surprised."

"Let's just say it's a long way from Paradise."

The humor left his eyes. The gold-flecked irises darkened with compassion. "It is, Anne. But not so far from Houston."

"That's true. I'm not little Annie Jo Baker anymore."

His smile turned wistful. "I think I might have liked her just as much as I like Anne Baker."

Maybe even more, Anne thought as she waved goodbye and headed back toward the house. Annie Jo would have stayed in Paradise and kept her daughter with her. She would have tried to make it on her own. Anne sighed.

Who's to say what would have been right? She could make herself crazy thinking about it.

She entered the kitchen. After collecting the vegetables she would need, she started chopping onions. A quick glance at the clock told her that if she was in Houston instead of on Jake's ranch, she would probably be knee-deep in meetings right about this time.

"If they could see me now," she said as she peeled the second onion. The pungent smell began to burn her eyes.

Where would she be if she'd stayed in Paradise? She would never know if she'd made the right decision or the easy one. But she was here and she'd better make the best of it. Not everyone got a second chance.

Her stomach lurched, surprising her. She stopped chopping and swallowed. Suddenly she didn't feel so great. She washed her hands, then drank a glass of water. If anything, the liquid made her feel worse. Almost nauseous. Was it the onions? She stared at the cutting board. They'd never bothered her before.

She started to take another sip of water when her stomach heaved. She set the glass on the counter and ran to the bathroom.

When she was done throwing up, she washed her face and sat on the closed toilet seat lid. Could it be the flu? Anne pressed a hand against her midsection. She hadn't felt this bad in years. She blinked. Thirteen years. She blinked again.

No. It wasn't possible. It couldn't be possible. Jake had said he was sterile. But it had been the middle of her cycle, at her most fertile time. Oh, God.

She ran through the kitchen and into the hallway. The Explorer keys hung on a hook. Jake had told her she could use his truck anytime she wanted. She grabbed the keys and her purse and headed out the front door. The closest drugstore was about five miles down the road. She had a couple of hours before Laurel got home from school. She could pick up the kit and be back in plenty of time. Then all she had to do was wait until morning. Then she would know for sure.

Chapter Nine

Jake drew the razor along his jaw. The master bath off his bedroom was big enough not to get steamy. The eight-foot-long mirror reflected his image, the double sinks and the stall shower in the corner. Behind him was the Jacuzzi. He glanced at the tiled monstrosity and wondered what on earth his grandfather had been thinking of when he'd ordered that. Jake had never bothered to fill it up and turn on the jets. For all he knew, the sucker didn't even work. There were a lot of luxuries in the house he considered unnecessary. But his grandfather had passed away about three weeks after construction had started. Jake had been too devastated to do more than let the contractors continue with their work. It had been easier than planning a new house. He realized now that in the back of his mind he'd always figured on coming here and building up the horse ranch.

He adjusted the towel around his waist before wiping away the shaving cream. He'd barely finished drying his face when the door to his bathroom flew open.

"You bastard!" Anne said as she stormed into the room. "You damned bastard." Her voice was low and controlled but there was no mistaking her anger.

"What the hell is wrong with you?" he asked, as confused by her rage as by her presence in his bathroom. It was barely six in the morning. "Don't you believe in knocking?"

"Interesting choice of words," she said. In her left hand she held a slender plastic wand. She raised her right and pointed her index finger at him. "How dare you? How *dare* you? Was it fun, like playing a game? Did you think you would risk it and let me pay the consequences?"

Her emotions flooded the room. He leaned one hip against the counter and folded his arms over his chest. "Are you going to tell me what you're talking about or do you want to rant some more?"

Her skin was pale, but her eyes flashed fire. Under her white cotton gown, her breasts rose and fell with each breath. He realized the filmy fabric was see-through. The darker circles of her aureoles and her puckered nipples were clearly visible. He hoped the towel was thick enough to hide his instant reaction.

"What is it about cowboys?" she asked, as if he hadn't spoken. She lowered her hand to her side and started to pace the room. She walked to the shower, then back in front of him to the closet door. On the return trip she glared at him. "Is it the jeans? Is it the button fly? Why can't I resist a tight butt in denim? Am I cursed or just stupid?"

"If you're looking for an answer, I sure as hell don't have one. I don't know what you're talking about. And keep your voice down. You'll wake Laurel."

"Wake her? As if you thought you could keep this a secret?"

She stopped in front of him and leaned close. He could feel the heat of her body and smell her scent. Her short hair was tousled from sleep. He wanted to touch the shiny strands and run his fingers through her curls. He wanted to pull her close and kiss away her anger. He wished she would get to the reason for her tirade because his groin had swelled past the point of uncomfortable, and his daughter's alarm wasn't scheduled to go off for another half hour. It wasn't as much time as he wanted to make love with Anne, but it would be enough to ease whatever ailed her.

"Fine," she said, poking his chest. "Play dumb. Just answer me this. Why? Why did you do it?"

"Do what?" he asked, his patience beginning to evaporate. "What are you talking about?"

"This." She tossed the wand onto the counter. It rolled until it came to rest against a box of tissue. He'd been wrong. It wasn't all white. One end was bright blue.

He looked from the device to her. "This is supposed to mean something?"

She stared at him as if he were as dumb as a stone. Then she shook her head. When she spoke, she enunciated each word carefully. "I'm pregnant."

He knew they didn't have anything close to a relationship, but his first emotion was heart-stopping betrayal. She'd told him it had been years since she'd been with someone and he'd been fool enough to believe her. His gaze dropped to her belly, and the triangle of reddish curls below.

"You lying bitch," he said softly. "What's next? You have some disease that you forgot to tell me about?"

"Disease?" Her brows drew together. "Lying? You're the one who lied. You're the one who promised you were sterile. Did you get a kick out of playing God? I even told you it was the middle of my cycle. What were you trying to prove?" She poked him in the chest again. "What is it? That you're too macho to use a condom? This is the nineties, buster. Only fools are unprotected. Okay, I was a fool. I admit that. But I'm pregnant!"

He tried to control his breathing, but he couldn't do anything except feel the red thick rage that flowed through him. His hands tightened into fists. He fought to relax them because he was afraid he would have to pound the wall over and over until she stopped torturing him. A child. She taunted him with a child.

Michael's words returned to him. "I'm sorry, son. The problem is with you. The problem is with you. With you. With you." The words echoed.

"No!" Jake said loudly. "No!" he roared. "Dammit, no!"

Anne backed away from him. He advanced on her. She grabbed for the door, but first she accidentally bumped it with her heel and it slammed shut. Her blue eyes widened with fear.

"Stop it," she commanded.

He froze in his tracks and fought the demons. With conscious effort he relaxed his muscles one by one. He turned from her and returned to lean against the counter. Slowly sanity replaced rage. With awareness came humiliation. She'd used him.

"You will not pawn another one of your bastard children off on me," he said softly.

A gasp was her only reply.

He didn't wait for more, he simply continued. "I don't know if this is what you did with Bobby. Was he Laurel's real father or did you try to trick him, too? Or are you such a slut you can't remember who knocked you up?"

"What's wrong with you?" she asked, coming up and standing next to him. "Why would I lie about this? Why would I pass another man's child off as yours?"

"So you could stay here, with Laurel." He turned suddenly and grabbed her arms. "It won't work." He shook her. "By God, it won't work."

"Stop it," she cried. "Just stop it."

He let her go and stared at his hands. What was wrong with him? In all the years he'd been married to Ellen, he'd never been this angry before.

"I'm not lying," she said. A lock of hair fell into her face. She brushed it back impatiently. He saw the tears in her eyes. "I swear, Jake, I'm not lying. My last relationship ended about four years ago. I haven't been with a man since. Why are you doing this? Why won't you believe me? You were there. You know what happened."

"Because I'm sterile," he said. "I can't father children."

The tears spilled over and ran down her cheeks. She squared her shoulders. Strength flowed through her. He could see it in the way she raised her head and tilted her chin. She defied him. "I've been honest with you from the beginning. I've been willing to accommodate myself to you and your wishes. I've tried to be fair with Laurel and with you. Not once have I lied or used my position against you." She wiped her face with the back of her hand. "You and I made love almost three weeks ago. We were irresponsible and didn't use protection. I'm pregnant. The child is yours, Jake. Believe me or not. There's nothing more I can say to convince you." She walked over to the bathroom door and opened it. Before she left, she turned back and stared at him. "Did it ever occur to you that the doctor made a mistake?" The door shut behind her.

He looked around for something to throw. He needed to vent the rage inside him. How dare she try to pawn off some man's bastard. What kind of a fool did she take him for?

He gripped the counter, squeezing tight until his hands ached. The doctor might be wrong. Hell, what other piece of goods would she try to sell him? Maybe she wanted him to start digging for gold in the paddock. The doctor might be wrong. Why not say the doctor lied? He closed his eyes and exhaled sharply. Even as he tried to forget, Michael's words returned, getting louder and louder. "It's your fault. Your fault. Yours."

God, it was a waking nightmare. He couldn't escape from the past. That lying, cheating, no-good bastard. Of all the people to give him the news. Why had he been the one?

Michael lied whenever it suited him. That was one of the reasons Jake hadn't wanted to continue doing business with his father-in-law. Michael had been willing to cheat anyone out of a buck. The only person in the world he cared about was Ellen. He would have done anything to protect her. Anything at all.

Suddenly Jake straightened and met his own gaze in the mirror. Disbelief and the desire to make it true battled with reality. It couldn't be that simple, could it? Just one lie in a long line of lies? He walked out of the bathroom and headed for the phone sitting on the floor by his bed.

Anne washed the red apple, then wiped it dry. She placed it in the paper bag and folded over the top. "Laurel, you're going to be late," she called.

The teenager slowly entered the kitchen. Anne glanced up at her. "You're going to be late," she repeated, then realized Laurel's eyes were red. "What's wrong?"

"I heard you and Daddy fighting," she said softly.

Anne's heart stopped. Oh, no, anything but that. She swallowed hard. "What did you hear, honey?" she asked, praying it wasn't as bad as she thought.

Laurel shrugged. "Nothing you said. I just heard you yelling at each other." She blinked several times, but the tears still escaped. "Don't fight with my dad. Don't go away."

"Oh, baby." Anne moved close to her and wrapped her arms around her slender body. "Hush. I'm not going away." At least not yet, she thought, wondering what on earth she was going to do. "We were just arguing. Grown-ups often do that. Sometimes it gets loud but it doesn't mean we hate each other." Anne gave her a reassuring smile even as she knew she was lying. Jake thought she was a slut, and she thought he was a weasel bastard. Not a great basis for a relationship. Still, none of that had anything to do with Laurel.

The teenager moved away and went to pour herself a bowl of cereal. Anne didn't want to think about food. Not this early. She couldn't even face coffee, she thought, turning away from the pot. Good thing because caffeine probably wasn't healthy for the baby.

Baby. Her knees grew weak and she had to grab a hold of the counter. She was going to have a baby. All last night she'd been frantic with worry, wondering if her suspicions were correct. She'd had to wait until this morning before she could take the test. Then she'd been so furious with Jake for lying to her that she hadn't had time to absorb the news. She was going to have a baby... another baby. She pressed her hands to her stomach as if she could already feel the fragile life growing inside of her.

"You okay?" Laurel asked from her place at the table.

"What?" Anne stared blankly at her. "Oh, sure." She was going to have a baby. A second chance to do it right. On the heels of joy came confusion. What was she going to tell Laurel? What was she going to do with a newborn? What about her promotion? What about her career? What about Jake? Why did he continue to lie to her? Why didn't he think the child was his? Had he been telling the truth when he said he was sterile? But he couldn't be—she was *pregnant,* and he was the only man she'd been with. What if he never believed her? What if—

"Annie, you're not listening to me," Laurel complained.

"I'm sorry." Anne forced herself to take a seat at the table. Questions swirled through her head. She tried to ignore them and concentrate on Laurel. "What were you saying?"

"School pictures are next week. I need you to help me pick out something to wear."

The request was light-years away from what Anne wanted to think and talk about. Scratch that, she thought suddenly. She certainly couldn't tell Laurel she was pregnant. Not yet. And certainly not until she'd figured out what was going on with Jake.

"Okay, a school picture. What about that red blouse you bought in Houston? You could wear it with your black pants."

Laurel shook her head. "I don't like the collar. It puffs my hair out."

"Then your cream sweater with the pink flecks. That would photograph well."

Laurel slumped in her chair. "What would I wear with it? It only looks good with jeans."

"The pictures are from your chest up, aren't they?" Anne asked, struggling to keep her patience. "What's wrong with wearing jeans?"

Laurel rolled her eyes. "It's picture day. We're supposed to dress up. Mom always told me to wear a dress."

Mom this, Mom that. Anne drew in a breath. She was trying to be understanding. Really she was. But every time she turned around she heard yet another truism from the sainted lips of Ellen Masters, as voiced by her daughter. *My* daughter, Anne thought defiantly.

"I can't deal with this now," Anne said, standing up.

"But the pictures are next week."

"Fine. Then we have the weekend, don't we?" She pointed at the paper bag. "Your lunch is ready. The bus will be here in about ten minutes. Please don't be late for it." She started walking up the stairs.

"Where are you going?" Laurel asked, trailing after her.

"My room."

"Why?"

Anne didn't bother answering. Why was she going to her room? Because she was tired, pregnant by a man who refused to acknowledge even the likelihood of his paternity, in a strange house, possibly risking her job, definitely risking her promotion, and sick to death of hearing what "Mom" would have done about any situation imaginable.

Anne taped several wallpaper swatches next to the window in Laurel's room. She'd promised the girl she would help her there first. The delicate floral prints belonged to different color schemes. One was rose, the other a pale blue. She'd already narrowed the selection down to several bedroom sets. Laurel could pick the one she liked best.

Anne walked across the room and looked at the samples, trying to get a feel for which would be more attractive. It was possible that Laurel would hate all of them. She stared at the patterns, then hurried back and touched their smooth surfaces. Pink and blue. A boy or a girl. She swallowed. She was having a baby.

Her legs grew weak and she sank to the bare floor, pulling her knees up close to her chest. A baby. She closed her eyes and allowed the feelings to wash over her. Regret. There was so much regret. She remembered the terror almost fourteen years ago when her period had been late. She'd waited and waited, praying every night and morning that God would make her not be pregnant. She'd waited until her clothes hadn't fit anymore before going to her mother and confessing her horrible secret. By then she'd been over four months along.

Anne hugged her knees closer. Life grew inside her. Precious life. A tiny being who would grow into her child.

She could remember the pain of labor. Of how she'd tried not to cry out. She'd been young and healthy, and it had ended quickly. But they hadn't let her hold her baby. They'd whisked the infant away, then judged her—the unwed mother—with their cold stares. Most of all, she remembered the emptiness of her heart. How she'd cried all night after her own mother had gone to the motel next door to rest. She'd tried to console herself with thoughts of college and a new life. She tried to imagine what the young couple would be like and how they would treat her baby. But it had been hard to think of anything but the pain inside her and how her arms had ached to hold her child.

She raised her head and looked at the posters Laurel had on her walls. There were a couple of young men from a popular TV show and a few of rock stars. Teen magazines lay around the floor and across the bed. Tubes of lipstick, the only makeup her father let her wear, were scattered on the single dresser.

Laurel was almost grown-up. Soon she would be entering high school, then college. Anne picked up a small tattered teddy bear and held it in her hand. The poor thing had lost most of its fur. One eye was gone and the threads that made up the nose were coming loose. She hugged the bear to her breast. This toy was as close as she would come to the child she'd lost that summer. She would never know what Laurel had been like as an infant or a toddler. She would never see that first step, hear those first words. She would always wonder.

She clenched her stomach tight. Was this new life an exchange for what she'd already lost? Or was it more punishment? How could she be happy about being pregnant now? Her world was turned upside down. What was she going to do with a baby? What about her job and her promotion? What about child care and labor and maternity leave? How could she live in Houston if Jake lived in Colorado?

What about Jake? He was acting crazy. What if he never believed it was his child? Did that matter?

She looked at the bear and smiled at its worn face. No, she told herself firmly. It didn't matter. She would have this child on her own. She would figure out a way to make it work without Jake. She would find her own answers and go forward.

But what was she going to tell Laurel?

She dropped the bear and lowered her forehead onto her knees. How could she explain to the child she'd given up, that this time she wanted to keep her baby? There were plenty of logical reasons why she could now keep her child, but she had a feeling none of that was going to matter to Laurel.

The sound of a car stopping by the house followed by a door slamming shut brought her out of her reverie. Jake was back. She hadn't seen him leave, although Laurel had mentioned something about it when she'd yelled her goodbye.

Anne scrambled to her feet and walked out into the hallway. She didn't know if she should go into her room and lock the door behind her or go confront him. She shook her head wearily. What was she going to say to him? She'd told him the truth. If he didn't believe her before, no new words were going to change his mind.

She was almost to her room when she heard him calling her. She walked to the top of the stairs. He stood at the bottom, his black Stetson in one hand.

He looked different, she thought, wary of his intense gaze. The lines of his face had deepened and his mouth pulled straight. There was an aura of controlled energy about him. Something hiding just under the surface, as if he fought with an emotion he couldn't quite control.

"Would you come down and join me?" he asked, pointing to the living room. His voice gave nothing away.

Anne hesitated for a second, then placed her hand on the cool wooden railing and slowly walked down the stairs. When she reached the bottom, Jake held out his hand, indicating she should precede him. She walked to the far couch and sat down on the edge of the cushion.

He tossed his hat on the other sofa, then stood in fron of her. He braced his feet apart and rested his hands on hi hips. Even with all that had gone on between them tha morning, it was difficult to ignore the way he made her feel Just seeing his long, powerful jeans-clad legs made her gla she was sitting. The proud set of his shoulders and hea made her want to cling to him and borrow his strength. A fierce feeling of gladness stole through her. It didn't mak any sense at all, but she was pleased he was the father. He child would be strong because Jake was strong.

The silence between them lengthened. She glance around the empty room, but there wasn't anything to lool at so she found herself returning his intense stare. Sh wanted to ask what he was thinking, then realized she wa too chicken to really want to know. What if it was awful What if he still thought she'd lied?

At last she cleared her throat. "You took off withou giving the men instructions," she said. "When they cam looking for you, I didn't know when you'd be back. I tol them to take care of their normal chores, then continu with what they were doing yesterday."

"Thank you for that," he said, never taking his eye from her face.

"It's nearly noon," she blurted out. "I didn't know hov long you were going to stay gone. I didn't know what to tel Laurel. She heard us fighting this morning." Concer flashed across his face. "Not what we were saying," sh added hastily. "Just the loud voices. I told her it was a argument and it didn't mean anything."

Jake shoved his hands into his pockets and paced to th window. When he reached the wide expanse of glass, h turned and walked back to her. He reached down an pulled her up next to him.

She stood reluctantly, prepared to step away if he starte yelling at her again. But he didn't say a word. He touche her face with the back of his hand. His knuckles moved u and down against her cheek. His thumb brushed across her mouth. The softness of the brief contact made her want to lean forward into his embrace. But she held herself straight and waited.

He rested his hands on her shoulders and looked down at her.

"You're pregnant," he said quietly.

"Thanks for the news flash, but I believe I already told *you* that."

He smiled and reached down toward her stomach. She started to back up, then stood still. Slowly, tentatively, he pressed his hand against her belly. She felt the warmth through her jeans and panties, all the way to her quivering skin. Heat flared and traveled with her blood until every part of her body hummed from the contact. Her breasts tightened. She didn't dare look down to see if her nipples were betraying her state of arousal. He was treating her with all the reverence of a worshiper at a shrine, and all she could think about was having him touch her more.

His hand moved back and forth, creating delicious friction. She glanced at his face. He had the strangest expression, as if he'd just discovered something wonderful. Their eyes met, and he smiled.

"You're pregnant," he repeated. "And I'm the father."

Chapter Ten

Anne folded her arms over her chest. "You seem surprised."

She sounded angry. Jake didn't blame her. After all the things he'd said to her that morning, everything he'd accused her of, she had every right to be furious with him. He left his hand on her belly, absorbing the warmth of her body. Somewhere under her soft skin, a tiny life was growing. A child. His child. He grinned.

"Surprised as hell," he admitted. "And very happy."

She stepped away and turned her back. "I really wish you'd quit looking at me like that. We haven't discovered something miraculous. Even farm animals can reproduce."

"I didn't know I could."

She spun back to face him. "You want to explain that to me? Because I sure don't understand it. I'm not even in a relationship with anyone. The way we fight, you'd be at the bottom of my list. The last thing on my mind is having a baby. After I gave up Laurel, I wasn't sure I'd ever have another child. I certainly didn't plan on having one like this."

He reached for her hand. She jerked her arm back, but he patiently held out his palm until she sighed and placed her fingers on his. He led her to the center of the sofa and urged her to sit down. She glared at him.

"If you're going to get all weird on me, we aren't even going to be able to talk," she said.

He sat next to her, angling his body so that his knees touched her thigh. "Define weird."

"You have this dopey look on your face."

Jake was sure he did look as stupid as the village idiot. He didn't care. Nothing mattered, nothing could get to him. After almost fourteen years of wondering why, of raging against God, of feeling like half a man, he was going to be a father. He wanted to reach over, grab Anne and pull her close. He wanted to feel her body next to his. He wanted to lay his head on her bare stomach and listen for the sounds of his child. Oh, he knew he wouldn't be able to hear anything, but that didn't matter, either. He was going to be a father. He was going to have a baby.

He contented himself with reaching over and touching her cheek. She jerked her head away from him.

"There you go again," she said impatiently. "Grinning like a sheep. This is *not* a happy occasion."

"Why? Aren't you happy?"

"I—"

He leaned forward and took her hands in his. They were inches apart. He stared into her blue eyes. "Don't you want this baby? Don't you wonder what he's going to look like? Will he have your hair, my eyes, your freckles, my dad's build? It's a miracle. One I thought I'd never see. Sure there are going to be problems, but we'll work them out."

The anger in her gaze faded a little at his words. Her full mouth turned up in a smile. "It's not that I don't want the baby, it's just so unexpected."

"It's wonderful," he said, leaning those last few inches until their mouths touched.

She was soft and sweet, tasting of heat and promise. Her lips parted instantly. He swept inside her mouth. Passionate need flamed to life inside. But when he would have gathered her closer, she broke the kiss.

"Not so fast," she said, the stern expression returning to her face. "You have a lot of explaining to do. Three weeks ago when I warned you I had the fertility of a rabbit, you promised it was safe. I guess that one ranks right up there with 'the check's in the mail.' I want to know what happened, Jake. You can be as happy as you want about the baby, but the reality is my life has just been turned on its ear."

He let go of her and leaned back on the sofa. She was right—he owed her an explanation. "I don't know what to say without sounding like a complete fool."

"Risk it," she said, glaring at him. "On a scale of crummy things to do to a woman, this ranks right at the top. A number ten. Or maybe even an eleven. Dammit, Jake, I'm thirty-one years old. I have a life that I enjoy. I've just barely begun to connect with a daughter I gave up for adoption thirteen years ago. On top of that, I now have to deal with an unplanned pregnancy." She covered her face with her hands. "Why can't I learn to say no to a good-looking man in jeans?"

"Oh, Annie." He touched her hair. It was soft, like silk. The wavy strands slipped through his fingers.

"Don't touch me," she said, not looking up at him.

"Why?"

"Because it feels good, and I don't need any more trouble."

His heart went out to her. Despite his own feelings of elation and wonder, he knew she wasn't as happy as he was. He almost couldn't blame her. But that didn't stop him from wanting to spin her around the room.

He moved his hand until he cupped her jaw, then he nudged until she raised her head. "I'm sorry," he said. "Not about the baby. I couldn't be sorry about that. But about the rest of it. I didn't trick you. I didn't lie." He grinned. "Actually, I guess I was lying, but I didn't know about it at the time."

"Stop looking so damn happy."

"Okay." But he was still grinning.

She cuffed him on the arm. "You're impossible. If you can't stop being happy, fine. But tell me what happened."

He drew in a deep breath and tried to organize his thoughts. Everything was a jumble. He held on to the joy and happiness of the moment because he knew cold, ugly rage hovered on the horizon. Ellen's father had committed the ultimate act of selfishness. It was all Jake could do not to hunt the bastard down and kill him like the lying, cheating scum he was.

"I told you Ellen and I grew up together," he said, finally, figuring it was better to start at the beginning.

Anne nodded and drew back from his touch on her face. Her eyes grew wary. He couldn't blame her. He, too, had heard Laurel going on about "Mom" this and "Mom" that. Anne was probably sick of hearing about his late wife.

"Bear with me," he said. "It's relevant."

"All right."

She folded her arms over her chest and angled toward him. Their knees bumped. He rested his hand on her leg. Her muscles stiffened as if she was going to pull back, but she didn't.

"Ellen only wanted two things in life—to be the perfect wife and mother."

"From what I hear, she was remarkably successful at both," Anne said. There wasn't a hint of sarcasm in her voice, but he saw the flash of fire in her eyes.

"We were best friends," he continued, remembering the good days, at the beginning, before it had all gone wrong. "I loved her." He drew in a deep breath. "I still miss her. Anyway, our fathers were partners in a large construction firm. When Ellen and I were friends and then started dating, it was understood that we'd get married. Joining the empire. We were young and in love. Everyone was happy. After the wedding, Ellen wanted to get pregnant right away. We tried for months, but nothing happened."

Now came the hard part. He shifted on the sofa until he was facing forward, his elbows resting on his knees, his hands clenched tightly together. "We both went to a doctor. He was a good friend of Michael's and a specialist. I didn't really think about it one way or the other. Ellen was hysterical, terrified the problem was with her. I thought we should wait a little longer before having a baby, but neither she nor Michael were interested in my opinion."

"Michael is Ellen's father?" Anne asked.

He nodded. "About three days later Michael called me into his office and sat me down. He told me that the test results were back and that the problem was with me." The shame of that moment swept over him. Michael's words began to echo inside of him. He stood suddenly. "I was stunned. I'd never thought about fault or blame. I'd assumed we were trying too hard or something. I didn't expect to find out I wasn't man enough to father a child."

He walked over to the window and braced himself against the wooden frame. "Ellen never said a word, but I could see it in her eyes. I was depriving her of the one thing she wanted in life. A child. My folks were shocked. I walked around in a daze. Then one day Michael called and said he'd found us a baby. A teenager in west Texas had gotten herself in trouble. She was due any day. We drove to El Paso and waited for you to give birth to Laurel."

He drew in a deep breath. "Ellen held her and told me she was enough. But I could see the truth in her eyes. She wanted a child of her own." He laughed harshly. "I did, too. I wanted a son." He paused, staring out the window at the grass and trees lining the long driveway. "I used to think God was punishing me for wanting a son. I figured if I hadn't cared so much, he wouldn't have made me sterile."

He turned around until he was facing her. She sat forward on the sofa, leaning toward him. Compassion battled with confusion in her pale blue eyes. In this light, with his child growing inside her, he wondered how he'd ever thought Anne Baker anything but beautiful.

"You never knew otherwise?" she asked.

"How would I? I believed what Michael told me. I was a faithful husband. There was no way for me to know the truth. Not until you. I called the doctor's office in Houston this morning. He pulled the test records and said that I was fine. Ellen was the one who couldn't have children."

She shook her head. "I don't know what to say. I'm stunned. I can't believe one man would be so horrible. That he would lie like that to you."

"I'm not surprised. Michael would have done anything for Ellen or money. He'd drive his truck over a puppy if it would give him an extra buck. Lying to me was probably just an inconvenience in his otherwise full day." Jake shoved his hands into his pockets. "After Ellen was gone, I lost it. We all did. When I finally figured out I couldn't keep mourning her forever, I realized Michael was getting worse and more careless in the ways he made his money. He was circumventing safety precautions on job sites. When I called him on it, he told me to keep my mouth shut." Jake shrugged. "I couldn't do that. I reported the violations, filed a complaint with the appropriate authorities and gave him my resignation that same day. Then I packed Laurel up and moved her out here."

"She wasn't happy about it, was she?"

"No. I can't blame her. After Ellen died, I withdrew." He pushed off against the wall and walked slowly toward the couch. He remembered those dark days when the house had seemed so empty and Laurel had been so lost. He hadn't known what to say to his child, so he hadn't said anything at all. He'd been too caught up in his own pain and guilt. He was angry at Ellen for dying before he could finally leave her. He'd wanted to face her and say she couldn't keep him in the marriage by throwing her own sacrifice up in his face. He remembered all the times they fought and she'd reminded him that if she'd left him for someone normal, for a real man, she would have children of her own.

He sat down on the cushion next to Anne. He'd hated Ellen then. When she'd died, he hadn't mourned the bitter, hostile woman she'd become, so concerned with appearances that she wouldn't even discuss a separation. Instead he'd ached for the loss of his friend. The young girl who had shared his childhood adventures. The teenager he'd squired to school dances. The woman with whom he'd learned about passion. That was the Ellen he loved and missed. But she'd been gone much longer than two years. Sometimes it felt as if she'd been gone a lifetime.

"Michael doesn't want anything to do with Laurel?" Anne asked.

"No. I've kept that from her, but I can't cover for him forever. I'm terrified she'll pick up the phone to call her grandfather and he'll tell her."

"It sounds like a mess all around."

He shifted on the seat cushions until he was facing her. "I'm sorry about the way this all happened, and everything that's been thrust upon you, but I'm not sorry I'm going to have a baby."

Instantly her expression hardened and her blue eyes flashed fire. She jutted her chin out. "*You* aren't having a baby."

He felt as if he'd been sucker punched. He grabbed her upper arms and squeezed. "Damn you, woman, I won't let you get rid of this child."

"Let go of me." She broke free of his grasp. "What is wrong with you?" she demanded, glaring at him. "I'm not saying anything about getting rid of the child. I wouldn't do that. I was pointing out the fact that your part in this is over. You might be the father but I'm the one who is actually having the baby."

He gulped in air, as relief swept over him. He would have done anything to make sure she had his child. "I know this is going to upset your life."

"Upset isn't exactly the word I'd use. I have a job I love, a career, a life-style, a condo in Houston. Everything I want is there except for Laurel. We can't even talk about her without yelling at each other or—" She stopped talking and clamped her lips together.

Or making love, he finished silently, remembering the explosive passion of that night. He smiled. He'd never done it outside like that before. Not since he and Ellen had experimented in the front seat of his car. Location aside, he'd never experienced anything that powerful before. They'd both been out of control, past reason and sanity.

"We've had some conversations that went well," he said.

"Maybe three," she said glumly. "Now there's a baby to deal with." She rose to her feet. "I can't do this." She held up her hands as if warding him off. "Don't go ballistic on me. I'm not talking about doing anything to the baby. I'm going to have this child. I just can't think about this anymore. Over a month ago, I didn't even know who you were. Now I'm living in your house, trying to establish a relationship with a thirteen-year-old girl I gave up for adoption. I have no friends here, no support system. I'm pregnant." She rubbed her temples. "Pregnant. How am I supposed to explain this to Becky Sue?" She groaned.

Jake laughed.

She glared at him. "Oh, fine. You can afford to think it's funny. It's not your life."

"It *is* my life. It's my child, too." He stood next to her. "I'm here for you, Anne. I'll be your support system. I'd like to think that I'm already your friend."

Her smile was shaky. "You think so? After what we said to each other this morning? I'm not convinced."

"We can make it work." He wasn't sure what he was promising, but it didn't matter. He would do anything to keep his baby. Hot damn. A son.

"Can we?" she asked. "A few minutes ago you called me Annie. Now you're back to saying 'Anne.' As long as there's a difference in your mind, I don't think we can make it work." She turned and left the room.

He stared after her, not sure if he should let her be or follow her and make her understand. What did it matter what he called her? She was having his child. A son. Somehow he knew it was going to be a boy. The Masters name would go on. He would have a son to leave the ranch to. He would teach him to ride and throw a baseball. He'd teach him about life and women and girls and...

Girls. He stared out the living room at the brightly colored sweater hanging over the banister. Laurel's sweater. The daughter of his heart. How was he going to explain all this to her?

"This is me in the first grade. Yuck, that hair. What was Mom thinking of?" Laurel pointed to the picture and grimaced.

Anne smiled. "You look adorable." She glanced from the photo to the teenager curled up next to her. "I like the ringlets."

Laurel shuddered. "She must have been mad at me or something. At least the dress is cute." She turned the page. "Oh, this is better." She peered at the writing under the pictures. "Second grade. Look at my report card. I got all *A*'s."

"Impressive," Anne said. She had one arm around her daughter, the other supported the photo album. It was early evening. She could hear the sounds from the kitchen as Jake finished cleaning up. He'd volunteered to do the job. When she'd protested, he glanced at her stomach and raised his eyebrows. Perfect, she thought with a sigh. She was about three weeks pregnant and he was already driving her crazy. Imagine what would happen when she actually started showing.

She kissed the top of Laurel's head. She wouldn't show for several months, and her visit here was almost half over. She wouldn't be around much longer for Jake to pester. She wondered if he'd thought of that.

Laurel continued turning pages in the album and narrating the events of her life. Anne tried to pay attention, but she couldn't. One reason was she kept thinking about the pregnancy. Another was that it hurt so much to see all she'd missed when Laurel had been growing up.

"Look, this is me with my grandfather. He took me to Disney World in Florida. We stayed for five days. It was great." Her smiled faded. "It was right before Mom died."

Anne leaned forward and studied the snapshots. The man standing next to a shorter, younger Laurel was tall and handsome in a hard sort of way. His dark hair held only a hint of gray. Brown eyes stared coldly at the camera. A shiver raced through her and she rubbed her arms against the chill. He sure didn't look like the kind of person who would take an eleven-year-old on vacation. Still, the pictures proved he had. But how had he been able to turn his back on Laurel right after that? Didn't she mean anything to him?

Anne wanted to pull her daughter closer and hold her until all the bad things in the world were gone. She settled on making a comment about the mouse-print T-shirt and turning the page in the photo album. She couldn't protect her from the world. That was part of growing up. Learning to deal with pain and uncomfortable circumstances. She could only be with her through the hard times, offer advice and a shoulder to cry on. The rest was up to Laurel.

But what about the pain *she* was going to inflict on her child? What about Laurel's reaction to the coming baby? Anne didn't want to think about that right now.

Jake came out of the kitchen wiping his hands on a dish towel. "Anybody want dessert?"

"I do," Laurel said, scrambling to her feet. "What are we having?"

"Anne baked a chocolate cake," he said, and winked at his daughter. "Your favorite."

"Cool." Laurel smiled. "With custard filling?"

Anne stood up. "No, honey. With chocolate filling."

"Oh. Okay." Laurel headed for the kitchen, her excitement noticeably diminished.

Great. Yet another in a long line of failures, Anne thought as she trailed behind. Once again she hadn't lived up to the memory of Ellen Masters.

Jake stopped her before she went into the kitchen. "It's going to be okay," he said, looping an arm around her shoulders. "She didn't get custard filling in her chocolate cakes all the time. She really does like you."

"I know," she said, leaning against him. "It's just hard to have everything I do compared with a memory. Especially when I keep coming up short."

"You're doing a great job with her. I appreciate it. And you."

He felt warm and hard as she leaned against him. The scent of his body swirled around her, seducing her with musky fragrance. His waist was lean where her fingers rested on his side, his thighs long where they brushed hers. She hadn't realized how much she needed a hug until he squeezed her against his chest. She rested her head on his shirt and listened to the comforting sound of his heartbeat.

This was the Jake she liked best, she admitted to herself. When they were just being together. Sharing, getting to know each other. She wished he could have been like this at the beginning, even though she understood why he'd been reserved at their first few meetings.

He kissed the top of her head and let her go. She smiled up at him, then walked into the kitchen. Laurel was already cutting up the cake.

"It's good," the girl said, taking a swipe at the icing and licking off her finger.

"Thank you," Anne said, and waited for the inevitable comparison. Someone was on her side that night because Laurel was mercifully silent.

Jake and Laurel took their dessert to the cow-print table by the window. Anne leaned against the counter and nibbled on her slice. Her stomach was a little shaky with the strangest foods, so she was cautious with what she ate. The first bite went down okay, so she risked a second.

"Annie and I are going to be planning my bedroom," Laurel said. "Could you come up and look at the wallpaper samples, Dad?"

Anne expected him to refuse the request, but he surprised her by agreeing.

"Really?" Laurel seemed equally amazed. "Then would you look at the catalogs with me? I've got a couple of bedroom sets that I like and I'm trying to decide."

"No problem. Want to do it now?" he asked.

"Yeah, when we're done here." Laurel dug into her dessert.

Anne stared at him. Why was he being so cooperative? In the past week she'd tried several times to engage him in conversation about decorating the house. He simply shook his head, told her he didn't care what she did as long as there weren't daisies in his bathroom or cow prints all over the place. What had changed his mind?

She set her half-eaten plate on the counter and reached for a glass of water. Jake was at her side in an instant.

"You okay?" he asked.

"Fine, why?"

He glanced at her stomach, then back to her face. "You didn't finish your cake. I thought you might be—" He shrugged. "I just wanted to make sure you're feeling okay."

She slammed the glass down, not caring that water sloshed over the side. "I couldn't be better," she said curtly.

He looked at her as if she'd just grown a second head. He didn't get it. She could have wept.

"You ready, Dad?" Laurel asked, oblivious to the undercurrents in the room.

He gave Anne one last hard stare, then followed his daughter out.

She leaned against the counter. She'd been a fool. Worse, she'd been taken in by a good-looking cowboy in a pair of jeans. Again. Not five minutes ago, he'd hugged her and she'd let him. She'd allowed herself to believe that he cared about her, that their time together might actually begin to mean something to Jake. She'd even been foolish enough to hope he thought she was special. Wrong. It was a lie. A smoke screen for what he really cared about.

The only thing he hadn't been faking was the sexual attraction. That was real and bigger than both of them. It would never be enough, she told herself, even as she realized any relationship with Jake Masters was out of the question. Even if she did like him and enjoy his company. Even if she admired the way he cared about his business and fought to protect his daughter. None of that mattered because no matter how much he wanted her, his heart still belonged to Ellen. He'd told her that himself.

"I appreciate you," she said, mocking his low voice. Lies, all lies. He didn't care about her. He only cared about the baby. That's why he was being nice. He didn't want to upset her. He was probably humoring Laurel for the same reason. She was going to be shattered by the news of the child.

Anne wondered what she'd done to deserve all this. How had her life gotten out of control?

Before she could find an answer, the phone rang. She answered it.

"Masters' residence," she said wearily, hoping it wasn't one of Laurel's new friends. If it was, Laurel would take the call, leaving Jake free to trail after her asking if she was feeling all right.

"Annie, hi, it's Heather."

A friendly voice at last. Anne pulled out one of the chairs and sank into it. "Hi. It's great to hear from you."

"I hope it's not too late to call."

Anne grinned. "Actually your timing couldn't be more perfect. What's going on?"

Heather brought her up-to-date with the current projects. "I had a meeting with the RCR people today," she said.

"How did it go?"

Heather chuckled. "Great. I even surprised myself. They are putting Houston to the top of their list for relocation. The president said she'd get back to me by the end of the week."

"Good for you."

"They haven't signed yet," Heather warned. "If they do, you deserve all the credit. You'd already done the research and prepared the report before you left. I just had to present the information. The proposal really sold itself."

"Don't you dare ignore your part in it," Anne said, and grinned. "It could have easily gone the other way. You did a great job." She bit back a laugh. Now she was sounding like Jake. Maybe she should tell Heather that she appreciated her.

"I do have some other very interesting news," Heather said. "It concerns a certain man in the office down the hall."

Anne groaned. "Let me guess. Tim the Turkey got the promotion."

Heather giggled. "Not exactly. It seems as if Tim's reputation and wandering hands finally caught up with him. He came on to one of the new secretaries in legal. She's here temporarily while she's waiting to start law school. When she turned down his offer for a date, he tried to fondle her. She beaned him with a law book, which broke his nose. Then she filed formal charges of sexual harassment. When word got out, twelve other women came forward and filed their own complaints."

"You're kidding?"

"Nope. Turns out those rumors we'd been hearing were true."

"I wish someone had done something sooner," Anne said. "Or that Tim had come on to me. I would have filed so fast his head would still be spinning."

Heather laughed. "He would never have tried it with you, boss. You might be pretty, but you're tough and that would have scared him to death."

"I don't feel tough right now," she said, touching her stomach and remembering everything she and Jake had to deal with. "This isn't going to look good for Tim when the vice president's job opens up." She couldn't help but be pleased. "Looks like my competition isn't going to be so tough after all."

"You could definitely say that."

Anne frowned. "I recognize that tone of voice, Heather. What are you telling me?"

"They fired him. I'm sure the boss is going to be sending you a formal letter, but the rumor is you have no competition, Annie. When your leave of absence is up, come on back to Houston because the promotion is yours."

Chapter Eleven

Jake heard the cursing even before he entered the kitchen. He grinned. Anne swore again, then something hit the floor. He walked to the entrance and leaned against the doorframe.

Bowls and dirty utensils were scattered on all the counters. Pots covered the stove. The sink was filled with dirty dishes. Anne stood with her back to him. She wore an oversize shirt and jeans. Thick socks covered her feet. A headband held her hair off her face. She turned to grab something and he saw a streak of red sauce on her cheek.

"You want to talk about it?" he asked.

She shrieked and dropped the spoon she'd been holding. "Don't do that," she said, spinning toward him. "You scared me to death. I didn't hear you come in."

"That's because you were cussing too loud."

She flushed and stared down at the counter. "I'm having a little trouble with this recipe," she said, motioning to an open cookbook.

"So it would seem."

"Oh, stop it," she said, and went back to her mixing. "I know what you're thinking, and you're wrong."

He moved into the kitchen and pulled out one of the cow chairs. After turning it around, he sat straddling it and resting his hands on the back. "What am I thinking?"

Her shoulders raised and lowered in an exaggerated sigh. "That I'm trying to compete with a paragon. Sainted Ellen." The spoon clattered into the bowl again. She turned toward him and covered her mouth with her hand. Her eyes widened in horror. "Oh, Jake, I'm sorry. I didn't mean to say that."

He waited, wondering if he would get angry with her. Nothing. He prodded his heart, the broken part that still missed Ellen. There wasn't any pain. He knew he would mourn her always, but the woman he missed had died so long ago. The wife he'd lost two years before had little in common with her save name and appearance.

"It's okay," he said, and was pleased to find out he meant it. "Ellen could be a little intimidating for all of us. She had this thing about her world being perfect."

Anne glanced around at the disaster that when he'd left that morning had still been a kitchen. "She probably kept things clean, too. I just never learned how to cook neatly. I know you're supposed to wash as you go. Put things away when you're done with them." She picked up a jar of spices. "I try to, but then I get caught up in the recipe or something boils before it's supposed to and then I can't do anything but handle the crisis." She frowned. "You probably think I'm completely incompetent, but really, I'm good at my job."

"I believe you," he said, liking this flustered woman much better than the controlled, competent stranger he'd met in Houston. He liked her in jeans instead of tailored trousers. He liked her sleepy in the morning because she'd stopped drinking coffee. He liked the way she started projects and didn't complete them.

Laurel's room was almost finished. The walls were done, but the furniture hadn't been delivered. Anne had already tackled the living room and the library together. Samples of wallpaper were tacked up in the front room. Between the bookshelves she'd dabbed bits of paint so they could "live" with the color. She'd taught Laurel some needle craft and pieces of embroidery floss littered the floor. She'd found an old sewing machine and was making curtains for the kitchen. He glanced at the scraps of fabric on the far counter and cringed at the cow print. She'd convinced him that they would blend with the table and chairs, but he sensed that he'd been had.

Ellen had kept his house orderly. Rooms had been decorated one by one, and kept closed off while the work was being done. She'd rarely appeared out of their bedroom without makeup. He liked the chaos; it reminded him that he was alive.

"What are you cooking?" he asked.

"Lasagna," she said, then looked at him. "Let me guess. You hate it."

"It's one of my favorites."

"Ellen had a secret family recipe?"

He shook his head. "To the best of my knowledge, she never made it."

"Thank God." She motioned to the mess on the stove. "I decided to make the sauce from scratch. Then I wanted to use fresh tomatoes instead of canned and well, it all got out of hand."

"This isn't a competition," he said softly.

"I know. I tell myself that. Most of the time, I almost believe it."

"I was worried when I moved out to the ranch. I didn't think I'd measure up to what my grandfather did."

"Really?" She looked over and smiled. "You hide it well. I can't picture you not being the best." She bit her lip and ducked her head as if she regretted the compliment.

"Michael told me I was a fool for leaving the company. That I'd never amount to anything." He shrugged. "I tried not to let it get to me. There was plenty of money, so I didn't have to make the ranch pay, but it wasn't about finances. I wanted to build something of my own. My grandfather talked about his dreams for this place. He never saw them realized. After hearing about them, they became my dreams, too." He stopped, suddenly, feeling self-conscious. "That sounds pretty dumb, huh?"

"Not at all." She pulled a lasagna noodle out of a large pot and placed it in a casserole dish. "I think it's wonderful. I hope you get everything you want. I just don't understand your father-in-law's part in all this. Why was he so creepy?"

"I don't know. I tell myself it doesn't matter anymore, except as it relates to Laurel."

"Do you think—?" Anne concentrated on layering the cheese.

"What?" he asked.

"I— Don't get mad, but do you think Ellen knew? About the sterility thing, I mean?"

"No," he said quickly. She looked at him. He squeezed the back of the chair. "I don't know. I want to believe she was an innocent party in all this. The woman I loved would never have been that dishonest." But the woman he'd loved had been gone so long, it was hard to remember what she was like. The other Ellen, the woman she'd become in later years, she would have kept that kind of secret if it had meant holding her perfect world together.

"I'm sure you're right," Anne said, spooning sauce into the dish.

He studied her, trying to see if she was humoring him. She gave him an impatient glance.

"I mean it," she said. "You and Ellen grew up together. You knew each other very well. If she'd been hiding something that big, you would have been able to sense it. Besides, she would have been devastated by the news. I doubt anyone would be able to hide that kind of pain."

"Did you hide the pain of losing Laurel?" he asked without thinking.

She slowed in her work, then stopped all together. "I don't know." She placed her hands on the counter and stared at the casserole dish. A spot of sauce lay on the tile. She wiped it with her finger, then cleaned herself on her jeans. "I gave birth in August, and I was leaving for college about four weeks later. I don't remember much about that time except sitting in the shade and reading book after book. I just wanted to get lost and forget everything that had happened. My mother knew of course, so I didn't bother hiding it from her." She reached in the large pot and drew out a lasagna noodle to start the second layer. "At college—" she shrugged "—it took me a while to make friends, so I didn't have to hide it from anyone because they wouldn't have known in the first place." She looked at him and smiled. "You're right, Jake. Ellen couldn't have known. As much as you and Laurel loved her, she couldn't have been that cruel."

"Thank you for that," he said, rising to his feet and walking over to stand next to her. He leaned on the counter. "I know this hasn't been easy for you."

"If you tell me that you appreciate me, I'll attack you with this sauce spoon," she said, waving the utensil in the air.

"I do appreciate you."

"I warned you." She reached into the smaller saucepan and scooped up a spoonful of thick red sauce.

He backed up, holding his hands out in front of him. "I take it back," he said, and smiled. "I don't appreciate you at all."

She eyed him for a moment, then dropped the spoon into the pan. "Better," she said. "At least we're a little closer to the truth."

"What does that mean?"

"You're being nice to me because of the baby."

"I—" His denial died before he finished speaking it. Was he? "I'm excited about the baby, Anne. I'll admit that. I've never had a child before. If I'm a little crazy and overprotective it's because I'm concerned."

"About the baby?"

"Yes."

"I'm the one who wanted you to be honest." She reached for the cheese and began smoothing it in place. Her shoulders were hunched as if she carried a heavy weight.

He tried to figure out what he'd said to upset her. "I'm not like Michael. I won't say or do anything to hurt you. I haven't lied to Laurel about you or tried to influence her against you."

"I know that. I appreciate it." She chuckled. "I can't seem to get away from that word."

"Then what did I say?" he asked, confused by her sudden change in mood.

"Nothing, Jake." She looked up at him. "Forget it. I understand that you're feeling protective. I am, too. I worry about Laurel, about what's going to happen when she finds out about the baby."

He glanced at her stomach, but the oversize shirt she wore hid it from view. "Were you big with Laurel?" he asked, trying to picture her swollen with his child.

She shrugged. "Not huge, but it did get pretty uncomfortable. Especially in Paradise in the summer. We didn't have an air conditioner. I lived in front of the fan. My feet puffed up like water balloons." She grimaced at the memory. "I was a lot younger then. It probably won't be so easy this time."

He moved closer to her, eyeing her waistline. "How long until you felt the baby move?"

"I don't remember. Four or five months, I think. I'll ask the doctor when I see her."

"Have you made an appointment?" He moved behind her.

"Not yet. I thought I'd wait until— What are you doing?" she asked as he nestled against her and slid his arms around her waist.

"Nothing. Just go on with what you're doing."

"I can't."

She tried to twist away from him, but he wrapped his arms around her and held on. She felt warm and smelled like flowers and Italian seasonings.

"Jake, what on earth are you—?"

He slipped one hand under her shirt. "Hush. I want to feel my baby."

"Don't be silly. There's nothing to feel," she said, but her voice had gone strangely soft.

He rested his cheek against her ear and murmured soothingly, as if gentling a skittish mare. Her body stiffened in his arms, then relaxed. He ran his fingers up her jeans to the snap. After unfastening it, he pulled the zipper down, then slipped his hand inside. He rubbed back and forth against her cotton panties. Her breathing increased slightly. He, too, was becoming aroused, but this wasn't about sex, he reminded himself. It was about the baby.

He moved his other hand down so both his palms cradled her stomach. Her cotton panties were too much of a barrier. He pushed them away so that he was touching her soft skin.

"You're having my baby," he murmured.

"If you start singing that damn song, I'll slug you. I hate that song."

He chuckled. "You are one feisty woman, aren't you?"

"You got that right."

He squeezed her tight. "I wish I could feel him moving," he said, rubbing back and forth along her skin.

"That'll happen soon enough. Then I'll look like I swallowed a basketball. My skin will stretch, my back will ache. I won't be able to sleep."

"Is it really going to be that bad?"

She drew in a deep breath so that her back pressed more against his chest. Her round buttocks brushed his groin. He was as hard as a rock, but he reminded himself this wasn't about sex.

"N-no."

It was the stutter in her voice that warned him his roving fingers had slipped lower on her belly. He felt the tickle of soft hair. It had been dark when they'd made love. Suddenly he wanted to see the color of the curls protecting her female secrets.

Don't be a fool, he told himself. But one finger moved lower to the dip at the apex of her thighs. Heat enveloped him. He wanted to plunge in and feel her moistness. He wanted to touch her most sensitive place and bring her pleasure. He wanted to raise her up on the counter and bury himself inside of her.

Before he could do any of that, she grabbed his wrist and pulled his hand up from her jeans.

"Let's hold off on the baby feeling until there's something more there, okay?" she said, her voice controlled.

But he heard the quiver underneath and knew somehow it had become about sex. What was there about Anne Baker that turned him on? He had to figure it out. When he could think straight.

He backed up. While he was trying to think nonarousing thoughts, she fastened her jeans and pulled up the zipper.

"Annie, I didn't mean—"

"It's okay," she said curtly, and went back to work on the lasagna.

"But I don't want you to think—"

"It's *okay*. I understand."

He wished he did. Instead of resuming his seat on the chair where his straddled position would flaunt his erection, he leaned against the counter. Her face was flushed bright enough to blend with the tomato sauce on her cheek.

"What are we going to do?" he asked.

"About what?"

"The baby? What else?"

"Oh." She swallowed. "I don't know. Our first concern should be for Laurel. I don't know how to tell her. She's going to hate me when she finds out."

"She won't hate you."

Anne laughed, but the sound wasn't pleasant. "That's easy for you to say. You get to come out perfectly in all this. I, on the other hand, am going to be the bad guy. Thirteen years ago I gave her up for adoption. Here I am, a single mother once again, but this time, I'm keeping my child. How is she going to feel about that?"

"Our child," he said, not liking her possessive tone.

"What?"

"The baby is mine, too."

She dropped the spoon she was holding and turned toward him. "It's not even real yet. The baby, our baby, if that makes you feel better, isn't going to be here for over eight months. Laurel is here right now. I don't want to have to lose her because you finally figured out you were fertile." She glared up at him, apparently unintimidated by the discrepancy in their size.

"So what do you want to do?" he asked.

"I don't know." She picked up the lasagna and put it into the oven. "But I'm not losing her now. Not after getting this second chance. You may not want to admit it, Jake, but Laurel is as much my daughter as this baby is your child."

He didn't have to like it, but she was right. "I know."

She raised her eyebrows. "That's quite an admission. I expected more of a fight."

"Why? It's true." He started to walk out of the kitchen, then paused by the doorway. "You don't want to lose Laurel, I don't want to lose my son."

Anne watched him walk toward the barn and his office. Great. Now what were they going to do? Part-time parenting? She would keep the baby for six months, he would have Laurel, then they would switch? That wasn't going to work. Would he give up his precious horses and come live in Houston? She shook her head. Of course not. She didn't want to move, either. She finally had the promotion she'd been working for since the day she graduated from college. As much as she enjoyed her time being in the house, decorating, baking, even sewing again, she couldn't move to Colorado. What would she do here? Act as the housekeeper?

The perfect solution, she thought sarcastically, wondering how many fights they could possibly get into each week. She started carrying the dirty pots and pans over to the sink. There was another reason living near him would never work, at least not for her.

Passion. Pure, simple, animal passion. When he'd touched her... She braced her arms against the edge of the sink and bit back a groan. She couldn't believe how quickly she'd gone from embarrassment to desire. She'd been ready to make love with him right there on the kitchen floor. She glanced over her shoulder toward the cow table. That would have worked as well.

Her stomach clenched tightly as she thought about his gentle hands on her belly. He'd stroke her reverently, searching for a hint of their growing child. Then he'd moved lower. Her hips flexed involuntarily. If he'd brushed against her center just once, she probably would have climaxed right there. Even thinking about it was making her blood hum through her veins.

"So stop thinking about it," she ordered herself and started cleaning the kitchen.

She'd almost finished washing up when she heard the school bus stopping in front of the driveway. About three minutes later the front door opened and slammed shut.

"I'm home," Laurel called.

"So I hear."

The teenager flew into the kitchen. "Something smells good. What are you cooking?"

"Lasagna."

"Great." She gave Anne a hug, then reached for the cookie jar, in one fluid motion.

"How was school?" Anne asked.

Laurel shrugged. "Good. I talked to Terry and that party is still on for tomorrow night."

"This is another sleep-over, right?"

"Uh-huh," Laurel mumbled, her mouth full. She filled a glass with milk and gulped down half of it. "But first there's a real party. With boys." Her hazel eyes gleamed with excitement.

"Boys?" Anne felt faint.

"Don't panic, Annie. Terry's parents are going to be there."

"That's something at least. Does your father know about boys being at the party?"

Laurel nodded. "He threatened to send me to a convent until I'm twenty-five, but I told him to lighten up. I'm a teenager now."

"Oh, well, that would make all the difference in the world." Anne smiled. "So you're excited about this then?"

"Sure. Lots of people are going to be there. The best kids, you know."

"So you're part of the 'in' crowd."

Laurel sat at the table. She rolled her eyes. "You are so old. 'In' crowd. That's dumb." She sat up straight and raised one shoulder. "If you're asking me if I'm popular, the answer is—" She paused dramatically. "Yes." She dissolved into giggles.

Anne filled a glass with water and took the seat next to her. When Laurel offered her stash of cookies, Anne refused. Her stomach hadn't recovered from Jake's tender caresses.

"Is this the same girl who kicked and screamed about moving away from Dallas?" she asked.

"I never kicked."

"But you did scream."

"Maybe a little." Laurel's smile faded. "I still miss my friends, but it's kinda okay being out here. I get to ride my horse a lot. Most of the kids are nice. Some of the boys are cute."

Jake walked into the kitchen. "You're not allowed to think boys are cute," he said. "I thought I explained that to you."

"Da-ad."

"See, you're already too grown-up to call me Daddy." He bent down and kissed the top of her head, then gave Anne a wink.

Laurel flipped her long hair over her shoulder. "Dad, you're so immature."

"And you're the queen of maturity. How was school?"

"Fine. We're talking about the party. I have to have something perfect to wear."

Anne held her hands up in front of her. "I'm not getting involved with that one again."

"What one?" Jake asked.

"We had a slight disagreement about what Laurel would wear to school pictures."

"I was thinking about my red dress," Laurel said. "The one with the lace sleeves."

"Isn't that a little dressy?" Jake poured himself a glass of milk, snagged the cookie jar with his other hand and sauntered over to the table.

He often joined them in the kitchen when Laurel got home from school. Anne told herself it didn't *mean* anything. But she couldn't help remembering how his hands had felt on her body. Of how his chest had burned into her skin, and the hardness she'd felt when her rear had brushed against his pelvis. A heated blush climbed her cheeks and she quickly looked down. As the conversation flowed around her, she traced the outline of a black spot on the table.

"When will the curtains be done?" Laurel asked, pointing at the window beside the table.

"In a couple of days," Anne answered.

"Cool. I can't wait to see them up. It's going to be totally together looking, don't you think, Daddy?"

He shook his head. "I never thought I'd have a cow kitchen."

"Yeah, Mom would have croaked, huh?" Laurel grinned. "Everything was always so perfect in our old house. It looked nice, but—" she shrugged "—sometimes I just wanted to mess things up a little."

Glory be, Anne thought, staring at her. Would wonders never cease? She'd been compared to the Sainted Ellen and actually come out ahead. Who could have thought?

"I liked Becky Sue's trailer," the teenager continued. "It was a place you could have fun in. You didn't have to worry about breaking stuff."

"It is a long way from Dallas," Anne said, risking a glance at Jake. He was studying her. Something in his gaze rankled her, as if he were weighing the factors of her life and finding them wanting. She squared her shoulders. "What are you staring at?"

"You. We come from very different worlds."

"You've just now figured that out? We've never had anything in common."

She wanted to bite back the words as soon as she said them. Jake's gaze instantly dropped to her stomach. She resisted the urge to fold her arms protectively over her midsection.

"You have me," Laurel piped up.

Anne broke free of Jake's intense gaze. "You're right, honey. We have you."

"And I have a party." Laurel stood up. "Come on, Annie. Help me pick out what to wear. I *promise* I won't get yucky this time."

It was as close to an apology as she was going to get. Anne rose to her feet.

"What time does it start?" Jake asked. "I have the vet coming out tomorrow afternoon. If I'm not done with him in time, Anne, would you drive Laurel?"

"I have a ride," Laurel said. "Brad is picking me up."

Brad? Anne struggled to keep her jaw from dropping. "You are friends with a boy old enough to have his driver's license?"

"No." Laurel shook her head as if she was dealing with morons. "His dad is taking us."

"I'm taking you," Jake said. "You're too young to go to a party with a boy."

"But boys are going to be at the party."

"I know that. I've already talked with Terry's mother. The boys are all going home at ten-thirty, then you girls are having your sleep-over. That's fine with me, but I'm driving you."

"Da-ad. Come on. Everyone else is going with a boy." She bit her lower lip and tried to look pitiful.

"No." Jake stood up and folded his arms over his chest. "Either I drive you or you don't go."

"Annie, would you please explain to him that he's going to make me look stupid in front of all my new friends?"

Anne had been hoping to escape without having to choose sides. She didn't look at either Laurel or Jake. She placed her hand to her stomach and prayed to be anywhere but here. God was busy.

"Jake, I—"

"See!" Laurel said, triumphantly.

Anne touched her daughter's arm, hating to see the hope in her hazel eyes. Hope that was about to be dashed.

"I was going to tell your father that I have to agree with him on this one, honey. You're too young to drive to a party with a boy."

Laurel's victory faded into bitterness. Her dark eyebrows drew together and her mouth started to tremble. "Annie, no. That's not fair. Everyone will make fun of me. You have to let me go. You have to."

"The decision is made, young lady. Either accept it gracefully or you're not going to the party at all."

"Laurel, I'm sorry," Anne said, gently squeezing her arm. "I hope you can understand—"

"Understand?" She jerked her arm free. "Understand?" she shrieked. "No, I don't. You can't do this to me."

"I'm sorry."

"No, you're not. You don't care about me at all. I hate you. I hate you." Tears flowed from her eyes and a spot of color stained her cheeks. "You don't care about me. You never cared about me. That's why you gave me up. You never wanted me. I'll always hate you."

She spun and raced out of the room. Anne stared after her. The words echoed over and over until she knew she'd hear them forever.

Chapter Twelve

Jake stared after his daughter. His first impulse was to catch her and shake some sense into her. His second was to pull Anne close and hold her until the pain was gone. Before he could make up his mind, Anne turned and started picking up the dirty glasses from the table.

"I'm sorry," he said, and realized he meant it. A few weeks ago he would have been grateful that Laurel wasn't getting along with Anne. He'd been so afraid of losing his daughter. But he'd changed in the short time Anne had been with them. He'd learned that as much as he might deserve otherwise, Laurel would love him forever. She would also love Anne. "She didn't mean it."

"I know that," Anne said as she put the milk back into the refrigerator. She sounded surprisingly calm. "She's just a child. She's lashing out at me because I'm convenient. Next time it might just as easily be you."

"I think I can handle it easier than you can," he said, coming up behind her and placing his hands on her shoulders.

She jerked free. "Don't touch me, Jake. Not again. I can't take any more today."

"I'm sorry," he repeated, and wished he knew the right words to say. "I mean that. Not because you and I have things to work out, but because you've made a real effort with Laurel. I know she means a lot to you."

"Of course she does. She's my daughter."

She moved around him and picked up the cookie jar. After returning it to the counter, she rested her elbows on the tiled surface and her head in her hands. He wondered if she was going to cry. He wouldn't blame her. He moved closer so that he would be ready to comfort her, but she surprised him by turning around and glaring at him. Her eyes were dry, her chin set in a determined tilt.

"She misses her mother, Jake."

He didn't want to hear that. "It's been almost two and a half years. She's gotten over it."

"My mother's been gone eleven years and I still miss her." She turned and in one fluid motion pressed against the counter and raised herself until she was sitting on the tile. "You miss Ellen. You told me you've never loved anyone the way you loved her. Laurel will never get over her loss. I think you know that, deep inside. But hiding away your feelings, pretending it never happened, not letting her talk about her pain isn't making her better. Don't you think it's odd that when she's with me all she does is compare me to Ellen?"

He shrugged and wished he'd stayed in the barn. He didn't want to talk about this.

Anne pulled off her headband. Her pale red hair tumbled into her face. She brushed it back impatiently. She wasn't wearing any makeup. The color had fled her face, except for the freckles dotting her complexion.

"At first I thought she was subconsciously telling me I would never be as good as her 'real' mother." She pulled one knee up close to her chest and hugged it. "God, that hurt. I just wanted to fit in. I didn't expect to take Ellen's place, but I thought there might be room in Laurel's heart for both of us."

"There is," he said. "I know Laurel loves you."

She went on as if he hadn't spoken. "I've finally figured out the problem. It's not about me at all. She was talking about her mother because I had given her permission to. I told her it was okay. You made her bottle everything up inside. That's the reason she started in with that bad crowd. I'm convinced of it. She wanted to get your attention. She wanted you to see she was hurting. She wanted you to let her deal with her pain."

He leaned against the sink. "I don't know what to say."

"Good. Then listen." She jumped off the counter and approached him. She raised one hand and poked him in the chest. "Ellen is dead. Nothing is going to bring her back. Not guilt or silence or hoping it's all going to work out. Your wife is gone, but you still have a daughter who needs you very much. Don't abandon her anymore. Deal with it, mourn, do whatever you have to, then get on with your life. Please. For all our s-sakes." Her voice got more and more shaky until it cracked on the last word.

She backed away suddenly and covered her mouth with her hand. Before he could catch her, she sank to the floor. He was beside her in an instant.

"Talk to her," she said, clutching his shirtfront. "Please. You've got to talk to her about Ellen. Otherwise she *will* hate me forever." Tears flowed down her cheeks.

"I'm sorry," he whispered, pulling her close. "It's all my fault."

It was. He'd known for a long time that Laurel was trying to make him see her pain. He'd ignored it and her because he didn't know what to do. He didn't have the words.

He was so raw inside, he could barely hold himself together.

Anne was wrong about one thing, though. He wasn't missing Ellen. At least not Ellen as she'd been in the end. Maybe that was why he'd shut down. Maybe it had been guilt instead of mourning. Maybe some of it had been anger and disgust with himself for holding on to a relationship that had long been over. He should have left years ago. He'd always told himself he stayed because he couldn't leave Laurel, but maybe it was more than that. Had he stayed because Ellen had stayed? He'd hated the way she would throw his sterility up in his face every time he talked about a separation, but maybe he'd agreed with the logic of her arguments. Maybe he'd secretly believed that he did owe her for staying with someone who was only half a man.

Anne's tears soaked through his shirt. Shudders racked her body. He murmured soothingly and held her close. Slowly the tears slowed.

"Why are you being nice to me?" she asked, her voice muffled against his chest. "You don't even like me."

"You always say that. But you never say the second half of the sentence."

She sniffed and looked up. Her eyes were red and her face was blotchy. He used his thumb to brush away the moisture on her cheeks.

"What second half?" she asked.

"That you don't like me, either."

"Oh." She sniffed again.

One of her hands rested on his shoulder, the other lay on his thigh. She was half leaning against him and her breasts brushed his chest. "Do you like me, Annie?"

"I'd better start to if I'm having your baby." Her watery smile broke as a sob caught her unaware. "I can't do this much longer," she said.

"What?"

"Pretend it's not eating me up inside. Pretend I don't care about being compared to Ellen. I hate it." She rubbed her face with the back of her hand. "I know that makes me a horrible person."

"I don't think you're horrible."

"Not now." She sniffed. "You called me Annie again. But soon you'll shut down and I'll be alone in this house, with Laurel hating me, and you wishing me gone. I'm falling apart here. Why is all this happening now?"

"I don't know." He kissed the top of her head, then moved her bangs off her forehead and kissed her skin. "We'll figure something out."

"Like what? What are we going to do? Jake, I'm pregnant."

She looked weepy and fragile and in need of comforting, but he couldn't help grinning.

She glared up at him. "Stop it. You always get that look on your face when I mention the baby."

"What look?" he asked, even though he knew.

"The one that says 'look what I can do.' It's disgusting." She wiped her cheeks.

"Disgusting?"

"Well, maybe that's a little strong. But it's silly. How much does it take to have a baby?"

"More than I thought I had."

"You're right." She straightened some, but didn't move out of his embrace. "I'm sorry. I'm sure that was hard for you."

He shrugged. "It doesn't matter now. I'm finally going to have a son."

She reached up and touched his jaw. When he was looking into her blue eyes she said, "Listen to me carefully. You keep saying 'him' and 'my son.' You don't know if it's a boy or not. Unless that doctor who messed up the tests could tell you only had little boy sperm swimming in your sample, there is a chance that this baby is a girl."

Never taking his gaze from hers, he slowly shook his head. "I know it's a boy."

"You are the most stubborn man."

"I know that, too." He studied her face, counting the freckles on her nose.

"What are you staring at?"

"Your freckles. They're finally starting to grow on me."

She sighed impatiently. "You're not taking this seriously enough, Jake. Dammit, we have—"

But he never heard what they had to do. Instead he lowered his mouth to hers. She was shocked by the kiss. He knew by the way she stiffened in his arms. He thought she might want to escape his embrace so he loosened his hold on her and prepared himself for the disappointment.

Instead of pulling away, she nestled closer to him and put her arms around his neck. Her breasts flattened against his chest. He remembered their heavy weight in his hands and the way he'd caressed her nipples into hard attention. He groaned low in his throat.

Wrapping his arms around her waist, he held her as he lowered himself backward toward the floor. When he was stretched out, she lay on top of him, her pelvis pressing against his, her legs between his thighs. She was in control. He wondered what she would do with her power.

She didn't disappoint him. She cupped his jaw and angled her mouth on his. Soft pressure gave way to heated kisses. Her tongue swept across his lips, once, twice, before he parted for her. She tasted faintly of Italian spices, and he grinned as he pictured her sampling the sauce.

As their tongues touched and stroked each other, he moved his hands lower to cup her rounded derriere. He flexed his hips so that his hardness pressed against the soft skin he had touched earlier that day. She rotated in response. A sharp flame of desire licked along him. He caught his breath and resisted the impulse to experience his release right there. He hadn't come that close to embarrassing himself since he was about fourteen.

She held his head and rained frantic kisses on his face.

"Oh, Annie," he breathed.

He felt something moist on his cheek. He opened his eyes and saw her tears.

"Tell me this is about more than the baby," she said softly.

"The baby?" He hadn't even been thinking of their child. "No, it's about—" He flexed his hips again. "Hell, I don't know what it's about. It seems anytime you and I get within two feet of each other, we risk going up in flames."

She rolled off of him and sat cross-legged on the floor with her back to him. "Jake, this is a cosmic joke or something. Do you like me?" she asked without turning around.

He thought about all she'd done around the house and with Laurel. He thought about the knack she had for driving him crazy. He'd been more angry since he'd known her than he'd ever been in his life. He'd also laughed more, and hungered with a passion he'd never believed possible. She made him feel alive. He hadn't realized how much he needed that until just this minute.

"Yes, Annie. I like you."

"I hope it's enough." She scrambled to her knees, then turned to face him. The tears were gone, but the sadness in her eyes just about tore his heart in two. "I hope we can work this all out. Laurel and the baby. But it's going to be hard. I have less than a month left here."

He didn't like being reminded about the temporary nature of her visit. He hadn't minded before. In fact he'd been waiting for her to leave. But everything had changed since he found out she was pregnant.

"You don't have to go," he said, then wondered what the hell he was thinking of.

"Heather, my assistant, called me. The promotion is mine. I've worked hard for the job. It's what I want for my life. You have your dreams, Jake, and I have mine. They don't connect in any way. I don't deny I want you, but does that mean anything?" She rose to her feet. "I'm lost. I don't know what to do. Laurel already hates me. What's going to happen when she finds out about this?" She placed her hand on her stomach. She swallowed. "I wish—" She drew in a deep breath. "No. I can't wish I'd never met her or you. What I do wish is that someone, anyone, would tell me what on earth I'm supposed to do about all this."

Jake stayed in the kitchen long after Anne had left. He thought about all that she'd said, about her tears, and the way her kisses made him feel. He remembered how he'd hated and distrusted her when they'd first met. He remembered his fears about losing Laurel, and the way he'd resented the changes in his life. In a few short weeks, he'd come so far. Now he trusted Anne. He liked and admired her. And he agreed with her. He wanted someone to tell him what he was supposed to do, as well.

She was leaving. There was nothing he could say to stop her. The thought of her going back to Houston carrying his son was enough to rip his guts out. Yet he had no right to ask her to stay. God, but he wanted to. He wanted to see her growing big with his child. He wanted to hear the infant's heartbeat and feel him kicking. He rubbed the back of his neck, then slowly rose to his feet. First things first. As Anne had pointed out, the baby wasn't going to be arriving for eight more months. However, Laurel was here and a part of their lives.

He walked up the stairs and to his daughter's room. He knocked. Her muffled answer was unintelligible, so he opened the door.

Laurel lay huddled on her bed, her knees pulled up to her chest, her back to the door. Her long hair spread over shoulders that shook with her sobs. All the women in his house were crying today. How much of that was circumstances and how much of it was his doing? He didn't want to know.

He sat on the edge of the mattress and pulled Laurel close. She didn't fight him as he'd feared; instead, she burrowed close, hanging on desperately.

"Oh, Da-addy." She sobbed against him.

"Hush, baby. It's going to be fine." But was it? He didn't have any answers. He wanted Laurel and Anne to work this out. They had to. There were even bigger problems to face.

As he held and comforted his daughter, he wondered if he were a worse bastard than he'd thought. Would he be willing to smooth things over if Anne weren't carrying his child? If it weren't for the promised trauma ahead, would he care that they weren't getting along? How much of his desire to play peacemaker was purely selfish?

He didn't have those answers, either. He would like to think that he would have done the right thing no matter what. Anne wasn't the conniving, selfish bitch he'd thought her to be. Thirteen years ago she'd made a mistake. Now he knew how easily that could happen. He also understood her ambivalence about the adoption. There weren't any easy choices anymore. She was sweet and loving, doing more than her part to make it all work. He owed her for that, regardless of what else happened between them.

Laurel's sobbing slowed to an occasional hiccup. He rocked back and forth, smoothing her hair from her face, murmuring her name over and over. He searched for the right words, then realized all he had left was the truth.

"I miss your mother, too," he said, for the first time in two years voicing the words aloud. "I think about her a lot. I think about the way it used to be."

"I want Mommy back," she said, clinging tighter. Her face pressed against his chest and her tears dampened his shirt.

"I know, sweetie. But I can't make her come back. No one can. You must remember that Mommy loved you more than anything in the world."

"I m-miss her."

"I know. And she knows. She'll always know how much you love her."

Laurel raised her head and looked at him. "Does she?"

He nodded. "I promise." Her bangs hung in her eyes. He smoothed them back and smiled. "She's not the only one who cares about you. Anne cares."

Laurel frowned. "No, she doesn't. She's never cared. She's just pretending. I hate her."

"All right. I'll tell her to leave first thing in the morning. Then you'll never have to see her again."

As he'd suspected, Laurel's anger gave way to more tears. "I don't want her to go."

"But if you hate her, why do you want her here?"

"Oh, Daddy." She hugged him tight. Her slight frame shook with the agony of her sobs.

"Hush, baby." He squeezed and rocked her. "I know you're confused. I'm confused, too." He drew in a deep breath. There was nothing left to lose. "When you first told me you wanted to meet your birth mother, I was very angry." She stiffened in his arms, but he continued rocking her, occasionally smoothing her hair. She was so young, too damn young to deal with this. "I was afraid I'd lose you."

She raised her head and looked at him. Her hazel eyes swam with tears. Hazel eyes. Anne's mother's eyes. It didn't matter what set of traits had created them, he realized. They were his daughter's eyes and they were beautiful. He kissed her cheek.

"How could you lose me, Daddy? I promised I wouldn't run away again."

He smiled. "Not that way, silly. I thought you'd love her more than me. You wanted to live with her in Houston, remember?"

"Yeah." She wiped her face. "I like it here, now. I want to stay. I want Annie to stay. But I was so mad at her." She glanced down. "If I don't hate her, why did I say that?"

"I think you're confused because you really like Anne. It's okay to like her. It doesn't mean you love your mother any less. There's plenty of room in your heart to love both of them."

"And you?" she asked, smiling.

"And me." He touched her cheek. "Anne was only four years older than you are now when she got pregnant, Laurel. That's not very old to make a big decision about what to do with an unexpected baby. I can't be sorry she gave you up for adoption. I know that probably makes you feel funny inside, but it's true."

Her smile faded. "You're glad she didn't want me?"

"I think she wanted you very much. But if she'd kept you, your mother and I wouldn't have been able to adopt you. I wouldn't give you up for anything."

Her smile almost blinded him. She flung herself at him, but this time there weren't any tears. He held her close and realized he'd spoken the truth. Even with all he'd had to go through because of Michael's lies, the one thing he couldn't regret was Laurel. She was his daughter in every way; she made the heartache worthwhile.

He held her shoulders and eased her away. When their eyes met, he smiled. "You and Annie share something very special, something you could never have with your mother. You and Annie are blood relatives. That's a bond that can never be broken."

She cocked her head. "We *aren't* blood relatives?"

He shook his head. "I could prick our fingers and mingle the blood if you'd like."

"Oh, Daddy, gross." She laughed and rolled away from him. Bracing her elbow on the mattress, she propped her head up on her hand. "Thanks for talking to me. I feel better."

"Good."

"Can I—?" She picked at the blanket. Her bedspread and matching curtains hadn't arrived yet. "Can I still go to the party?"

He tried to frown, but he was too relieved to even fake it. "Sure, but only if I take you and then pick you up the next morning."

She thought for a moment. "Okay."

Anne rolled dough into long strips. She brushed the entire length with egg white then loosely knotted it. With a spatula she placed the roll on the cookie sheet next to four others.

"I can't believe I'm making bread by hand," she muttered. "For a bunch of ingrates who won't even notice."

She felt her anger slipping, but she hung on to it. If she didn't stay mad, she would start thinking about what had just happened with Laurel. Then she would cry, then she would want to leave. At this point, leaving wasn't an option, so she couldn't think about it or her daughter's angry words. She'd already figured out the tears didn't accomplish anything, but that didn't stop her eyes from burning.

When had everything become so complicated? She wanted to say that it had all started when Jake had first walked into her life, but she suspected that wasn't true. There had to be a reason she was so susceptible to his formidable masculine charms. It couldn't just be the jeans. Maybe she'd spent too much time alone. Maybe her life was so out of balance with all her energy focused on work that when a good-looking man turned up in her office, she completely lost it.

She rolled out another piece of dough and wished it were that simple. Her reaction to Jake wasn't just because he was good-looking. She knew lots of handsome men, had even dated some of them. But no one had tempted her the way he did. It had to be chemical. Or maybe it was the fierce way he'd protected his daughter from the very beginning. Maybe it was his willingness to admit he'd made a mistake. Whatever the reason, Jake had gotten past her barriers and deep inside her heart. She wanted not to care about him, but it had been too late for that for days.

She was moving the roll to the cookie sheet when she heard a noise behind her. She recognized the light footsteps, but didn't turn around.

"Annie?" Laurel said softly.

"Yes."

"I'm sorry I said those things to you. I don't really hate you."

Anne pulled off another length of dough and started to roll it. "Thank you for apologizing. I know you don't hate me, honey."

Laurel moved close until she was standing next to the counter. Anne didn't want to look at her, but she couldn't resist a glance. Her daughter's face was pale, her eyes wide and red from tears.

"You're still mad, huh?" Laurel asked.

"I was never mad." Anne hesitated, then decided she was tired of all the lies in this house. She was through with walking around on tiptoe so that no one was offended. The teenager was old enough to hear the truth. "I'm still hurt, Laurel. I appreciate the apology. I'm not going to punish you by pretending to be angry or not talking to you, but I can't act as if nothing happened. Saying 'I'm sorry' doesn't take away the fact that you hurt me."

"I'm sorry." Laurel's lower lip started to quiver.

"I didn't say that to make you feel badly," she said, putting the last roll on the cookie sheet then wiping her hands on a dish towel. "I'm pointing out a fact of life. If you say mean things to people, if you lash out without thinking, you're going to hurt people. They have to live with what you said, and you have to learn to live with hurting them." She placed her hand on Laurel's shoulder. "I have to live with the fact I chose to give you up for adoption. It wasn't a decision I made easily. I have regrets, but I'm not sure it wasn't the right decision. We'll never know. I was very young, but I did the best I could."

"Daddy said that you were only four years older than me when you got pregnant."

"That's true," she said, faintly surprised Jake had been defending her. "I had a college scholarship I didn't want to lose. I talked about what to do with my mother. We decided that giving you up to a nice family would be best for everyone." She squeezed Laurel's shoulder, then lowered her hand to her side. "There hasn't been a day that I haven't thought about you, wondered where you were, what you were doing, what you looked like. Especially on your birthday."

Laurel smiled. "You remember when it is?"

"Of course. It's my birthday, too."

"Really?"

Anne nodded. "You were born on my eighteenth birthday." She remembered that it had been the first time in her life there hadn't been a big family celebration with her mother and Becky Sue. She'd been in that small hospital labor room, fighting the pain in her body as she gave birth, and the pain in her heart as she realized she was going to have to give up her child.

"Did you cry when they took me away?" Laurel asked, staring at the floor.

Anne reached out and touched the girl's chin, forcing her to look up. She could feel the tears forming in her eyes. She didn't try to blink them away.

"They wouldn't let me hold you," Anne said softly. "I begged them to. They said it was for the best. Later, one of the nurses told me that you were already gone. I felt as if there were a hole inside of me so big I'd never fill it up. And I didn't. Not until I met you." She swallowed and brushed away the moisture on her cheek. "Ellen is your mother. She raised you, taught you, was there when you were hurt or sick. She'll always be your mother. I'm your mother, too, in a different way. I'll always love you, no matter what you say or do. You can be mean to me, if that's what you have to do to survive, Laurel. You can't make me hate you."

"Oh, Annie." Laurel threw herself into her arms. "I love you."

"I love you, too, baby," she said, holding her close. "Always. No matter what."

They stood like that for several minutes. Finally Laurel eased back and grinned up at her. "I guess I have two moms, huh?"

"I guess so." Anne returned her smile.

"I promise I won't say anything mean again. And if I mess up, I'm sorry."

"It's okay." Anne tapped her daughter's nose. "Don't you have a party to get ready for?"

"Yeah." Laurel started from the room. When she reached the doorway, she turned back. "You're the best," she said and ran down the hall.

Chapter Thirteen

Anne started to turn the page of her book, only to realize she hadn't read a word in the last half hour. Normally she could get lost in a story, forgetting her own troubles with someone else's, but tonight it wasn't working.

She paced the bare living room and listened to the sounds of the evening. The hoots from an owl were drowned out by a car engine, then the engine was shut off. She heard a door slam followed by footsteps on the porch. Jake walked into the house.

"Did Laurel get to the party all right?" Anne asked, settling back on the sofa.

"Yeah." He walked into the room and sat down next to her. He shook his head and grinned. "It turned out that none of the girls were going with boys. This Brad fellow thought he might be able to convince Laurel to go with him because she was new in town. Instead of his father driving, it was his big brother."

"You're kidding? I can't believe he would lie like that."

"Neither could Laurel."

"What did she do?"

He turned until he was facing her. His mouth relaxed into a huge grin. She could see his pride in his daughter's actions. "She gave him a piece of her mind, and his older brother, too. Told Brad he was a lying creep and she never wanted to have anything to do with him. Several of the other girls applauded her. Brad was allowed to attend the party after apologizing. I took him and his brother aside and had a few words with them."

"You threatened him, didn't you?"

Jake didn't even have the grace to look ashamed. "Of course. I told Brad and his brother that if they ever bothered Laurel, I'd hunt them down and beat the—" He paused. His grin got bigger. "Let's just say they got the message."

"The macho solution."

"Hey, it worked, didn't it?"

She shrugged, then gave him a smile. "Time will tell."

He was wearing a long-sleeved white shirt rolled up to his elbows. As usual, jeans and boots covered his lower half. She wished she could look at him without wanting him. She wished he wasn't so protective of Laurel and such a good father. It would be easier to dislike him, and ultimately easier to leave.

Slowly the atmosphere in the room changed. The air grew heavy as if charged with electrical current. Without Laurel in her room playing music or flipping channels on the TV, the house seemed strangely silent. Laurel was spending the night with her girlfriend. Which meant, Anne realized with a sinking feeling, that she and Jake were going to be alone.

She cleared her throat, then didn't have anything to say. She glanced around the room, at the book she'd thrown down, at her athletic shoes, at Jake's boots. The latter was dangerous. She wanted to gaze at his long legs, then his chest, then his face. But that would be a mistake. She could feel it.

"We have to talk," he said. "We have to come to some sort of resolution to our problem."

"Our problem being?"

"Laurel and the baby."

Oh. Of course. It wasn't about them or the desire flickering between them. There was no "them," Anne reminded herself. Jake was barely admitting that he liked her. As for the sexual feelings between them, so what? The sex hadn't been that special.

She cringed in her seat and waited for lightning to strike her dead. It was about the biggest lie she'd ever told. The sex between them had been hotter than a bonfire. She could still feel the heat. But that wasn't what he wanted to talk about.

"I don't see a resolution," Anne said. "You and Laurel live here on the ranch. I'm going back to Houston in a couple of weeks. What do you suggest? I want to stay in touch with Laurel. I thought she could spend time with me in the summer, and maybe on school holidays."

"She'll want to see more of you than that."

"I know. I want to see more of her. But alternating weekends are impractical. They'll also disrupt her life. But that's not what you're worried about, are you?" She risked meeting his gaze.

His brown eyes had been shuttered to conceal his feelings, but she saw the hints of pain in the straight line of his mouth and the tight set of his jaw. A lock of dark hair tumbled onto his forehead. His shoulders were stiff, his hands balled into fists.

"No," he admitted. "I know that you and Laurel will keep in touch. I think it's a good idea. As you pointed out before, she's going to need a woman in her life. It's unlikely that I'm going to remarry any time soon. I trust you to do right by her."

"Thank you," she said. "So the real question is what are we going to do about the baby?"

His gaze dropped to her midsection. Her oversize shirt hid her body from view, not that there was anything to see. Her stomach looked the same as it always had—not quite as flat or as firm as she would like—but there wasn't any sign of the baby.

He opened his mouth to speak, then closed it and looked away. She ached for him. He wanted so much. But she couldn't give him this.

"I'm keeping the baby with me," she said. "I'm sorry, Jake. I know you want him." She shook her head. "Now you've got me talking like I know it's a boy. I gave up one child. I'm not giving up another one. I know that hurts you, but I don't have another choice. You don't know what it was like wondering all the time. Wishing you could be there, just see your child, or touch her. I missed everything about Laurel. I missed her learning to crawl and walk and talk. I missed her first birthday, her first day at school."

"Now I'm going to miss all that."

Her breath caught in her throat. She hadn't thought of it that way. Oh, God, what were they going to do?

He read the question in her eyes. "You could stay here."

"No." She stood up and walked to the window. When she reached it, she held on to the wooden frame. "I can't. It's not fair to ask me. I've spent my whole life working for what I wanted. I finally have it. I have the job I want, I have friends, a life I'm very content with. I'm not going to give that up and come live here."

"I can't raise horses in Houston," he said. "This is my grandfather's land. It belonged to his father."

"So we're back where we started," she said slowly. "Nowhere. Neither of us happy with the situation." She leaned her head against the cool glass. "You realize we haven't figured out what we're going to tell Laurel."

"I don't want to think about that."

"We have to. There has to be some perfect sentence to explain it and keep her from being hurt." She turned slowly. "Jake, please don't let her hate me."

"She doesn't." He frowned. "I thought she apologized to you for saying that."

"She did. That's not what I mean. When this whole thing comes out about the baby, she's going to be very upset. She's going to feel betrayed. I gave her up for adoption, but I want to keep this child. She's not going to understand that. Be on my side."

"There aren't sides to this. We're all in it together."

"I wish that were true." She walked over to the coffee table and bent down to pick up the photo album. "I've looked at all the pictures. I've seen the evidence of her growing up, but it's not the same as being there. I missed so much." She looked at Jake. He sat on the edge of the sofa, his elbows on his knees, his hands laced together. "I don't want to deprive you of that. I swear I don't. I just want to do what's right for both of us."

"I wish I knew what that was."

"Me, too." She tried to smile, but her mouth wouldn't cooperate.

He stood up and held out his hand. "Come with me."

"Where are we going?"

"Trust me."

He had that peculiar expression on his face again. The one he'd had when he'd first realized he had fathered her child. She set the photo album back on the coffee table and placed her hand in his. His skin was warm to the touch. Instantly his fingers closed around hers. She felt safe and secure, which was insane considering what they still had to deal with. But she couldn't shake the feeling, so she gave in to it. When he smiled at her, she was able to smile back.

He paused by the downstairs rest room and snagged a box of tissue. "What's that for?" she asked.

He pulled her down the hall. "It's kind of how the day's been going around here. Just in case."

They stopped in the study. He stood her in front of the leather sofa and placed both hands on her shoulders until she sat down. Then he walked over to the bookcase beside the VCR. After fumbling through a shelf of tapes, he pulled one out and put it into the machine. He rejoined her on the couch.

"Ready?" he asked.

She nodded. He settled back next to her, then shifted and dropped his arm over her shoulders. She thought about resisting his embrace, then figured that she was already pregnant. She could hardly get in more trouble.

The scent of his body surrounded her. She liked the musky fragrance of man and heat and horses. He was hard to her soft. They meshed. She remembered the cold stranger who had come to her office such a short time ago. The result of their chance lovemaking had forced them to deal with each other on a much more immediate basis. She wondered what their relationship would have been like if she hadn't gotten pregnant. Would Jake still be trying to hate her? Would she be doing her best to ignore him? Or would they have become friends with the passage of time? Had they interfered with or created their own destiny?

A soft cooing sound caught her attention. She looked at the TV screen. A gasp escaped her. She sat up straight, her body stiff, all her attention focused on the flickering picture in front of her.

A toddler, two, maybe three, ran through a petting zoo. The assortment of goats, lambs and ponies didn't frighten the little girl. Brown hair tied into pigtails bounced with each step. Her pink shorts and ruffled shirt were covered with dust, as were her tiny white tennis shoes. The girl reached out to pet a duck, but the bird ran off. She looked up and laughed out loud.

"Almost, Mommy," Laurel said to the camera. "A duck."

"You okay?" Jake asked, and placed his hand on her leg. "You said you missed seeing her grow up. It reminded me of these videos. If it's too painful to watch..."

"No!" She gave him a quick glance. "I want to see everything. It hurts, but it's not a bad pain." She turned back to the screen and smiled. "I can't believe how beautiful she is. And so small."

The video continued, showing Laurel enjoying her day with the animals. She petted most of them, chased the duck, all the while quacking. Anne laughed with her, vaguely aware that Jake kept his arm around her in a protective gesture. She wanted to tell him that she was fine, that the ache in her heart came from bittersweet joy. She couldn't undo what had been done, but these films allowed her to see pieces of Laurel's life that she had only imagined.

The picture flickered, then changed to a picnic scene in a park. Laurel still looked young, but her clothes were different. The camera panned across the green grass to the little girl playing with a ball. Suddenly a woman stepped into view. Anne's breath caught in her throat. The woman was tall and slender, with stylish short dark hair. She walked barefoot across the grass, her narrow hips swaying provocatively. When she reached Laurel, she crouched down beside her, then looked up and smiled.

"That was Ellen," Jake said.

"I figured."

Anne wanted to glance at him to try to read his emotions, but she didn't dare. She didn't want to know how much he still loved his late wife. She stared at the figure on the TV screen. The photos in the library hadn't done Ellen Masters justice. She was pretty in a still shot, but in motion, she was pure elegance. Tasteful jewelry glittered from her ears and around her neck. Her summer dress exposed well-shaped tanned arms and legs. She had the long neck and elegant carriage of a fashion model.

Some people joined the picnic, but Anne couldn't take her eyes off Ellen and Laurel. The woman chatted with her friends, but kept most of her attention on her child. When Laurel toddled off out of the camera range, Ellen hurried after and brought her back. The child's smiles threatened to turn stormy, so Ellen tickled her belly and blew on her neck until the little girl was giggling.

The scene shifted again. Now the family was at the beach. This time Jake played with his daughter. A younger Jake, looking sinful in swim trunks. The little girl ran toward the waves, then shrieked when the water lapped against her toes. The picture tilted as the camera exchanged hands. Now Ellen appeared, her lean body displayed by a two-piece bathing suit. She took Laurel's hand and led her to the waves. Laurel was afraid of getting her face wet. Ellen crouched down and patiently encouraged her to try until the child was laughing and playing in the surf.

"My mother always did that," Anne said, staring at the screen. "She always told me to try and that it was better to face the fear than let the fear win."

"I wish I'd met your mother," he said, from his seat beside her. She could still feel his heat and inhale his scent; he still turned her on with his mere presence in the room. Despite that, she was less inclined to pursue a physical relationship. Not after seeing Ellen in a bathing suit. She glanced down at her large breasts and generous thighs. She'd never thought of herself as heavy, but she did have curves. Ellen had been a fantasy woman, long and sleek, elegant and well dressed. Anne worked hard to be put together for the office, but at home, she just couldn't bring herself to care if her shorts and T-shirt were in perfect condition or if her bra and panties happened to match. There were too many important things to worry about. But even saying that over and over to herself didn't stop her from wondering if Jake missed Ellen's perfection in his life.

The video came to an end. Jake got up and changed it. When he came back to the sofa, he stared at her.

"You're not crying."

She smiled. "You sound surprised. I'm really enjoying these. You've given me something I thought I'd never have—a chance to see Laurel grow up. As for the tears—" She shrugged. "I think I'm all cried out right now."

He reached for the remote but didn't use it. "There's a bunch of tapes. Help yourself whenever you want to watch them."

"Thanks, I will." She angled toward him on the sofa. "The three of you were a real family. Laurel was well loved, happy and with a good home. I'm glad she had Ellen." Funny the truth didn't hurt as much as she'd thought.

He raised one hand to her face and brushed his knuckles across her cheek. His skin whispered against her, igniting tiny fires in her nerve endings. Then he dropped his hand and the tingling stopped. She wished he would touch her again.

"I admire your generosity," he said. "I'd like to think that I'd be the same, but I doubt it."

"What do you mean?"

"Bobby, her 'birth father' for lack of a better term. I'm not sorry he's gone. The last thing I need is more competition for Laurel."

"Why do you doubt yourself? You're a terrific father."

"You don't know what happened after Ellen died. I—" He shook his head. "I got lost. I missed her so damn much. I know Laurel needed me, but I couldn't put myself together enough to be there for her. She paid a big price for that."

"She's done fine, Jake. You've started to make your peace with Laurel. That will go a long way to making up for the past."

Anne briefly closed her eyes and wondered what it must be like to love and be loved that much. To be part of a family and so important that your passing would leave an empty spot that would last a lifetime. What had Ellen Masters possessed that made Jake unable to stop loving her even when she'd been gone for two years? Could he ever come to care about anyone else, for example her, as much?

The last thought shocked Anne. She didn't need Jake to care about her romantically. They had problems to work out, but none of them required more than a friendship.

Oh, but wouldn't it be perfect if they could just... Just what? she asked herself. Fall in love? Then she would have to make other kinds of choices. Besides, he couldn't love her—he loved Ellen. Even if she'd wanted a chance with him, it wasn't going to happen. There was too much baggage between them.

"What are you thinking?" he asked.

"I was wondering if you would have liked me better if we'd just met as strangers. If we didn't have Laurel between us." Or Ellen, but she didn't say that aloud.

His brown eyes met and held her own. The gold flecks in his irises glowed with a fire that made her want to squirm in her seat.

"Yes," he said, his voice husky. "I would have liked you too damn much."

Despite the tension building in the room, and the night around them and the fact that the house was empty, save for the two of them, she smiled. "How can you like someone too much?"

"Easy." He leaned toward her. "You expose your feelings and they use them against you. They manipulate you or make you feel guilty about something that wasn't even true."

She told herself she should pay attention to what he was telling her, that the information was important. But she couldn't think about anything except the fact that his face was getting closer to hers and his gaze had locked on to her mouth. She licked her lips in anticipation.

The good girl inside her, the one raised in a small Texas town by a conservative single mother, reminded her that this wasn't a good idea. It would only complicate the situation. He was going to kiss her. If he did there was no telling where this night might end. The two of them had a bad habit of burning out of control in each other's arms. The voice in her head mentioned all that, then told her making love could easily turn into *being* in love. She needed that complication even less. Jake was still in love with Ellen. She would regret this come morning. Loving him would make it harder to leave. She *had* to leave. She owed it to herself to follow her dreams.

As if he sensed her hesitation, Jake hovered above her mouth. His breath fanned her face. One strong hand gripped her shoulder, but she could have easily pulled back. The voice in her head ordered her to do just that.

"Go away," she whispered to the voice.

Jake froze.

"Not you," she said, and slipped her hand behind his head.

But he didn't kiss her. He straightened and rose to his feet. Passion burned in his eyes, giving him the hungry, powerful expression of a predator. He paused and extended his hand.

"I want to make love to you, Annie Jo Baker," he said. "In my bed, with the lights on. I want to touch and taste and see every inch of you."

Instantly moisture dampened her panties. Her breasts tightened. If he'd been touching her anywhere on her body, she would have climaxed right there. Her breathing stopped altogether, then started in short ragged breaths. Their eyes met. He neither pleaded nor warned her away. The decision was hers. It was as inevitable as the tide.

She placed her fingers on his palm and allowed him to help her to her feet. She thought they would walk calmly up the stairs, then undress like civilized people. She'd been wrong.

He pulled her hard against him. Her breasts flattened against his broad chest. Before she could think, he claimed her mouth. Even as his tongue caressed hers, his fingers fumbled with the buttons on her shirt. He didn't bother pulling it off, instead he left it hanging open and expertly unfastened her bra. When her breasts were free to his touch, he lifted them in his hands and used his thumbs to tease her nipples into delicious hardness.

Her thighs trembled, her knees threatened to give out. She had to wrap her arms around him to keep from falling. He tasted of coffee and something masculine and heady. His hair slipped through her fingers like raw silk. She kneaded his shoulders, then gripped him as his fingers plied their wondrous touch on her sensitive skin.

He raised his head and stared at her. "Tell me you wanted me this afternoon. When I touched your belly."

"I wanted you."

"And now?"

"I want you more."

He groaned low in his throat, then bent down and locked his arms below her buttocks. He raised her so he could suckle on her sensitive breasts. His tongue circled around each tip, leaving a moistness that cooled quickly in the night air. The contrast of hot and cold, wet and dry, made her blood run faster. She rained kisses on his head, then wrapped her legs around his waist. Her most sensitive spot rubbed against his erection, the thick fabric of their jeans the only barrier to their mutual pleasure.

He moved out of the room and toward the stairs. On the third step he released her and let her slide until her feet touched the carpeted flooring. He was one step below her so they were almost at eye level. He kissed her mouth, then sucked her bottom lip. She clutched at his shoulders. Her shirt and bra hung open. She wanted to press bare skin to bare skin, so she reached for his front buttons. He reached for her jeans.

He couldn't pull the denim off over her shoes, so he sat her on the stair and took them off. Her socks followed, then he slipped the pants down her legs. He knelt between her thighs and ran his fingertips along her bare skin. From ankle to calf, from knee to hip. Shivers raced through her. She braced herself on the stair and watched him. Their eyes met and he smiled.

"What happened to making love in your bed?" she asked.

"We'll get there." He touched the elastic band of her panties and followed it from her hips to between her legs. "You're wet. I can feel it through these."

Before she could be embarrassed, he bent down and nipped at the skin right below her belly button. She jumped, then laughed because it tickled. Even as he licked her belly, he moved to one side and pulled off the scrap of damp cotton.

He stared at the exposed femininity. "Auburn," he said, as if he'd just made a wondrous discovery.

"I have red hair. What did you expect?"

He looked up and winked. "Just checking. You have freckles." He touched her chest, then her legs. "And curves." He touched her breasts.

"Jake, we're on the stairs."

"I know where we are."

"But what if someone finds us?"

He slipped his fingers into her damp curls. "The doors are all locked."

"But I—"

"You're talking too much. I must be doing something wrong."

With that, he bent down and kissed her thigh. With his fingers, he gently stroked her waiting heat, then urged her legs farther apart. Despite the stairs and the remote possibility of discovery, she complied with his silent command. Every touch led her closer and closer to her release. When he lowered his head and brought his mouth to her tiny place of pleasure, she had to bite her lip to keep from screaming. He knew exactly what to do, exactly how fast—her breath caught—then how slow—she gasped—to move against her. His tongue slipped over and around, then dipped inside, mimicking the act of love. He left her hanging on the taut edge of ecstasy, then gently sucked her to oblivion.

Jake knew the precise moment she began to climax. He kept his ministrations moving in time with her contractions. When her body ceased to tremble beneath his, he pulled her close and held her. Only when her breathing returned to normal, did he pick her up and carry her to his bedroom.

The place, the bed itself, everything was new. He firmly closed his mind to any memories that might wish to intrude on this perfect time. He placed Annie on the bed, then quickly pulled off his own clothes. She was slick with perspiration. He wiped her with his shirt, then slipped in next to her. Her small hands reached for him, cradling his arousal. Instantly his hips flexed.

She looked up at him. "Something tells me that if I mentioned I had some mending to take care of right now you'd be most unhappy."

"Most," he agreed, and kissed her. Her mouth opened without urging. Their tongues mated, causing him to harden even more. The pressure was uncomfortable, but he didn't want his release yet. He liked being tempted to the edge.

He rolled onto his back and pulled her up against him. Her full breasts burned into his chest. God, she felt good. He traced her hips, then gripped her rear, squeezing the rounded flesh. He liked the curves and the way she tasted. He liked—

He gasped. She suckled his nipple as he had hers. Her fingers brushed his chest, then ran down his belly, tangling with the thicket of hair. His hardness flexed in anticipation. She moved her fingers lower to his thighs, then brushed delicately against his testicles. He parted his legs to allow her to explore that part of him he'd always thought useless. Aching need grew, but he held back, waiting, letting her lead the way.

She raised her head and smiled at him. Moving slowly, she straddled his midsection. Her moist center dampened his stomach. Bracing her arms on the mattress, she slipped back until the tip of him teased at her.

Before she could continue, he gripped her waist and tumbled her to her back. He poised between her legs.

"So you want to be in charge," she teased, her eyes bright with anticipation. Her pale red hair fanned out on the pillow. Her generous breasts moved with each breath. He wanted to kiss each freckle, discover every inch of her, as he had promised, but first he had to be inside her or he would die.

"I can't wait," he said, by way of apology.

"Then don't." She tilted her hips toward him, bringing his erection in contact with her waiting warmth.

"Ah, Annie, how do you do this to me?" He slowly slipped home.

It was as explosive as that night in the desert. There was no time to discover a mutually satisfying rhythm, no conscious thought left to deal with finesse. There was only the feel of her around him, the heat and the need. Her legs embraced his hips. His fingers held her breasts, her hands urged him closer.

When her eyelids slipped shut and her mouth parted, he forced himself to slow enough to take her with him. At her moment of climax, he held back a heartbeat. As his body shuddered and expelled his seed, he reveled in the power of knowing this is how he had created their child. This mystical act that bonded the generations. This moment from which he'd felt excluded and so much less than a man.

As she cried out his name and her nails bit into his arm, he knew that there would never be a more perfect feeling than her body rippling under his, and his echoing the passion.

As clearly as the sensations filling him, he knew the solution. It was so simple he wanted to laugh.

So when their breathing returned to normal and she lay next to him, her head on his shoulder, he took her left hand in his and spoke five words.

"Annie, will you marry me?"

Chapter Fourteen

Annie immediately moved away from him and reached for the sheet. After she pulled it up to her shoulders, she brushed her hair out of her face and slowly sat up. "You don't mean that, do you?"

She didn't sound overly enthused, but he wasn't worried. "Come on, Annie," he said, raising himself up on one elbow. "It's the perfect solution. You can stay here and be with Laurel and the baby. We won't have to worry about custody or visitations. I know the ranch isn't making any money yet, but when I sold out of the construction business, I made a mint. Not to mention the stocks my grandfather left me." He shrugged modestly. "What I'm trying to say is that finances will never be a problem."

She shook her head. "This isn't about money." She stared at him. The color fled her face leaving behind pale skin and the dark spots of her freckles. "It was never about money. It's about different lives and goals. You don't love me."

He fingered the cotton sheet that covered her. "Is there someone else? Is that why you don't want to marry me?"

"No," she said quickly.

He was surprised to find out he was relieved that there wasn't another man in her life. "Then don't you see?" he said, taking her hand. "It'll be good between us. We get along. We both love Laurel. I think we're pretty damn hot in bed." He raised his eyebrows. "Marriages have been built on less."

She sighed impatiently. "You can't marry me just because it's convenient and we happen to have a chemical attraction."

He leaned close so that he could nibble on her shoulder. "Sure I can. Why not?" Her skin grew hot under his touch and her eyelids slipped closed. He watched as her grip on the sheet loosened. The white cotton slipped lower until her breasts were exposed. He stretched so he could gently lick a puckering tip. "It's magic, Annie. It's never been like this before for me."

"Me, too," she said softly. "Jake—" Her voice became a moan as he continued his ministrations.

She tasted sweet, almost like peaches, he thought, deepening his kisses, drawing more of her breast into his mouth. She squirmed, then pushed him away and pulled the sheet up to her neck.

"Stop it," she said. "I mean it. You've made your point about the sex. It's very powerful. But that doesn't prove anything. I'm not interested in getting married so that I can have a good time in bed."

It seemed like a fine idea to him. The first few years with Ellen had been fun, but there had never been this instant heat between them. "Why *are* you interested in getting married?"

"Oh, Jake, don't do this." She drew her knees up to her chest and hugged them close to her body. "You think getting married makes it all work. You get a housekeeper, a lover, another parent to help with Laurel and the baby. You make it sound so easy."

"Why does it have to be difficult?" He rolled off the bed and stood up. "Dammit, Annie, can't you see this is the best solution for both of us?"

"No." She shook her head. "It's the best solution for you. I still have a life of my own back in Houston. What about that? What about the job I've worked so hard for? It's been nine years coming. I deserve this chance and you don't have any right to keep me from it." Her blue eyes flashed with fire, but it wasn't fueled by the heat of passion.

"Are you saying you don't like it here? I know it's not a high-powered job, but neither is trying to make the horse ranch pay. It's different, and in a lot of ways, better."

"That's your dream. Mine is different."

"But it would make everything—"

"No, it wouldn't," she said, cutting him off. "You aren't listening. I won't take the easy way out again. I did that once. My mother and Becky Sue both told me giving up Laurel was the best thing for the baby. I believed them because I wanted to. I was seventeen, and terrified of being alone with an infant. I had a future I didn't want to mess up." She drew in a deep breath. "I'll regret that decision until the day I die."

That got his attention. He stared down at her. "You never told me that," he said softly.

"I never wanted to admit it to myself. I did what was simplest and best for everyone. Or so I thought. I'm not doing that again. I'm happy about the baby, but not thrilled about the circumstances. It was an accident, and we'll find a way to deal with it. That doesn't mean we have to get married."

He braced his hands on his bare hips. "I'm beginning to think there are no accidents. You're not going to marry me, are you?"

"Not like this."

He sat on the mattress and pulled on his jeans. It had been the perfect solution. All his elation faded away, leaving him feeling old and tired. Nothing was easy, that was one thing he could count on. He thought about all the years with Ellen, and the way they'd fought at the end. He thought about the baby. His son. He turned on her.

"Dammit, woman, you're not taking my child away from me. You have no right."

She stretched her legs out in front of her, then raised her head and looked at him. He'd expected her to be angry, or at least defiant. Instead her mouth trembled at the corners and her eyes looked very sad. "Don't worry, Jake. I'll make sure you get everything you want."

Anne threaded her needle and picked up a square of fabric. The ultimate handicraft, she thought, knowing it would be faster to use the sewing machine. But she wanted to make this quilt by hand. She wanted to touch the cloth. She wanted to feel the different textures and have it grow slowly from unconnected pieces to a complete whole.

The late-afternoon sun poured in through a freshly washed window. She glanced down at her hands. When she'd first arrived on Jake's ranch, her skin had been smooth, her nails long and elegantly rounded. Now she had a few healing cuts from run-ins with the potato peeler or a paring knife. Her index finger was pricked from sewing. She'd long since cut off her nails. When she got back to Houston, her manicurist was going to have a fit.

She picked up the square of fabric and knew that her scarred hands weren't the only changes since she'd left her white-on-white condo. Not by a long shot. She was pregnant. That was certainly a change. And she was hurting.

She'd thought she'd experienced her worst pain when she'd given birth to a baby she'd never been allowed to see. The death of her mother had also been hard. Meeting

Laurel, dealing with Jake—that, too, had added to the amount of pain she'd experienced. But none of these events compared to his proposal for a marriage of convenience.

If she lived to be a hundred, she would never forget the flash of joy following his words. Marriage. In that second when she'd stared at him, she'd allowed herself to hope. Worse, she'd allowed herself to admit that she'd come to love him. The thought that he might care about her had been too wondrous to be contained. But she'd forced herself to hold back, even when she had wanted to throw herself into his arms. She'd bitten her tongue until she could get out words other than "Yes, yes, a thousand times, yes." She'd asked if he was sure.

He was. He wanted to marry her because it was convenient, the best solution to their mutual problems. Not because she was special, not because he loved her, but because it was easy. He would have everything he wanted, and she would be left with nothing.

She sighed and began stitching the cow-print fabric. That wasn't completely true, she admitted to herself. He wasn't the only one who would gain by their marriage. She would get to be with Laurel all the time. That would be lovely. She would be part of a family, something she'd longed for ever since she was a little girl.

But what about her career? What about the job she'd worked for all these years? Could she walk away from it? She could find other work, but relocating big companies to Houston, Texas, wasn't exactly a job she could do here on the horse ranch. Would she be willing to give it all up because a man loved her? She shook her head. No, not for that.

She glanced down at the squares of fabric she'd already cut. Several were from the cow-print curtains hanging in the kitchen. A few had been part of a dress Laurel had stained and torn. Five came from fabric samples for curtains now hanging in the mostly decorated house. She hadn't made a quilt in years. Not since high school. She also hadn't baked or sewn or made lasagna from scratch. She wouldn't have given up her job just because Jake loved her, but she might have given it up to stay home with her new family and experience a different, maybe even better, life. She'd never been a full-time mom before. It sounded challenging and more rewarding than any contract. Of course that could simply be a case of wanting what she couldn't have.

She glanced at the clock. Laurel was out riding with her father. They would both be back soon. She put down her sewing and walked into the kitchen. She had a chicken ready to go in the oven. She checked the temperature, then slid the pan inside and set the timer.

It had been a week since she and Jake had made love. A week since he'd proposed and she'd turned him down. A week since they'd had a conversation that was anything but impersonal. She pulled out a bag of potatoes and put several on the counter. If she didn't know better, she would say his feelings had been hurt by her rejection.

That wasn't possible, she reminded herself as she reached for the peeler. He didn't want her; he wanted a solution to his problems and full custody of his child. She could have been anyone and he would have come to the same solution. He didn't care about her. He didn't love her. Thank God he hadn't figured out she loved him.

In another week it wouldn't matter, she thought, peeling the first potato, then dropping it into a bowl of water. She would be gone. Back to her real life. She paused in mid-stroke and dropped the vegetable onto the counter. She didn't want to go.

Anne leaned her forearms against the counter and closed her eyes. She had to admit the truth to herself if to no one else. She wanted to stay here and be a mother to Laurel and the baby. She wanted to plant a garden and watch it grow. She wanted to make all her mother's favorite recipes, and can berries in August. She wanted to be a part of a family.

She wanted to love Jake forever. Most of all, she wanted him to love her back.

The front door opened, then slammed shut. She straightened and blinked to make sure her eyes were completely dry.

"The mail is here," Jake said, walking into the kitchen. "They left a package." He set a large box on the kitchen counter.

Anne glanced at the label. "It's from the company that made Laurel's bedspread. It's probably the throw pillows."

"I'm sure she'll be pleased," he said, his voice as impersonal as it always was these days.

She almost wished he would get angry at her. Then at least there would be something to react to. This calm, cool stranger had nothing in common with the Jake Masters she knew. He was not the same man who had stood in her office and passionately reminded her she had no legal rights to Laurel. He wasn't the man who had made love to her on a rock beside a trailer park in Paradise, or reverently touched her skin searching for proof of his child. Some of the memories she would carry with her were wonderful, some very painful, but in each, Jake was vibrantly aware of her. He wasn't distant and uncaring.

"What time is dinner?" he asked, picking up the box.

"About five-thirty."

"What are we having?"

"Baked chicken, broccoli and scalloped potatoes."

"I'd prefer mashed potatoes," he said, and walked toward the door.

She almost said fine. After all, she didn't care about the potatoes. But something inside of her snapped. She was tired of being ignored and treated like hired help.

"No," she said, and set down the peeler. She wiped her hands on a dish towel.

Jake stopped dead in his tracks. His eyes met hers. For the first time in a week, something flashed in the brown depths. Something alive and passionate. Even if this fire was fueled by anger, she didn't care.

"Excuse me?" he said.

"No." She smiled. "I'm not going to make mashed potatoes."

He drew in a deep breath, then spoke slowly, as if dealing with a recalcitrant child. "We always have mashed potatoes with baked chicken. Both Laurel and I prefer it that way."

"I figured as much. That's why I'm going to do something different." She folded her arms over her chest and raised her chin defiantly.

He set the box down and approached her. When he was about two feet away, he braced his hands on his hips. "Don't start something you don't intend to finish."

"Oh, but Jake, I *do* intend to finish this. I'm tired of you ignoring me. You want mashed potatoes?" She tossed one of the unpeeled vegetables toward him. He caught it in his left hand. "Go ahead and make them yourself. But if you want me to cook, we'll do it my way. I refuse to live up to the memory of a saint."

"You leave Ellen out of this."

"How can I? She surrounds all of us. To the best of my knowledge, the woman never even lived in this house, yet her presence is everywhere. If you want to live your life in homage to the dead, go ahead, but that's not part of my deal. I'm tired of being compared and found wanting."

"Then maybe you should do a better job."

She told herself he was just lashing out and that it didn't mean anything, but she felt the sting of his remarks all the way down to her heart. She squared her shoulders. "I'm doing a fine job. I've been better to you and Laurel than either of you deserve. I've done my best to fit in. I'm not playing that game anymore. If you want an Ellen clone, go find yourself one. Some dark-haired beauty with the right manners and a perfect pedigree. I'm just Annie Jo Baker, from a trailer park a little east of nowhere." She leaned forward and glared at him. "I'm also Laurel's mother, and nothing is ever going to change that."

She was finally getting through to him. She could tell by the veins throbbing in his neck. His muscles tensed. "You shouldn't mind being compared to Ellen. After all you're the one trying to take her place in Laurel's heart and my bed."

"That's a lie, and you know it. You're the one who wants me to be a replacement. You're the one who wants to get married because it's so damned convenient for you. You're the one insisting I stay. Have you thought about that, Jake? Do you ever wonder why you're so scared of me? I'll tell you why."

She moved until they were inches apart. Heat radiated from his body. She knew its source was rage, but that didn't stop her body from responding to his. She had to dig deep for her own temper to find the courage to tell him the truth.

"You don't trust anyone to love you enough to stay. You hold on to Laurel so tightly, I'm not surprised she ran away. You're afraid of losing her. You don't have the guts to admit you might need me, so instead of trying to keep me here by caring about me, you talk about 'the perfect solution.' More than that, more than anything, you're afraid of losing your baby." She touched her belly. "It's my child, too, Jake. I'm the one carrying him, and possession is nine-tenths of the law."

The silence nearly deafened her. Jake's eyes gave little away, save a growing ugliness directed at her. "Damn you," he growled. "Don't you threaten me. I'll never let you keep my son."

A soft sound made them both turn. Anne saw Laurel standing in the door. She must have come in from the barn without either of them hearing her.

"Daddy?" she said, her voice shaking. She turned her hazel eyes on Anne. "Annie? Are you having a baby? A baby you're going to keep this time? How could you?" The question came out as a scream. "How could you?" She turned and ran from the room.

Chapter Fifteen

Jake took off after Laurel, but she beat him to her bedroom. He heard the door slam, followed by the click of her lock.

"Let me in," he said, then pounded on the wooden door. "Dammit, Laurel, I'm not kidding about this."

"Go away," she screamed. "Just go away."

Her voice shook with sobs. He wanted to break down the barrier between them and hold her until this all went away. Instead he leaned against the doorframe and closed his eyes. It wasn't going away. He'd put off thinking about Laurel and how this would affect her. In his happiness about the baby, he'd deliberately ignored her feelings. He hadn't wanted to think about the problems and had instead concentrated on the reality of actually being able to father a child.

"Laurel," he called through the door. He deliberately spoke softly. "Please, honey. We have to talk."

"I don't want to talk to you. Go away, Daddy. Leave me alone."

If she'd claimed to hate him, he would have felt better. Her emotional outbursts never lasted very long. But this uncontained agony was more than he could stand. Determined to give her the time she needed, he turned to leave. Anne stood behind him on the top of the stairs.

"I hope you're happy," he said, pushing past her. "You've just destroyed your daughter's life for the second time."

"Don't you dare blame this on me," she said. "I've wanted to discuss telling Laurel from the very beginning. You're the one who wouldn't listen. You're the one—"

But he didn't wait to hear his part in the problem. He continued down the stairs and out to the barn. He started to go into his office, then realized the last thing he needed was to be cooped up. Emotions bubbled through him. Frustration at the situation, anger at Anne, regret for hurting Laurel, determination to keep his son. They boiled through him until he wanted to put his fist through a wall.

He jogged out of the barn and around to the side. Logs had been stacked, ready for splitting. It was late October. The first snowfall would come with the next storm. They needed the wood for their fireplace. He eyed the ax and the huge pile of wood. Perfect.

He took off his wool work shirt. The late-afternoon breeze cut through his cotton T-shirt, raising goose bumps on his skin. He didn't care. It wouldn't take long for him to warm up.

He positioned a log, then picked up the ax. His stroke was sure and true. The wood split down the center. He left the halves where they fell and reached for another piece.

The rhythmic motions raised his body temperature and cooled his temper. Random thoughts filled his mind. Why the hell couldn't Anne be more cooperative? If she'd just agreed to marry him, everything would have been fine.

They could have put off telling Laurel about the baby until she was ready to hear about it.

He must have done something wrong. He hadn't used the right words or something. He would have thought after all those years of living with Ellen and watching her get her way in everything, he would be better at manipulating people. God, he'd hated living in her perfect world. That damned house in Dallas. He grimaced remembering the matching wallpaper and drapes, the furniture that looked beautiful, but untouched. The rose-colored lace in their bedroom. He remembered how she always took so long to get ready to go out, it wasn't usually even worth the trouble to go. Ellen couldn't just take off to the movies or a picnic. Everything had to be perfectly choreographed.

Not like in the early days. His ax cut through the logs, one by one. Sweat broke out on his back and forehead. He remembered when they first had Laurel and had both stayed up all night. Neither of them had known what her crying meant. They'd stared helplessly at their newborn and prayed for someone to give them some guidance. He remembered the afternoons he'd rushed home from work so he could be with his wife and daughter. Of the times they'd spent at the park.

He stopped in midswing and took a breath. The air was crisp and clean, smelling faintly of pine, freshly cut wood and horses. When had she changed? Had it simply been a function of time? Was it when they'd moved to the big house? Had it started the night he'd said they should think about a separation?

Laurel had been five, maybe six. He'd finally realized that even though Ellen was his best friend and he loved her, he didn't want to stay married to her. He sensed there was something missing. Their friendship and youthful feelings hadn't matured into something that would last. Had it started then? Had she changed to keep him, not knowing that by turning into the perfect wife and mother she had killed what he had loved about her? He remembered the pain in her eyes and the way she'd defied him to leave her. She'd said that he owed her—she had stayed with a man who couldn't give her the one thing she'd wanted most in the world. He was the reason she couldn't have a baby.

He'd stayed because leaving had been too hard. He'd allowed her words to build a paper cage around him, closing him inside with a lock fashioned from guilt. He raised the ax and drove it through the logs, one after the other, hating Ellen for what she had done to him. Cursing her name, her memory.

When his muscles trembled and he couldn't raise his arms high enough to split another log, he sank onto the tree stump and struggled to catch his breath. The sweat on his body evaporated, leaving him chilled, but he made no move to reach for his shirt. He prayed she would burn in hell for what she had done to him. She had used him to her own end. And he had let her.

He started to stand up, then sank back to the log. *He had let her.* He dropped the ax on the ground and slumped forward, resting his elbows on his thighs and his head in his hands. Dear God, he had *let* her manipulate him. She hadn't made him stay. He could have left, but he didn't.

Images from the past flooded him. Of course, he thought, startled by the realization. Staying had seemed like the right thing to do at the time. It had also been easier to stay in the life he knew than risk starting over. He'd done what everyone wanted. Just as Annie had done when she'd given up Laurel. But unlike her, he'd done it out of fear. She'd been right when she'd accused him of being afraid of losing it all. If he'd left Ellen, he might have lost Laurel. If Anne went back to Houston, he would lose his son. He would also lose Annie, and he couldn't bear to think about that.

He raised his head up toward the sky, but found no answers in the coming night. He had chosen his own path and now he had to live with the consequences. As Anne had to learn to do. She had chosen this path as well.

He shook his head. No, that wasn't fair. He'd been the one to get in touch with her. He'd been the one to bring her out to Colorado because he hadn't wanted to take Laurel back alone and risk her not forgiving him. He'd been the one who wouldn't discuss the realities of the pregnancy, because he'd been afraid of what would happen with Laurel. Annie wasn't the guilty party. Yet her innocence did nothing to change the fact that they had both hurt Laurel.

He had lost his best friend years before when Ellen had changed. Then he had lost his wife. Annie would be taking away his unborn child when she returned to Houston. He could very easily lose Laurel because he'd put off dealing with the truth. He would be left with nothing, and he had no one to blame but himself. None of this would have happened if he hadn't withdrawn after Ellen's death. If he'd only thought about his daughter instead of himself. But the realization came two years too late. He didn't know how he was supposed to make it all work now.

Anne sat in the hallway and leaned her head against Laurel's door. She hadn't heard anything for almost ten minutes. She didn't know if that was good or bad. It didn't really matter, she thought sadly. She had to try to make Laurel understand.

"I'm sorry you found out this way," Anne said, raising her voice so she could be heard through the door.

"Go away."

At least she hadn't said she hated her. Maybe that was something. "I can't go away until we talk."

Laurel's response was to turn up her stereo until the music pounded through the walls, blocking out any possibility of conversation. Anne waited. She tried to gather her thoughts together and figure out what she was going to say. She should have told Laurel before, when she'd wanted to.

At least then she could have planned her words in advance and tried to soften the blow. To hear the truth that way, blurted out in anger.... She winced. She wasn't even sure what she and Jake had been yelling at each other, but she would bet it had been ugly and unsuitable for a thirteen-year-old to hear.

Oh, baby, she thought, touching the door between them. If only it had happened differently. If only she and Jake hadn't made love that night in the desert. She touched her stomach. No, that's not true. She wanted the baby. She wanted Laurel. Her mouth curved up in a slight smile. She might as well finish the list and go for it all—she wanted Jake. But not like this. Not with everyone bleeding inside. She'd come here to make a difference, to make it better. Instead everything was going wrong.

In a few minutes the music stopped. She drew in a deep breath. "You will always be my daughter, Laurel," she said, hoping the girl would at least listen. "I still love you and want you in my life."

The door flew open. Laurel glared at her. "No, you don't. You want your b-baby." Her voice cracked. Her long brown hair hung down in two braids. With her warm plaid shirt and baggy jeans hiding her budding figure, she looked young and fragile.

Anne scrambled to her feet. "I'm sorry you found out this way."

Laurel glared at her. "You're not sorry you're pregnant, are you?"

"No."

"I knew it." Fresh tears formed in her eyes. "You never cared about me. That's why you gave me away. You never wanted me. You only came here because you wanted to get pregnant. You wanted the baby so you could keep it. You're going to keep it."

Laurel balled her hands into fists and struck out. Anne grabbed her wrists, holding her at arm's length. The girl thrashed for a few seconds, before going still.

"You didn't keep me. You gave me away." Her hazel eyes, so like Anne's mother's, accused her of the most heinous crime. "You were supposed to be my mother. Now you're going to be someone else's mother. I can't even hate you anymore. You made me want to have you stay here forever. But it was lies. You lied to me."

Anne pulled her close. Laurel resisted at first, then sagged against her. She wrapped her arms around the sobbing girl and murmured soft, meaningless phrases. "Hush, honey. Hush." She led Laurel over to the bed and sat next to her. "I'm sorry."

"No, you're not."

"I am. I swear." Anne reached out and brushed her daughter's face with her fingers. Laurel flinched at the touch, but didn't pull back. "I wish I could explain, but it's very complicated."

"That's what grown-ups always say." Laurel sniffed. "It doesn't seem very complicated to me. You want this baby and you're going to keep it."

Anne shook her head. "I know this hurts you. It hurts me, too." She held up her hand to ward off her daughter's interruption. "Please listen, honey. I was seventeen when I got pregnant in the back of a boy's pickup truck. It was stupid and I knew better, but I did it anyway. I gave you up for adoption because I thought it was the right thing to do. If I could be that seventeen-year-old girl again—" She swallowed hard. "I want to tell you that I would keep you. I would, knowing what I know now. If I had been smarter, I wouldn't have gotten pregnant in the first place. But given the same set of circumstances, knowing there was a loving couple wanting a baby and not being able to have one, I would give you up again."

Laurel stared at her. Anne could see the pain in her eyes, and the need to believe, but she was afraid to have her trust shattered yet again.

Anne took one of her hands and held it tightly. "There's nothing you can say to me that I haven't said to myself. I never wanted to hurt you. Even though I wasn't with you all those years, I never forgot about you, or stopped wondering where you were or what you were doing. Your dad showed me some videos."

Laurel looked up, surprised. "He did?"

She nodded. "Of when you were little."

Laurel grimaced. "They're so dopey."

"Not to me. I thought they were very special. I got to see you playing and laughing. I saw you with your mom. I saw the way she held you and taught you not to be afraid to try. What would you do, Laurel? If the choice were yours, if you could go back, would you want me to keep you? Would you want to give up your mom and dad so that you and I could live in a trailer like Becky Sue and her kids? I never got married. You might never have had a stepdad. It would have just been the two of us. My mom is gone, and Bobby didn't have much family, either. Would you give up everything you've ever known and everyone who's loved you just so you and I could be together?"

Their eyes met. Laurel slowly shook her head. "No. I love my dad. I miss my mom. Sometimes I cry because I want her back so much."

"I know, honey." Anne rested her hand on her daughter's head and pulled her close. She rocked her back and forth. "I'm not asking you to decide. I'm trying to show you that we all make hard decisions. We do the best we can, then we have to live with it. I'm sorry the thought of my having a baby hurts you. But you'll always be my firstborn. We've found each other now. It's up to us to keep that relationship special or let it die. We can't change the past, but we can influence the future. I love you and want to be a part of your life forever. You decide what happen next." She held her breath and prayed for a miracle.

Laurel drew in a deep breath and sighed. She stiffened then shifted and wrapped her arms around her waist. Ann hugged her back.

"I love you, Annie."

"I love you, too, Laurel."

"I'll try not to be upset about the baby."

Anne touched a finger to her daughter's chin and urge her to look up. "You can be upset. I'm upset. This change everything. But we can make it work. I promise."

"I used to want a little brother or sister."

"Your dad is convinced it's a boy."

Laurel frowned. "If my dad's the father of your baby that means you guys—" She stopped talking and gri maced. "Oh, gross."

Anne bit back a smile. "Maybe it's best if you don' think about that part."

"I guess." Laurel wrinkled her nose. "Does this mea you're going to get married? Don't you have to be marrie to have a baby?"

"Obviously not," Anne said. "I had you."

"But that was different. If you marry my dad, tha means you'll stay here with me. Don't you want to?"

"It's not that simple."

Laurel sighed again. "That means no."

"I can't marry your father. He's still in love with you mom. That would make the relationship hard on every one. I don't belong here. I have a job, a promotion, wai ing for me back in Houston. All my friends. Everything there except for you." And Jake, but Laurel didn't need t hear that.

"But you have friends here, don't you? I think Dadd likes you a lot. Don't you have to like someone to, well— She glanced at Anne's stomach, blushed and looked awa

"I mean, I wouldn't mind if you married him. Dad says I can love you and Mom. That it's okay."

"Can't you love me if I don't live with you?"

Laurel thought for minute, then nodded slowly. "I guess."

"Good. Because I'll still care about you. We have something very special. It's not about geography or who lives where. I'll always be available to you Laurel. Just a phone call away. We'll work out some way to have visits together. Often, I promise."

Laurel stared at her. Her freckles stood out on her pale skin. Anne counted the dots on her daughter's nose and knew the number and pattern matched the freckles on her own face. They were tied together by more than blood, but it was nice to know the family connection was still there.

"You're leaving," Laurel said suddenly.

"You always knew that."

"But you're leaving now. You're not going to wait until the two months are up, are you?"

Laurel threw herself at her. Anne clutched her. Sometime in the last few minutes she'd made up her mind. It would be easier for everyone if she was gone. Jake and Laurel could get on with their lives, and she could make plans for her maternity leave. She would have to figure out how much time she should take and... She touched Laurel's hair. The details could wait. For now it was enough to hold and be held by the child she'd lost so long ago.

"No, honey, I'm leaving in the morning."

Jake stood on the top of the stairs. He heard the words but didn't want to believe what they meant. She was leaving him. The sharp pain in his chest surprised him. He hadn't realized how much he would care.

Laurel looked up and saw him. "Daddy." She ran to him and embraced him fiercely. "Annie's leaving. Don't let her go. Please make her stay."

"Laurel, I—"

She tore herself free and raced down the stairs. The fro door opened, then slammed shut.

He leaned against the doorframe and folded his arn over his chest. Annie sat on his daughter's bed. Her ey looked haunted.

"How much did you hear?" she asked.

"Enough to know that you're going to be one terrif mother."

Her smile looked a little ragged at the corners. "Thank I don't feel so great right now."

"Laurel knows that you love her. That's the most in portant thing. The rest of it can be worked out."

She folded her hands together on her lap. Her pale re hair had grown a little since she'd been here. It brushed h shoulders in an unruly mass of waves. The oversize swea shirt she wore dwarfed her, concealing her generous curve But he remembered them. He remembered how she taste and felt in his arms. He remembered the fire that co sumed them every time they got within two feet of ea other. He knew in his heart it would be like that forever. I thought about her gentleness, her humor, her quick wit a sharp mind. He thought about her half-finished cra projects, littering the house, and the cow curtains flutte ing by that damn cow-print table and chair set in t kitchen. He thought about how she had struggled to ma it work for all of them, and the fact that she put her nee last. He knew he would be a fool to let her go.

"I don't remember when I first met Ellen," he said qu etly.

She glanced up, her eyes wide. "Jake, I don't—"

"Please. Just listen."

She bowed her head and nodded.

"I guess we were babies. I don't remember a time in r life when Ellen wasn't there. We were best friends, all t way through high school. We both dated other people, b we hung out with each other. We could talk about ar thing. Then I went off to college while she was in her last year of high school. I came home for Christmas break, and something had changed. We thought we were in love."

Anne took a deep breath. "That sounds very wonderful," she said. "I'm sure your parents were pleased."

He wished she would look up so he could guess at what she was thinking, but she didn't. "They were. In retrospect, I know we weren't in love. I think the hormones kicked in and we didn't know what else to call it." He smiled, remembering their fumblings in the front seat of his sports car. It had been an awkward tight fit, but neither of them had minded. "We got engaged, then married. It took me several years to figure out something was wrong."

She looked up then, surprised. "What are you saying?"

"I didn't love Ellen the way you think I did. The woman I mourn has been gone a lot longer than two years. I miss my best friend, the girl I grew up with. Not the woman who died. I keep up the traditions out of obligation and maybe a little guilt. Also because they mean something to Laurel. Not because I care. I—" Now it was his turn to look down. He stared at the pale gray carpet newly installed in Laurel's room, then glanced back at Annie. "I used her memory to make you feel unwelcome. Maybe I used it to hide behind, as well." He shrugged. "I'm not proud of that, and I apologize."

She didn't say anything. He cleared his throat and continued. "I care about you, Annie. You've found your way into our lives. I can't imagine this house without you. I need you. Laurel needs you. We're not naked in bed, I'm not drunk or angry or desperate. Please stay and be my wife."

She reached up and tucked her hair behind her ear. "Because you love me?" she asked.

He nodded cautiously.

"Passionately?"

He smiled. "You can't deny the passion."

"No, I can't." She stood up and approached him. When she was close enough for him to inhale the sweet scent of her perfume, she placed her small hands on his folded arms. Her blue eyes stared into his. "I love you, Jake. I don't know when or how, but I do. I think it all started when you were so protective of Laurel."

A fierce gladness rose inside of him. The knot of tension in his gut released. It was going to be all right. She was going to stay. "Annie, I—"

"No." She reached up and touched her fingers to his mouth. Her hand cupped his jaw briefly, then returned to his forearm. "I won't marry you."

"But if you love me, why not?"

"Because you don't love me."

"I do."

She shook her head. "I'm not saying I don't believe your story about Ellen. I'm sure it's true. Actually it explains a lot of things to me. But your timing stinks. It's a little too convenient for my taste. I'm leaving in the morning so you happen to figure out that you haven't loved Ellen in years, oh, and by the way, you love me, too? I don't think so."

He could feel the panic growing. He was going to lose her. He knew it. "Dammit, woman, what do you want me to say? I've told you I love you, I've asked you to stay. Is it the idea of being married? We can live together, if you prefer. I don't like that, but I can be flexible. As long as we're a family."

"As long as you have your son." The sadness of her fact pierced him like a knife. "That's what this is all about. Whether you're willing to admit it or not, this entire discussion is because you're afraid to lose your son. If you can't intimidate me into staying, you're going to woo me into submission."

"That's not true," he said, but wondered if it was. Was he playing some kind of elaborate game with her? Was h that shallow and unfeeling? She was right about one thing. The timing of his confession did stink.

"I'll figure something out," she said, stepping away from him. "Visits, or maybe I'll look for another job close by. You'll be able to see your son, Jake. I promise."

He framed her face in his hands, then bent down and kissed her. He tasted her passion and her sadness. Had it been their destiny to break each other's hearts? "Despite what you think Annie Jo Baker, I do love you."

Tears formed, but she blinked them away. "Then let's stay friends. For both our children."

He pulled her close and held on tightly. Her body felt familiar against his. Familiar and so very right. "I'm sorry," he whispered into her hair.

"I'm not. I found Laurel. I've been gifted with a second chance and a second child. And I found you, Jake. You'll never know what loving you has meant to me."

Then why are you leaving me? he wanted to ask. But he didn't. There weren't any words left to convince her to stay.

Chapter Sixteen

The rain fell, obliterating all but the brightest lights in the Houston skyline. Anne stood at her window watching the storm. Through the glass she could feel the damp, cool air. It was early December. In Colorado, they had already had snow. She knew because she watched the weather channel's national report, as if seeing computer images of snow or rain would make her feel she was still living on the horse ranch with Jake and Laurel.

Her daughter also brought her up-to-date, she reminded herself. The twice-weekly phone calls lasted almost an hour with Laurel chattering about her friends and her plans for the weekend. When Anne called, Jake rarely picked up, and when he did, he politely asked how she was feeling, then handed her over to their daughter.

She'd been back over a month, so why didn't the beautiful white-on-white condo feel more like a home?

Anne turned from the window and walked toward her study. She'd brought work from the office, as she did most nights. Her new promotion carried with it a lot of responsibility. She wanted to be accessible to her team during the day which meant her paperwork had to be done in the evening. She had a big raise, stock options and use of the corporate apartment in New York when she went there on business. Heather had taken over her old job and was doing it very well on little more than forty hours per week.

"You don't have to kill yourself to be successful," Heather often reminded her when they went out for lunch. "I might not get the next promotion as quickly as you got yours, but I have a family to think of."

Anne did, too, but she hadn't told anyone about her pregnancy. As she entered her study, she touched her rounded stomach. All but the most formfitting of her suit skirts still fit. Still, she would have to think about buying some maternity clothes soon. And this condo. She glanced around at the perfect decorations. Maybe she would sell it and buy a small house with a yard. She had to think about hiring a nanny to take care of the baby while she was at work.

She sat behind her desk but instead of picking up the file on top, she reached for the photograph Laurel had sent her. It was her school picture. The teenager smiled out at the camera. Her hazel eyes hinted at laughter and a loving spirit that even difficult circumstances couldn't deny. Anne remembered the fight they'd had about what the girl would wear for the photo session. The screams that had led to tears and a deeper understanding of their relationship. There had been so many tears. Later, when Laurel had found out about the baby, and then at the airport, when they waited for her plane.

Anne closed her eyes to block out the visions of the past, but they intruded. Her flight had been late, giving them more time to stand around awkwardly promising to call and write. Jake had looked as if she was ripping his heart out by leaving, but that couldn't be true. He didn't really love her; he wanted his child.

But she still loved him. Not a day went by that she didn't ache for him. Her body needed for him to ignite and consume her passion, her mind and spirit longed to be in his presence, to hear his voice, to love him honestly, as a woman loves a man. She grew sick with wanting, then told herself it was the baby making her feel ill, not missing Jake. Besides she would be seeing him in a few weeks.

She opened her eyes and leaned back in her chair. How was she going to get through that visit? Laurel and Jake were coming to Houston for Christmas, then Jake was returning to the ranch right after the holiday, and his daughter was spending the rest of her vacation in the city. Anne had planned to take several days off. The holidays were always slow around the office. She and Laurel would see the sights; she even had tickets for a Houston Ballet performance. Then Laurel would fly home and Anne would be alone. Again.

But it wasn't the being alone that scared her. She would deal with that when it happened. It was seeing Jake. Being in the same room with him for three days. She only had one spare bedroom so he would be staying at a nearby hotel. When he told her about his plans she'd wanted to offer her couch, but she knew how easily that would lead to her bed, and then they would be back where they had started. She wouldn't be able to leave him again. She knew that now.

"I'm fine," she said, aloud, and reached for the top folder. After flipping it open, she stared at the page in front of her. But instead of words and numbers, she saw Jake's face, the gold flecks in his eyes, and the smile that could melt her bones.

"Stop it," she ordered herself. She didn't need a man in her life. She didn't need Jake. She and her baby would be fine by themselves. Just fine. After all, she'd worked hard for her career and this promotion. She deserved the chance to be successful.

She looked at her hands. Her nails had grown back and her skin was smooth again. Still she missed the baking and the sewing. The quilt she'd been working on lay packed in a box. She hadn't taken it out to finish it. She told herself she was too busy, but she knew the real reason was she couldn't face the memories.

Her gaze swept her desk to another framed picture. This one was of her mother. "You always told me to be the best," she said to the photo. "I'm being the best I can be, Mama."

Her mother had also told her to be happy. That happiness was the most elusive gift of all, and if she found it, she should hold on to it with both hands. Anne reached forward and touched the silver frame. She wondered what her mother would think if she knew her only daughter had settled for being just fine.

The flurry of present opening Christmas morning left the living room looking like a paper storm had blown through. Laurel sat on the floor in the center of the pile of presents. She opened yet another box and pulled out a pale pink wool sweater that matched a pair of corduroy pants Annie had given her.

"Cool," the teenager said, then leaned over and kissed Annie's cheek. "This was some Christmas."

"I think Annie and I both went a little crazy," Jake said, from his place on the white sofa. "We're going to have to be on our toes to keep you from turning into a spoiled brat."

Laurel rolled her eyes. "Da-ad. I'm the perfect child."

"Oh, please," Annie said, reaching for several torn sheets of wrapping paper.

"And you both love me," Laurel said confidently. She scrambled to her feet and crossed over to the couch. "Thanks for everything, Dad," she said. "I love it all."

He held her briefly as she kissed his cheek. If nothing else, she was right about one thing. He and Annie did love the girl. That's why they were going through these awkward three days together. For her sake.

"Is it okay if I call Terry and tell her what I got?" Laurel asked.

"Sure." Annie pointed down the hall. "You can even use the new phone in your room."

"Thanks." Laurel gathered an armful of presents. "Just so I don't forget anything," she said, then grinned and dashed toward the guest room. Her long brown hair fanned over the back of her bathrobe. From behind she still looked like a little girl, but Jake knew his daughter was very nearly a woman.

Annie rose to her knees and picked up several bows resting on the coffee table.

"Let me help you with that," he said, leaning forward. They reached for the same bow and their fingers brushed. He half expected to see sparks fly between them.

She jerked her hand back. "Sorry."

"It was my fault."

They stared uneasily at each other. It was about ten in the morning. Jake had come over early from his hotel room, but Laurel had slept in until almost nine. He'd sat in the kitchen with Annie, talking about the ranch and her work. Everything but what he really wanted to say. Now, alone in her big living room, with the remnants of the holiday around him, he still couldn't find the words.

"It looks beautiful," he said, pointing to the large decorated tree in the corner. "It must have been tough getting it up in the elevator."

She reached for a trash bag and began filling it. "There's a service elevator in the back. They use it to bring up furniture and that kind of thing."

"Oh. Convenient."

"Hmm. Yes, it is."

She sat on her knees, half turned away from him. Her profile was exactly as he remembered. The small nose, the full lips. The freckles. Every time he looked at Laurel's sweet face, he saw Annie's freckles.

A pale peach oversize shirt hung to midthigh. Peach stretch pants covered her lower half. He couldn't tell how much she was showing. He wanted to ask how she felt, but he was afraid she would misunderstand the question.

"It's hard without you, Annie," he said, because he was tired of pretending it wasn't.

She bit her lower lip. "I miss you guys, too."

"I've hired a housekeeper, but it's not the same."

"Yeah, she probably gives you everything you want."

He leaned forward and rested his elbows on his knees. "She does. It gets really boring."

She looked up at him. Her delicate brows drew together in confusion.

"There's no one to argue with," he said. "The house is clean all the time. No projects scattered around. No more sewing or baking."

"She doesn't bake?"

"I told her not to."

"Why?"

"Laurel and I agreed it would be better that way. We have too many memories of you already."

"Oh."

"How's work?" he asked, knowing he was a coward. He knew what he wanted to tell her, what he wanted to ask her, but what if his words weren't enough? How could he convince her of the truth?

"Fine." She grimaced. "I'm perfectly fine."

He swallowed his pride. Without her, what good was the damn thing anyway? "I'm not fine. I still love you, Annie, and I miss you. That house is big and cold without you in it."

"Jake, don't." She picked up a piece of paper and crumpled it. "I can't go through this again."

"I've finally figured out a way to convince you that I want you because I love you and not because of the baby." At least he hoped he had.

She looked up, skeptical. "Oh?"

Here goes nothing, he thought. "I'm going to sleep with another woman and get her pregnant."

"You're *what?*"

He fought back a grin. Leaning back on the sofa, he raised one arm to stretch along the back. "It's the only way. Then I'll have another child of my own."

"That's the most...the most..." She clamped her mouth shut and glared at him. "Don't you even think about it, buster."

"Don't you see? If I have another child and I still love you and want you to marry me, you'll believe me when I tell you it's not about our baby." Then he did smile. "You were right. I was trying to have it all without thinking about you. The timing for my confession was a little too convenient. I've had these weeks to think about all of it. Annie, I can have a baby with anyone. If that was all I was interested in, I'd go out and find a woman who wants to marry a rich rancher, then get her pregnant. I'm not the greatest guy in the world, but I think I'm a pretty fair catch. I'll admit at the beginning I was focused on the baby." His gaze dropped briefly to her midsection. "Our baby. But I've realized it's so much more than that. I want a child, but I *need* you in my life. I love you. Please marry me."

"Damn you, Jake Masters." She threw the crumpled paper at him.

"Is that a yes, Annie?" he asked hopefully. "Do you believe me, now?"

"Do I have a choice?" Her smile was shaky. "If I don't you're going to go knock up some bimbo."

"I have better taste than to choose a bimbo," he said, and held open his arms.

She moved to the sofa and bent down. Their mouths met in hungry exploration. He gripped her hips and lowered her so she settled on his lap.

He looked at her. "Was that a yes?"

She nodded. "Yes, Jake, I'll marry you."

She took his hand and slipped it under her shirt. He could feel the change in her shape, the growing roundness of her belly. He could feel something else, too. The heat of her body and the electricity arcing between them.

"I love you," she murmured, then touched her mouth to his.

"And I love you."

Her breasts flattened against his chest as she leaned against him. Her tongue dueled with his.

"Wow!"

They broke apart. Jake groaned low in his chest, then turned his head to look at his daughter. Laurel danced from foot to foot in the hallway. "You're kissing," she crowed.

"You're interrupting," he said.

"This is good, right?"

Jake looked at Annie. "Very good."

"So you guys are like getting back together?"

Annie smiled at her daughter. "We're getting married."

"All right!" Laurel made a pumping motion with her arm. "That's totally cool." She looked at them both, then her expression changed from childish happiness to adult amusement. "I think I'll leave you two alone and go make another phone call."

"Make it a long one," Jake called after her. He looked back at Annie. "Where were we?"

"Right here." She angled her head, then lowered her mouth to his.

Epilogue

"I told you he would be a boy," Jake said from his place on the side of her hospital bed. He reached out and touched the tiny infant's face.

"You were right." Anne stared down at her sleeping child. Her body ached from the six hours of labor and she wondered if she would ever lose the extra twenty pounds, but none of that mattered right now.

She closed her eyes and savored the feel of the small bundle in her arms. He felt so perfect there, as if they had been made to fit together. Joy filled her, tinged with a bittersweet realization. Almost fourteen years before she'd given birth in a small hospital like this one. It had been Texas, instead of Colorado, and she'd just turned eighteen instead of being thirty-one. But the experience had changed her as much as this child being born.

As she held their son, she fought against the tears. She'd lost this with Laurel and it could never be recovered. She glanced up at her beautiful daughter. "Are you okay?"

Laurel nodded, her eyes wide. "He's so small."

"It's hard to give birth to them full grown."

"I guess, but gosh, I didn't expect this." She peere down at the scrunched-up red face. "He's not very hanc some, is he? He's got monkey ears."

Anne laughed, then winced as the muscles in her ston ach protested.

Jake winked at his daughter. "It's just how you looke kid." He glanced at the sleeping baby. "Nah. He's bett looking."

"Da-ad." She leaned closer. "Can I hold him?"

"Sure." Annie placed her son in her daughter's arm.

The teenager held him securely and cooed. "Hi. I'm yo big sister. Laurel. Can you say Laurel?" She walked aroun the small room.

Jake touched Anne's face. "You feeling all right?"

"Never better."

"You did great in there. I'm really proud of you."

She leaned back against the pillows and sighed. "W make a good team."

"Well, I'm the team captain and I want to remind ye that you promised not to go back to work for six weeks.'

"Jake, I'll take the baby with me. The craft boutique h only been open a couple of months. I want to go in an keep an eye on things."

He frowned, then shook his head. "Why do I eve bother fighting you? You're more trouble than my mo stubborn brood mare."

"Speaking of brood mares, you knew this one was g ing to be a boy. What's the next one going to be?"

He took her hand and brushed his thumb against the d amond ring on her left hand. "You'd have another baby?

"Sure. I thought we agreed on three kids."

"I know, but I thought with the labor and all the wee you haven't been able to see your feet, you might chan your mind."

She looked at Laurel holding her brother. Then she stared at Jake. The love between them was as tangible as the world they lived in. She would do anything for him. Every day she loved him more. He trusted her with his heart, his soul and his flaws. If he wanted another child, she could deny him nothing.

"I liked our plan of three," she said, smiling. "So what is it going to be? A boy or a girl?"

He placed his hand on her stomach and thought for a second. "A girl."

"You're sure?"

"Yup."

"Okay. I'll stock up on pink." She touched his face. He was tired from staying up most of the night with her. The lines around his eyes had deepened, but he'd never looked more handsome to her. The transition hadn't been easy but they were together and they were happy. She couldn't ask for anything more than that. As her mother had taught her, she was holding on to their happiness with both hands.

* * * * *

Rugged and lean...and the best-looking, sweetest-talking men to be found in the entire Lone Star state!

Diana Palmer

LONG, TALL TEXANS

In July 1994, Silhouette is very proud to bring you Diana Palmer's first three LONG, TALL TEXANS. CALHOUN, JUSTIN and TYLER—the three cowboys who started the legend. Now they're back by popular demand in one classic volume—and they're ready to lasso your heart! Beautifully repackaged for this special event, this collection is sure to be a longtime keepsake!

"Diana Palmer makes a reader want to find a Texan of her own to love!" —*Affaire de Coeur*

LONG, TALL TEXANS—the first three—reunited in this special roundup!

Available in July, wherever Silhouette books are sold.

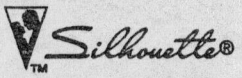

LT

This August,
Harlequin and Silhouette
are proud to bring you

by Request™

Baby *on the* Way

Pregnant, alone and desperate...

Strange things can happen when there's a **BABY ON THE WAY**

Relive the romance...

Three complete novels by your favorite authors—in one special collection!

THE VOW by Dallas Schulze
WILD TEXAS ROSE by Linda Turner
THE DADDY CANDIDATE by Cait London

**Available wherever
Harlequin and Silhouette books are sold.**

HARLEQUIN®

Silhouette®

SREQ894

ONE OF OUR OWN
Cheryl Reavis

Getting custody of her orphaned nephew was the hardest thing Sloan Baron had ever faced. She found herself on unfamiliar New Mexico territory, forced to battle stubborn Navaho policeman Lucas Singer. Lucas was as stubborn as Sloan was feisty, but soon she found herself undeniably attracted....

Don't miss ONE OF OUR OWN, by Cheryl Reavis, available in August!

She's friend, wife, mother—she's you! And beside each Special Woman stands a wonderfully *special* man. It's a celebration of our heroines—and the men who become part of their lives.

Don't miss **THAT SPECIAL WOMAN!** each month—from some of your special authors! Only from Silhouette Special Edition!

TSW894

WHAT EVER HAPPENED TO...?

Have you been wondering when much-loved characters will finally get their own stories? Well, have we got a lineup for you! Silhouette Special Edition is proud to present a ***Spin-off Spectacular!*** Be sure to catch these exciting titles from some of your favorite authors:

HOMEWARD BOUND (July, SE #900) Mara Anvik is recalled to her old home for a dire mission—which reunites her with old flame Mark Toovak in *Sierra Rydell*'s exciting spin-off to ON MIDDLE GROUND (SE #772).

BABY, COME BACK (August, SE #903) *Erica Spindler* returns with an emotional story about star-crossed lovers Hayes Bradford and Alice Dougherty, who are given a second chance for marriage in this follow-up to BABY MINE (SE #728).

THE WEDDING KNOT (August, SE #905) *Pamela Toth*'s tie-in to WALK AWAY, JOE (SE #850) features a marriage of convenience that allows Daniel Sixkiller to finally adopt...and to find his perfect mate in determined Karen Whitworth!

A RIVER TO CROSS (September, SE #910) Shane Macklin and Tina Henderson shared a forbidden passion, which they can no longer deny in the latest tale from *Laurie Paige*'s WILD RIVER series.

Don't miss these wonderful titles, only for our readers—only from Silhouette Special Edition!

SPIN5

Those mischievous matchmaking babies are back, as Marie Ferrarella's Baby's Choice series continues in August with MOTHER ON THE WING (SR #1026).

Frank Harrigan could hardly explain his sudden desire to fly to Seattle. Sure, an old friend had written to him out of the blue, but there was something else.... Then he spotted Donna McCollough, or rather, she fell right into his lap. And from that moment on, they were powerless to interfere with what angelic fate had lovingly ordained.

Continue to share in the wonder of life and love, as babies-in-waiting handpick the most perfect parents, only in

Silhouette
ROMANCE™

To order your copy of the first Baby's Choice title, *Caution: Baby Ahead* (SR #1007), please send your name, address, zip or postal code, along with a check or money order (please do not send cash) for $2.75, plus 75¢ postage and handling ($1.00 in Canada), payable to Silhouette Books, to:

In the U.S.
Silhouette Books
3010 Walden Ave.
P. O. Box 9077
Buffalo, NY 14269-9077

In Canada
Silhouette Books
P. O. Box 636
Fort Erie, Ontario
L2A 5X3

Please specify book title with your order.
Canadian residents add applicable federal and provincial taxes.

SRMF2